SUMMERTIME

RAFFAELLA BARKER, daughter of the poet George Barker, was born and brought up in the Norfolk countryside. She is the author of seven other novels, *Come and Tell Me Some Lies*, *The Hook*, *Hens Dancing*, *Green Grass*, *A Perfect Life*, *Poppyland* and *From a Distance*. She has also written a novel for young adults, *Phosphorescence*. She is a regular contributor to the *Sunday Times* and the *Sunday Telegraph* and teaches on the Literature and Creative Writing BA at the University of East Anglia and the *Guardian* UEA Novel Writing Masterclass. Raffaella Barker lives by the sea in north Norfolk.

Also by Raffaella Barker

RAFFAELLA BARKER

SUMMERTIME

B L O O M S B U R Y

LONDON · NEW DELHI · NEW YORK · SYDNEY

First published in Great Britain in 2001 by Headline Book Publishing
This paperback edition published 2014

Bloomsbury Publishing Plc
50 Bedford Square
London
WC1B 3DP

www.bloomsbury.com

Bloomsbury is a trademark of Bloomsbury Publishing Plc

Bloomsbury Publishing, London, New Delhi, New York and Sydney

A CIP catalogue record for this book is
available from the British Library

ISBN 978 1 4088 5065 7

10 9 8 7 6 5 4 3 2 1

Typeset by Hewer Text UK Ltd, Edinburgh
Printed and bound in Great Britain by
CPI Group (UK) Ltd, Croydon CR0 4YY

MIX
Paper from
responsible sources
FSC® C013604

For Lornie,
with love from Mum

MARCH

March 13th

Mother's Day begins badly. No one has remembered, and Lowly, the weirdo dog has found one of The Beauty's dirty nappies in the rubbish bin in the bathroom and has disembowelled it. Glistening white beads of indestructible gel are sprayed like polystyrene snow across the carpet, and there is a malodorous whiff in the air. Instead of lying in bed receiving trays of breakfast, heaps of compliments, kisses and lovely flowers like every other mother, I spend the first part of the morning vacuuming and spraying air freshener in a hygiene frenzy.

It is eleven o'clock and none of the children are visible or audible. This can only mean one thing – the Nintendo machine. Sure enough, I unearth a full complement of offspring in the playroom, their noses pinned to the television screen. Giles, aged eleven, should be old enough to know better by now, but in fact is the child most on the edge of his seat and is air-punching exultantly: 'Yessss, forty of them as dead as dodos, and we're on to the next level.'

Felix, who is nine, will never be old enough to know better – it simply isn't his way. He is draped elegantly along the back of the sofa, a line of squat metal lumps stretched like vertebrae before him to the other end of the sofa back. These are his army men, a cohort of Deathmasters and elves with whom he is locked in a Warhammer bloodbath. Perched next to him, and wearing her beloved purple tutu with red frill over her pyjamas, is The Beauty. She will be three in June, and doesn't need to know better as she is convinced that she always knows best.

'Mummy, *sit down*. Look! It's Dinosaur Death Run. Such fun,' she urges in her mad Enid Blyton way. Squalor in the playroom is extreme. Even though the curtains are drawn, I can see strewn orange peel and sweet wrappers all over the floor and also my eagle eye detects that Giles's toenails need cutting. Glorious sunshine has been barricaded out, but through the gap between the curtains I glimpse our two remaining Bohemian pigeons swooping on a spring breeze, and a twig of cherry blossom scratching at the window pane. The perfection of outside increases my rage one thousandfold. On the television screen some foul-looking dinosaurs are hopping about. Their bloodcurdling roars are nothing like as frightening as mine.

'Will you turn that thing off. You *know* it's banned until after dark. You *know* I hate it. And it's Mother's Day.'

Sit down on a small pink chair, squashing one of The Beauty's tiny tea parties which are set up all over the house, and burst into tears. Felix rushes to embrace me and Giles hastily removes all Nintendo equipment from within arm's reach – he is used to this scene, and knows that I may hurl vital components into the bin, or the fireplace, at any moment.

'We've got a surprise for you,' Felix soothes, patting my shoulder kindly. The Beauty hovers anxiously at his side, proffering a small white handkerchief, either in truce or to blow my nose on.

'Cheer up Mum,' says Giles. 'At least you aren't forty yet.'

Hadn't even thought of worrying about that milestone, but can now add it to my list of near-future neuroses.

The Beauty squats in front of me, peering interestedly. 'Don't cry. Blow your nose. And get off my cuppa tea,' she commands, ramming the handkerchief into my face. I have an overpowering sense of panic. I have forgotten how to manage my children on my own.

For the past year I have been mollycoddled and buffered from single motherhood by the presence of my lovely handsome tower-of-strength boyfriend David. Before he moved in I must have managed somehow. The children's father Charles used to have them for the odd weekend, and still does when he can fit them into his ghoulish schedule running a chain of pet cemeteries and, more recently, setting up an animal funeral service on the internet called deaddog?.com. More than two years on, I now quite like the poisoned dwarf Helena, and am indeed grateful to her for luring him away from our unhappy life together. Less sure about Holly and Ivy-Eff the Petridish twins, as they may jeopardise my own children's position. Their role so far has been gurgling and toddling, but last year's Christmas card from Charles and Helena (not, of course, sent to me, but shown me by a well-wisher) had Giles and Felix sitting crosslegged on the grass with The Beauty, the twin blobs propped between them. The Beauty's expression of disdain spoke volumes, as did the larger than usual alimony cheque which arrived for me in lieu of the frightful card. Charles always sends more money when he does something underhand: it is his saving grace.

It was on Christmas Day, when David and I borrowed a boat and chugged across the basin of sea at the head of the creek to Alborrow Sands for a bonfire and picnic, that we decided we would go away, just the two of us, in March. The children were with Charles, my first ever Christmas without them, and David made sure there was no time for me to brood. Up and out on an ice-grey morning to catch the tide, wearing a scarf as soft and pink and warm as midsummer rose petals which he wrapped round me saying, 'First Christmas present of the day,' when we reached the harbour. The second present was a bailing bucket, and scooping water from the floor of the leaky boat kept me warm as we crossed. The sun came out and sent dancing golden rays to race ahead of us on the still water and up on to the shore. 'Elevenses,' said David, and pulled a bottle of champagne out of the basket he had brought and wouldn't let me look into.

Fuelled by a cold glass, drunk with our arms round each other, looking out at the horizon, we gathered wood to build our fire on which we cooked steak and baked potatoes. He had even brought a Christmas pudding, and we lit it, holding it up to see the purple-pink sky through the smoky flame, then we ate it fast, with spoonfuls of brandy butter, before the sun went down and we returned to the twinkling fairy lights of the harbour town. And David shouted above the boat engine and the roar of the sea, 'Today was perfect. Let me take you away somewhere like this but warmer. Let's go at the end of winter. I'll organise it, I'll ask your mother to have the kids. All you will have to do is pack.' He cut the engine and we floated into the jetty. He climbed out and held out his hand to me. I jumped off the boat and he pulled me into his arms, and the skin of his cheeks was so cold it almost felt hot against mine. 'I promise it will happen. It's your Christmas present,' he whispered.

Huh! is all I can say. The end of winter came, and David got a brilliant job in Bermuda. An old friend of his was out there doing a fashion shoot and set it up. Now David is staying in a house called Pointy Fingers on Banana Patch Road, and will be there for weeks, no doubt. He is building a library for a bloated old screenplay writer, and now he's been asked to do

5

a colonnade too. Actually, for all I know the script-writer may be a lissom twenty-two-year-old, but I prefer to keep my mental picture very hideous. David's job makes me alternately paralysed with envy and incandescent with rage. Colonnades and librar-ies and kidney-shaped pools are a million miles from the scene here and now. Norfolk is charmless in March, soggy, grey and mud-ridden. My life has shrunk to a monotonous routine of school run, wash-ing clothes and digging drainage ditches. Cannot bear to think of David lolling next to turquoise swim-ming pools and sipping cocktails with film stars and moguls. Because he is working flat out, or so he says, I am not able to visit him, so am denied even the fun of being carpenter's assistant and thus achieving a version of a winter-sun holiday. It is all too much for Mother's Day.

Sense of ill use carries me into the kitchen to dispense cereal, and is utterly confounded. The chil-dren have laid the table with my favourite gold-lustre teapot and cups, and have created a vast cream-puff effect with bananas and yogurt as a breakfast centre-piece. Each of them has made me a card. The Beauty's offering is very contemporary, a piece of kitchen roll with felt-pen dots of pink and purple in one corner. Giles has drawn Betty Boop wiggling towards a sink full of washing-up which has a big red cross through it. She is batting her eyelashes at a giant balloon in front of her which says, 'Put your feet up, Mum. Let someone sane take the strain.' Not sure how to take this, but am overcome by Felix's vast pink square of cardboard, on which he has written a poem which begins with the couplet

You're as fast as a cheetah and as pretty as roses
I love you Mummy, everybody knows.

More mawkish weeping, and Giles gets out the ice cream to have with the banana Melba to celebrate. Become carried away, and introduce the boys to the inimitable Coke float, favoured drink of my childhood and certain death to teeth.

March 15th

Open the curtains to a grey morning with frost glittering on the branch of the lime tree outside my window. The view is wrapped in fine mist, and the air is brittle with cold, but the sun is rising. I open the bedroom window and lean out to enjoy the spectral loveliness of my knot garden. Frost is a definite improvement on rain, and the shimmer of the pink sun marbles the sky until it becomes iridescent, and a rainbow of colour drives back the mist and the grey to make a pink morning. Allow myself a few seconds of wallowing in missing David before closing the window and trying to muster enthusiasm for the pre-school rush.

David telephones at seven o'clock, just as I am going downstairs to make myself tea before waking the children.

'Hi gorgeous,' he says lightly, 'how are you?'

'Fine thanks.' Am suddenly aware of his voice, the first male voice I have heard for days. I close my eyes and pretend I don't know him, and try to imagine a face for the sexy voice.

'I'm about to go to bed, I know it's school time for you lot. I just wanted to tell you I love you, I miss you,' he says, and of course, I just imagine him.

'I miss you too,' I murmur. I am downstairs now, thanks to the cordless phone, and I want to curl up in the chair by the Aga to talk to him and try to seduce him home. He sounds sad, I bet I can get him to come back. I open the door into the boot room to get some milk from the fridge. Lowly has emptied the rubbish all over the floor.

Forget sodding seduction. Instead shriek into the phone, 'Buggering hell. Hateful Lowly swine hound! Now I'll have to clear it all up.' Become even shriller, not allowing David a moment to speak. 'Anyway. This really isn't the moment. I've got to get everyone ready for school and the car will be covered in frost. I'll speak to you later. When you get up, I mean.'

Put the phone down and wish to saw off my tongue. Absolutely no need to be foul to him, he is simply doing his job. He can hardly be blamed for the time difference which means that he is tucking himself up in bed when I am dragging the dustbins down the drive with the dogs licking their lips behind me.

Distracted from the dustbins for a moment by a patch of hellebores next to the front door, nodding graceful pale heads towards a small clump of vivid blue scillas. Remember that the white hellebore is the

Lenten rose, or is it the Christmas rose? Anyway, it must be Lent now because it's March. What shall I give up? Is it too late? Surely a little is better than none as far as self-denial goes.

Can't see the point of giving up chocolate as I undoubtedly will not be able to stick to it, particularly as the house is practically made of gingerbread like the witch's cottage in Hansel and Gretel, due to volumes of tuck required for the perpetually starving, always growing boys. Quite impossible to know biscuits, for example, are there in the biscuit tin and not sample one at elevenses or tea, now there is no one else in the house save The Beauty to check up. Biscuit life took a very dangerous turn last week on the discovery of some caramel-covered chocolate digestives on special offer in the supermarket. Stupidly bought them, pretending it would be a treat for the boys, then even more stupidly ate the whole lot.

Toy with the idea of abandoning alcohol until Easter. This too seems unwise, as I might have to attend a sales conference for Vanden Plaz hotels soon, in order to suck up and get more work writing their brochures. This annual evening of frightfulness is made bearable only by the very high quality of food and drink. Generally have about four glasses of champagne and start inviting people I have just met to stay. Last year I asked the whole corporate hospitality team, and the leader seemed very keen. It came to nothing, thank God. Allow myself to imagine the horror of entertaining six strangers for a weekend, and trying to produce food for them while looking like a top-efficiency copywriter who deserves a pay rise. Giving up alcohol may be my salvation.

Return to the kitchen from the dustbins to find the children running on peak efficiency. Giles is making scrambled eggs, Lowly and Digger, David's Labrador, are eating the eggshells under the table, and The Beauty has dragged a chair over to the sink and is doing the washing-up. Occupying another area of high ground is Felix, who is standing on the window seat watching the second hand of his watch.

'Well done, Mummy, you're back within the allotted time. Have you seen my goalie gloves?'

He jumps down, interrupting before I manage to say no.

'In fact, I think I may have left them in the hen house. Time me.' He chucks his watch at me and hurtles out of the back door and across the yard to the dilapidated hen house, crouching to open the nesting-box doors then vanishing save for his legs as he leans in to look for gloves, and I hope, eggs. The cockerel sticks his head out of the door to see what sort of day it is, and finding it to his taste, emerges on to the lintel, groaning and clucking to warn us all that he is about to crow.

In order to crow, he needs to feel tall, so he hops on to the handle of The Beauty's pink tricycle, and manages the first part of the triumphant morning call before losing his balance due to overexertion and splashing in a dust of feathers to the ground again. Felix scatters a few grains of corn and dashes back to the house. I refrain from sending him out again to give the bantams more than just the half-teaspoonful he has found adequate, because I want him to eat his breakfast right now, and because none of the hens has come out yet. There are only three, and I think they have all decided to be broody together, which is tiresome as we shall have no eggs this summer.

The sun breaks through and dispenses a weak dose of uplift as we pass the pig farm on the way to school. The pig farm is often a haven of picturesque loveliness, but not today. Something has happened to the muck heap, and it has avalanched across the road in front of us, so our path is steaming and pungent. Abruptly shut my window and attempt to drive through the slurry, but in moments the wheels are spinning and we are embedded.

'Phew, it stinks,' says Giles, turning the radio up, as if he thinks this will make a difference.

I rev the engine once more, to no avail. 'Hell and buggeration, we're going to be late.' Open my door and step out, heart sinking as feet do the same into warm manure. Have not worn my wellingtons, and as I squelch towards the barn, looking for a shovel, bits of straw and soft slime stick to the soles of my shoes and float in over the top to lie beneath my heel. Find a spade, and a broom, but no farmer to assist me, so stomp back to the road in a big rage.

My life seems entirely made up of shit-shovelling episodes, be it dogs, pigs, children or hens. Am fed up with it. Am fed up with David being away, and never being able to speak to him because it's always the wrong time of day. Whenever he does ring, it is a bad moment and I am in a rush or unable to concentrate and the conversation becomes dyspeptic, or dysfunctional, or just plain disagreeable. He will never want to come back at this rate. Must work out a way to improve this state of affairs, and also my appearance. This is foul, as a few moments in the bathroom after the school run demonstrate. Am loitering in front of the mirror, killing time while The Beauty busies herself with her babies whom she has lined up against the wall and to whom she is administering medicine and dabs of hand cream along with a kindly kiss on the head. This absorbing occupation gives me plenty of time to notice the leaden texture and pallid tone of my skin. Must implement a thorough purification regime forthwith. However, by the time I have wiped all the babies, put away the hand cream and restuffed the whole packet of baby wipes The Beauty has discarded and thrown into her sock drawer, I have lost interest in purification. Dump The Beauty in her cot, praying that she has forgotten that she now knows how to climb out, and retreat to my own bed, promising, 'I'll just lie down for ten minutes.'

Surface again at midday, flushed with the sense of achievement which comes from having read a whole Georgette Heyer at one sitting, and spurred by the merry dance of true love in *Cotillion*, to a more cheerful level of existence.

March 16th

Good cheer is beginning to drain away again as I stare out at the blank sky and try to decide whether it would be more ghastly to do my work or to go to the super-market. There is no loo paper, no cereal, no washing powder and no milk. After some consideration, choose to do my work, as the shopping option involves more than meets the eye: a multitude of chores will be unleashed by a visit to the supermarket, each one more urgent than the last. Also, it is one thing gliding up and down the aisles with The Beauty, humming away to piped music and wondering which Teletubbies video to buy today, but it is quite another to be back home, dragging vast, splitting bags of stuff out of the car, and into the house where the final insult still awaits in the form of unpacking and putting away, accompanied by a hovering and stamping Beauty who needs her supper. Work, on balance, is the easy option today.

Five minutes at my desk has me riffling through the waste-paper basket and then my diary in search of something interesting to take my mind off the Vanden Plaz Conference Catering brochure. Discover from my diary that Easter is almost upon us, and telephone my friend Rose in London to invite her to stay. She is out, so have to make do with her answerphone. Try telephoning my mother for a spot of work avoidance instead. She is at home and is sniffing back tears. Fortunately they are of joy.

'Oh, Venetia, it's so wonderful. I was just about to ring you. You will never believe this – never. Desmond has asked Minna to marry him and she has agreed.' There is a pause, and the deep intake of breath required for a huge puff on the celebratory cigarette crackles down the line. I am speechless. I must digest this extraordinary news. My brother Desmond is getting married. Surely he is not grown-up enough? He is certainly old enough, and has been for years, but old is not the same as grown-up.

'Gosh, that's fantastic. When? How? Where?'

Have a sense of urgency, and a potent desire to have the whole thing sewn up before Minna changes her mind. But perhaps she won't. After all, they have been together for nearly two years, which is certainly a record for Desmond. My mother's excitement is gathering force.

'Wait there,' she commands. 'I'll just pop into Aylsham for a bottle and I'll come over to tell you everything.'

She arrives with Egor, her bull terrier, hanging out of the passenger window of her car, yapping hoarsely. This sets Rags and Lowly off, and Digger joins in, so there is a hellish cacophony of dog reverberating through the house. The telephone rings, and I leap to answer it. Pick up the receiver but am distracted from saying hello by The Beauty, who has thrown herself at my mother and is warbling, 'Grannee, Grannee. Come and have a cuppa tea now.'

'No fear,' says Grannee, 'no tea for me. I'm celebrating with vodka and tonic.'

'Vodka tonic, vodka tonic. No fear,' parrots The Beauty.

'. . . CAN YOU HEAR ME, VENETIA?' blares in my ear. It is David sounding tetchy. Decide to punish him by pretending I can't hear him.

14

'Hello? Hello? Is anyone there? Oh, well, there must be something wrong. I expect whoever it is will try later.' I hang up and turn to greet my mother. She and The Beauty have settled at the kitchen table, and are watching in admiration as the bull terrier Egor and his idiot offspring Lowly run in circles of pleasure, holding one another's tails.

'Do look, Venetia. They are clever,' coos my mother, sloshing vodka into two glasses The Beauty has brought her from the cupboard. She sighs, leaning back in her chair, and muses, 'I must say, I always thought you would be married before Desmond. In fact, I never thought Desmond would be married at all. It's marvellous.' The telephone rings again and I battle with my better self, my bad fairy alter ego telling me not to answer it. Better self wins and I grab the phone.

'Hello, who is it?'

'Hi Venetia, it's me, David, missing you already today and I've only just got up.' Decide to ignore this, particularly in view of my mother's remarks, which have deflated me to the size of a worm. Almost burst getting the words I want to say out without sounding resentful or expectant.

'Guess what David, Desmond's getting married!' The silent jaw-dropping I can imagine down the line from Bermuda is as expressive as any exclamation.

'Darling, do get off the phone, I want to tell you everything.' My mother has tired of the dogs and is poised for a chat at the table, and The Beauty has found a straw and is making purposefully towards her glass.

I cut in on David's laughter and the tumble of questions he is asking. 'Sorry, David, I've got to go before The Beauty starts on the vodka. Call me later, darling.'

Barely hear his resigned 'OK then,' before hanging up and moving across to the chair opposite my mother and as far as possible from The Beauty, who is stripping off her red corduroy skirt in favour of a pair of Chinese trousers from the dressing-up box and a pink feather boa from my bedroom. Sip the first delicious mouthful of vodka and tonic, experience great dizziness and rosy glow of well-being, decide there is no room for resentment or jealousy today and get stuck into wedding details.

'Where are they getting married? I don't think Minna's got any parents, has she? What's she going to wear? When did he ask her? Oh, *God* it's so exciting.' Jump up, grab The Beauty and waltz around the room, dizzy with disbelief that this can be happening to the unmarriageable Desmond.

The ash on the end of my mother's cigarette has grown as long as a catkin, so lost has she been in silent musings. It is flicked off now, and a businesslike puffing recommences.

'No, she's an orphan. I don't know what happened to them, though. Do you?' My mother pauses to refill her glass, adding, 'Actually, I'd rather not know, if you don't mind. It might be gruesome. Anyway they want to get married here. And I've already asked dear Rev. Trev, who doesn't seem to mind that neither of them are spinsters of the parish.'

'That's because he's got a crush on you,' I remark cynically, but am ignored. My mother is in full sail, her black beret sliding towards her left ear and giving her the look of a crazed French Resistance officer.

March 21st

Easter weekend looms, and according to the weatherman it will be snowing for the whole four days. I don't care because Rose is coming to stay, along with her son Theo who is The Beauty's best friend, but without her husband Tristan, whom she referred to on the telephone as 'that snake-witted hell-hound'.

Am rather inspired by this moniker, but also worried, as I recognise it as similar to the abuse I frequently heaped upon my ex-husband Charles in the final stages of our marriage. Now I can simply call him dreary, which indeed he has become, and which is a vast improvement on being a hell-hound.

Chugging and loud banging on the front door announces a Parcel Force van with a lumpy package from David. The Beauty falls on it crying, 'It's my Happy Birthday,' and tears at the string and tape binding it shut. Inside are three vast balloons, one for each of the children, and three water pistols shaped like aliens. A note is attached to the smallest of the aliens: DO NOT SQUIRT YOUR MOTHER ON PERIL OF EXECUTION BY GREEN SLIME. The final item in the parcel is wrapped in pink tissue paper.

'I bet this is for you, Mum, it's all girly,' says Felix, handing it over. The tissue unfurls to reveal a pair of

sandals with velvet soles and purple and orange flowers garlanded across the top. They are enchanting. I
put them on and they fit me perfectly. Burst into
tears. Felix groans, 'God, don't start crying again.
What's the matter this time? Look, here's a letter from
David. It might cheer you up.'

Darling Venetia,
   I think I'll be home in a few weeks. I'm writing
this in my room. The windows are open and rain is
crashing on to the balcony, so work is off for the
afternoon. I've sent Desmond a pair of Elvis shades
from the market here to wear at his wedding.
They're Graceland rather than GI, and have thick
gold arms with squares cut in them for Desmond's
sideburns to stick through. I bought these shoes for
you to walk all over me in. Metaphorically. Mind
you, I wouldn't say no to literally . . . You are my
dreams, xxxx David xxx

Most pleasing. Almost worth him being away if this is
the sort of treatment I can expect. Float to Budgen's
supermarket on a cloud of pink pleasure, and still
wrapped in unreality, purchase seventeen long tubes
of mini Easter eggs for the Easter-egg hunt. Absently
proceed to eat two with Felix and The Beauty while
waiting for Giles to come out of school. This returns
me to earth with a thump of nausea. All of us feel
sick, and The Beauty has turned an unbecoming
caramel colour all over by the time I realise Giles
should be out, and I go into the school to look for

him. Find him in a darkened room with other low-lifers, playing on someone's Nintendo. Cannot understand how the school can allow this form of brainwashing to go on, and stand in the doorway muttering furiously while Giles and his automaton friends continue to perform thumb wars on their consoles. Giles waits until we are out of earshot of his friends before turning to me in raging contempt.

'God, you're so embarrassing. None of my friends have mothers who talk to themselves and ban Nintendo. Why can't you get a grip on your own life and stop interfering in mine?'

Very impressed by his astute summing-up of me, but dismayed not to be in the position of power. Have to regain the moral high ground. But how?

March 23rd

My position as mistress of any high ground, moral or literal, is becoming pronounced fantasy. Am paralysed with agonising pain in my foot, and cannot even drag myself to the doctor who is two miles away. The first twinges occur at lunchtime, after a strenuous morning in the garden with The Beauty. Our mission there is to glean lovely branches and wild flowers to create posies for the bedrooms and magnificent displays of twig and leaf for downstairs. However, it would seem that I have done this once too often. The garden looks as though a plague of locusts has visited it: all the trees are hunched and defensive, lifting their branches out of harm's way and well above my secateurs, and the few crocuses and grape hyacinths that have bothered to flower so far have been chewed by the hens and cower, soggy and downtrodden, in the mud. Am forced to hop and leap in order to grab a branch of pussy willow (not yet in leaf but in the warmth of the house it soon will be), and this may have contributed to the afternoon's foot disorder. The Beauty is entranced by flower-picking, and is clad as a mini land girl in pink shorts, knee socks and a T-shirt with a hula-hula girl on it which David sent her. Can't help feeling that she could do with tights and a cardigan as well, but bitter experience has taught me not to try to elaborate on her sartorial decisions once she sallies forth from her bedroom.

'Mummy. Do a wee like this,' she suggests, pulling her shorts down and squatting behind some daffodils in a very earthy fashion. Am saved from joining her by Lowly and Rags, who bustle over and lick her boisterously so she topples into long wet grass. Back in the boot room removing outer garments and tripping into the dogs' water bowl, I experience the first twinge of pain in my foot, then immediately forget about it in the search for vases, followed by the washing of same to erase terrible cabbage smell and internal coating of green slime. The Beauty has removed the heads from the few primroses and crocuses we have picked, so decide to go for the Zen look and float them in saucers of water. Playschool simplicity of this form of arrangement very pleasing. By the time all the flowers are roughly where they should be, and the house smells green and fresh like spring but still looks like a rubbish dump, the foot has taken over, and I hobble to the telephone to beg my dear kind friend Vivienne to bring the children home from school for me.

The doctor arrives at the same moment as the boys and Vivienne, and far from adopting the bedside manner and extreme discretion we all expect from our GP, he grins broadly and announces to the room at large that I have gout. I am outraged, mainly because Vivienne, and my mother who has material-ised quite unnecessarily, both start giggling. The doctor giggles too, eyeing Vivienne appreciatively, drinking in her rippling copper hair and short skirt above long, gout-free legs.

'I can't have gout. I don't drink port, and I'm not old.'

'Yes you are, Mum, you're very old,' says Felix, clearly believing these to be words of comfort, and a reasonable explanation for my condition. Giggling reaches a crescendo, my mother leading the field, delighted with this evidence of my depravity outstrip-ping hers.

'You'll have to wear slippers and carry a walking stick,' she crows, and The Beauty takes this as an order, and fetches my beautiful new sandals and an old cane with a curved handle from the chimney pot in the hall where all cricket bats, tennis racquets and other sporting implements live. She looks very much like Little Bo Peep with a shepherd's crook, as the stick is taller than she is.

Find myself having to gaze at the floor and set my jaw to stop hysterical laughter or tears brimming over.

Fortunately, Giles is hanging around, swinging on the Aga rail. He is hungry and also single-minded.

'Mum, if you can't walk, shall I make our supper?'

What a marvellous, responsible child I have produced, ready to step into the breach and be helpful.

'Oh darling, would you? You can have whatever you like if we've got it.'

Just about to turn smug expression towards my mother and Vivienne, and set up camp on high ground, when he adds, 'Great. We'll have pizza and ice cream, but I'll only do it if you let us play on the Nintendo afterwards. For an hour.' Outmanoeuvred. Last vestiges of strength depart and I feebly nod agreement, hoping none of the adults have noticed the depths to which I have sunk.

Smile sadly but bravely at the doctor as he leaves, hoping he will reconsider his verdict if I am saintly. He scarcely notices me, however, as he is buzzing around Vivienne. He shakes hands with her three times, looking at her as he tells me, 'You may find it improves tomorrow. If not, maybe a friend could bring you into the surgery and we'll sort you out with some medication.' He breaks off, scribbles something then looks over his glasses at Vivienne.

'You're a violin teacher, aren't you?' he says, without preamble. Vivienne nods, and the doctor is at a loss. He turns briskly back to me. 'Gout is a serious condition, so don't leave it without treatment. And no chocolate over Easter.' He wags his finger as if I am Bessie Bunter and Parson Woodforde rolled into one, and departs. I am hard put not to hurl my stick at him. Only prevent myself because I do not wish to seem any more dyspeptic than I already do. Wish my mother and Vivienne would stop carousing and become solicitous.

Later

After several hours in which I did not become resigned to having gout, I am miraculously healed. Don't know if it was the arrival of Rose, or the delicious behaviour of the children who put The Beauty to bed, and put on their pyjamas without being asked, or if it was the vile green stew of various herbs my mother concocted, or indeed the massaging effect of velvet-soled sandals, but something has cured me and I must send a postal order to Lourdes forthwith, or at least go to church. Church is probably easier, especially as Easter Sunday is the day after tomorrow.

Vivienne, my mother, Rose and I have eaten fabulous supper of mussels and brown bread. Mussels made even more delicious by the fact that I had no hand in their endless scraping, but sat and talked to Rose about my very unfulfilled New Year's resolution to find a new career, while my mother and Vivienne slaved over the sink, removing mussel beards and managing not to mention the word gout once. Rose and I decide that with training, I could become a part-time driving instructor, but otherwise am only qualified as a housekeeper, and not if they came and looked at the state of my laundry and storage cupboards. David telephones. I ask him if he thinks I would be better as a driving instructor or a house-keeper. 'Neither,' he says without hesitation. 'You should find something where you can make use of your skills.' There is something about his voice on the telephone that makes me feel we are having a steamy, intimate conversation, even when we are just talking about the weather in Bermuda.

Have to remember I am in the room with others. Cough and ask him, 'Well, what are they, and how do I fit them in between school hours and term time?'

He considers for a few expensive moments, then suggests, 'What about being a lifeguard?'

Choke with laughter and find I am missing him painfully, unless it's the gout. 'Oh, come back soon, we miss you badly. I'm wearing the shoes right now.'

'Well, if all goes to schedule, we'll be finished by the end of next month, so I'll be back then. I've got to go now, I should be at work.' He sighs, then speaks again, and it is as if he is right here, next to my ear. 'Anyway sweetheart, what else are you—' There is a beep and a click and he is cut off.

March 25th

Easter Sunday dawns with an uncanny heatwave. Bright sunshine beams in through all windows, high-lighting the Plimsoll line of fingermarks around the house at Beauty level. She and Theo, Rose's son, have been up since first light, and show no signs of flagging by church time, as they are engrossed in creating a small tinker homestead inside the dog's wooden castle. This folly, which David built a year ago when Lowly was small, fills the boot room and most of the hall. Lowly is now much too big to fit through any of its doors, but can be brought in over the battlements if bribed with cheese-flavoured crisps, his favourite form of nourishment. Anyway, The Beauty has made it her own, and I find her inside, with Theo and two pairs of chocolate ears, which suggest that bunny bodies have been devoured. Giles appears at another entrance as I squat and reach in, trying to grab a limb of either The Beauty or Theo, who have tucked themselves into the labyrinthine heart of the castle.

'Mum, please can I miss church, I just want to finish my book in peace.' Giles has put on his most long-suffering and yet wounded expression. I know just how he feels. In fact, I feel the same. Decide to be generous-spirited to him, as self must be sacrificed anyway.

'All right darling, go back to bed. But could you crawl in and get The Beauty out first?'

Squeaky laughter issues from the castle, followed by a cheery farewell. 'Bye bye Mummy, see you soon. Theo's such fun, isn't he?'

Suddenly perk up. I won't take her. She can stay here with Rose and eat chocolate. Church will be a sanctuary. A whole hour without toddlers or washing-up. See the light. This must be how people get religion. Find vast brown tweed coat of David's and put it on over my nightie. No time to get dressed now, and anyway, nightie is my favourite garment at the moment, as it is the only thing I have ever managed to dye, and is newly papal purple thanks to Dylon machine wash. Cannot believe that I have allowed so many years of my life to pass without experiencing the joy of dyeing clothes. In fact, I would have continued in this drab and grey existence, but for the happy accident which caused The Beauty to place a tub of dye in my shopping basket as I was selecting nails at the hardware shop. Great excitement and a ceremonial dipping followed, with each of us supplying one garment. Felix chose his school games shirt, and hurled it in before I noticed.

When discovered, he was defiant: 'It's the only white thing I've got. And anyway, it's too small so I can't wear it for school.' Giles tried not to join in at first, but was seduced by the velvet richness of the colour in the sink and brought a pair of boxer shorts to the dip.

'Fancy pants, fancy pants,' carolled The Beauty and Felix when we pulled the now violet underwear out on a wooden spoon.

The Beauty brought two dolls, a nappy, three vests and a pair of shorts to the laundry area, and managed to get all of them in and submerged without me noticing. Keep finding ultraviolet dolls lying around the garden looking as if they have had too much sun, or Ribena, or something. The nappy looks wonderful though. We dried it on the Aga and sent it to the manufacturers with a note saying, *Please can we have more like this one?* Have not yet received a reply.

Church with just Felix is a treat and we sing loudly and tunelessly at every opportunity. On the way out I force him to lend me his pocket money for the collection, and become convinced that a halo is budding above my head. Am moved to sing a Christmas carol in the car on the way home:

> Joy to the world
> And joy to you.

Particularly lovely to be singing as we whisk between hedgerows basking in the sunlit morning. Curling primrose leaves rise, new and crisp and green, from the banks, and also vivid spears of daffodil foliage and yellow trumpet flowers.

> Joy to the world
> And joy to you—

Erupting apparently out of the tarmac is a vast chrome-fronted truck; its bonnet rears above us and my foot flails for the brake. The truck swerves, tyres shrieking, engine roaring; my windscreen fills with bull bars and car bonnet, and all I can think is that this is just like the Dinosaur Death Run game in both mood and soundtrack. Felix bounces up in his seat, shouting excitedly, 'Look Mum, it's a Big Foot. Cool. Can we have one? Oww! Stop twisting my arm, we're quite safe, you know.'

Find I have involuntarily closed my eyes, and grasped Felix with one hand while wrestling to steer with the other, and maintaining a stream of foul language: 'Shit! Buggering hell and buckets of blood. Felix, are you sure you're all right? WATCH OUT!'

We have crashed. Not fatally, as we were only going about ten miles an hour, but firmly. Felix whistles under his breath. 'Yes Mum, I'm fine. Did you mean to do that handbrake turn? It was really excellent.'

The front end of the car is buried in the grassy bank, as if sniffing keenly at primroses, and the body of the car has slewed at ninety degrees across the road. The same has happened to the purple and yellow truck, but the front of his vehicle is facing the other way, so the driver-side windows are next to each other. We both lean out. I am shaking with shock, he is grinding his teeth, flaring his nostrils and flashing his eyes dangerously. In a minute I expect he will begin yanking his hair out by the roots. I say the first thing that comes into my head.

'Well I don't know why you're looking so angry. You could have killed us. And it's Easter Sunday.'

This is the wrong thing to say.

'Mum, it was your fault,' mutters Felix. 'You were on the wrong side of the road.'

Fortunately, the man does not hear this vital witness evidence as he is struggling to open his door and get out. This is impossible, as the vehicles are too close to one another. He hisses, 'Oh, for Christ's sake,' and slides over to the other side to get out of the passenger door. Hear him from beyond the truck cursing, 'This is absurd. How the hell did we get into this mess?'

He reappears in the driver's seat, and I notice that his eyebrows are long and thick and join in the middle like the bristles of an old-fashioned carpet sweeper. No wonder he looks so bad-tempered. He is also unshaven and has wild black hair sprouting around a thinly covered crown, and a very earthy-looking jacket with no sleeves, just trails of unravelling string around the armholes. Presume he is a son of the pig farmer down the road, and make a suggestion.

'What if you walk home and get someone to bring a tractor?'

'Why don't you?' he says, rudely.

Answer very reasonably, rather enjoying the sensation of maintaining calm good humour in the face of his wild wrath, 'Well, I haven't got a tractor, and anyway, your truck's in the way, and I wish you'd move it because I need to get home to cook lunch. We're having an Easter-egg hunt this afternoon.'

Felix has climbed out of the sunroof and is inspecting the bank behind me. I am certainly not getting out. A nightie is fine for church, but it's not my garment of choice for a traffic incident. Pull the tweed coat close about me, and wish it was fur. Would then feel grand and Cruella-like, and would be able to get the better of this rudester. His shirt is missing a couple of buttons and he has a melted-looking ring on his wedding finger. In fact, it looks very like one of the mourning rings made by Charles's company, Heavenly Petting. He grips his steering wheel and the skin on his knuckles seems to slide back until bone white shows. Decide not to ask him about the ring, he looks too cross. He leans towards me through the window again, eyes glinting, and says between clenched teeth, 'What makes you think I have a tractor?'

I am fed up with all this now, and just want to get home. Am beginning to think that this is not a junior pig farmer at all, but in fact a free-range psychopath, and am anxious to make my escape. Felix pokes his head in through my window like a traffic warden.

'Mum, if you go backwards first, you can do a three-million-point turn and get out. Hey, look. He's got one of Dad's Heavenly Petting rings. It's one of the ones I designed for small rodents. It costs three ninety-nine and you can buy it in Argos, Asda or any good pet shop.'

Felix is good on the Heavenly Petting sales mantra. I wonder if Charles gets him out on the road with him when he has the children for the weekend. I can just imagine him forcing Felix, Giles and The Beauty to wear ties and carry plastic briefcases full of his wares in order to go doorstepping in Cambridge. He wouldn't dare do it to the twins, Helena would never allow it, but as ex- rather than present wife, I have no power on weekends away.

Come back to the present to find Felix standing on the truck's running board, interviewing the driver about his dead animals. 'Oh, I see. It wasn't *your* guinea pig. It was your stepdaughter's. Did she get a ring for her cat when it died, or did she just go for a garden burial and nothing to commemorate? You know we've gone on the internet now. You can look it up. It's called deaddog?.com and I thought of it and we've registered it and . . .'

The psychopath is glowering and begins to mutter something about little bastards. It is time to go.

'Come on Felix, jump in,' I yell, and inclining my head graciously in a farewell gesture, I grind the gears to begin the three-thousand-point turn.

The psycho-pig starts and yells, 'Watch out. You'll tip over. You can't do—'

Oh, the joy of electric windows.

March 28th

The Easter-egg hangover lasted for three days, and I fear that flashbacks may occur for weeks. The Beauty, who has never been biddable, has become an addict. Her rear, clad in red polka-dot bloomers beneath her customary net tutu, is visible now from my window, as she sifts the garden stalk by stalk, on hands and knees, searching for yet more mini-eggs. Every so often she finds one, and there is a whoop of joy followed by a satisfied silence while she consumes it. This new-found greed makes the garden a wonderful giant playpen for her. She has no desire to follow Lowly and Digger on a dustbin trail, even though she generally enjoys this treasure-seeking mission, nor did she try to get into the postman's van this morning with Rags, who never likes to miss an outing.

I am able to achieve much domestic satisfaction by repainting the downstairs loo. It is now cream with garnet-coloured woodwork, and looks very Red Cross and businesslike. Become aware, when debating whether to wash the brushes or just leave them to rot in a jam jar of white spirit, along with twenty or so other paintbrush corpses in similar jars, that this is deluxe and advanced work avoidance. Usually find that a bit of mucking out in the kitchen is enough to keep me from my desk, but since Easter have begun to see that clearing up is as bad as work, so have left it and moved on. Hope vaguely that the debris will all just disappear eventually, in the way that unwashed hair goes through the greasy stage and comes out the other side renewed and full of vim. Wonder how long it takes?

March 30th

The Beauty sleeps late this morning, and I'm not surprised. From midnight until three a.m. she was busy reorganising my underwear drawer and conducting a one-woman fashion show. I tried smoothing the pillow for her and turning the light out, but was met with stentorian commands through the darkness at ear level.

'Light on now, Mummy, or else.'

Where has she learned this awful threatening vocabulary? Must encourage her to watch more improving television such as *Teletubbies*, I think.

Finally convinced her to lie down in my bed with me, and four lumpy, cold plastic dolls, her companions for every breath she takes at the moment. She spent the remaining small hours swinging her feet and then her knees and then her dolls into me with the regularity of a clock pendulum. I fell asleep as dawn broke, and just in time to be jerked awake by the alarm clock at seven. Not sure how the boys got to school, as head feels as if it is sewn on backwards today, but cannot go on allowing them to drink Coke and eat cheese on toast for every meal.

Have still not managed to clean the kitchen, and have thus lost the cheering Easter card David sent to all of us. It vanished beneath an avalanche of papers somewhere on the table, where a substratum of stickiness acts as a deterrent to any movement of stuff when the kitchen door is open and fresh, green-smelling spring air pours in. Housewifery has deserted me. Open the fridge and notice Giles's cricket socks in there. Just cannot think where else I might put them, so shut door again, leaving them there.

March 31st

All is not well. I suspect David of having found new love. Undoubtedly young, certainly without gout, and probably wearing a silver bikini and mirrored Moroccan mules with pale blue linings as seen in the magazine I am toying with in the hairdresser. I am in Blow 'n' Glow in Cromer, a salon famous among local pensioners for its tinted rinses, and entirely lacking in photographs of fabulous-looking models with cutting-edge hairstyles. I am not having a tinted rinse, although the notion is beginning to appeal, the longer I sit and look at my pale face, lugubrious expression and lank hanks of hair being teased into order by Cheyenne, the troll-like stylist. I have succumbed to middle age and am having a blow-dry. With hairspray. It is very awful to find myself doing this, but how else am I to look presentable for this evening? Vivienne and her husband Simon have asked me to go with them to the Hunt Ball. They are always invited because Simon is a farmer, but I have not done anything so recherché since I was in the Pony Club, and am looking forward to the evening with some dread. Tried to get out of it on the grounds that my mother is coming to stay, as she needs a rest cure from The Basket Weaver, a barefoot hippy who keeps a caravan in her garden, and who is hosting a workshop for the Pedal to Paradise lobby. But Vivienne just says, 'Good, she can babysit.' As if life is ever that uncomplicated. However, on this occasion, it seems to be.

'It's so ghastly,' moans my mother when she arrives, somewhat dishevelled and wearing only one shoe. 'I've had to leave home. And I couldn't find my other shoe. I think Egor must have taken it, he seems to be embracing fetishism in old age. Yes, of course I'll babysit, anything to keep me away from pious Peta.'

Egor, the bullet-brained bull terrier, bounces into the kitchen, his claws clicking on the tiles, his tongue lolling like a pervert, in search of sustenance as always. I shrink to the other side of the kitchen and continue to apply a layer of vibrant pink nail polish called Siren to my toes. Am trying to do this without being seen by The Beauty, who adores nail polish, and will want to do her own, and the toes of all her babies too.

'Egor's gone yellow,' notices Giles, who is passing through on his way to the larder, but my mother is too distraught to rise to this faint criticism of her beloved.

'I know, darling. It's age. We must try Biotex next time we bath him.' She unwraps a new packet of cigarettes with the practised ease displayed by a croupier opening a deck of cards in a Las Vegas casino, and lights one before continuing, 'That woman is a menace. She's trying to construct a basket-weave yurt for Desmond's wedding reception. I don't know how to stop her, and he particularly said he was having a perfectly normal tent, so he'll be rude to her, which I just can't stand. And when she's not designing that, she's busy bullying me to give up my car. She's found some hopeless man to be her boyfriend and she makes him dress up in a gold diving suit, with a helmet like a goldfish bowl, and sends him off to walk to Aylsham wearing a placard saying, *Cut out the car crap – pedal to paradise.*'

'So why doesn't she make him ride a bicycle instead of walking, Granny? Hasn't he got one?' Giles is back, eating a cold sausage and a hard-boiled egg, so he won't need supper in my view. Granny is much struck by this question. She turns to face Giles and fixes him with an intent, gimlet-like expression. The Beauty appears in the doorway like Isadora Duncan, trailing three pastel chiffon scarves and wearing a hair band with fluffy antennae, a small pink-headed doll clasped to her bosom.

'Oooh, Mummyyy, nails! Polish me. Polish my baby. Oooooooh, Mummmyyy,' she yells, charging towards me.

I leap like a limber goat or sheep on to the table, shrieking, 'Grab her, Giles. Quick.'

Granny remains impervious to the new layer of chaos in the kitchen. 'Why indeed, Giles? Why indeed? I think you've provided me with some ammunition to use against St Peta at last. Thank God. She keeps trying to make me ride that old bicycle of The Gnome's, and hiding the keys to my car. I was only allowed to drive here today because I told her Egor has a heart condition, and she's on every animal awareness committee in existence.' Granny pauses for a second, then adds a final lament: 'Oh, how I wish The Gnome hadn't gone to live on Uist, he was a much easier lodger. Planets are so much less annoying than baskets to have around the place. They take up so little room.' Granny takes a comforting puff of her cigarette and, like her dog, looks around for sustenance.

'The sun appears to be over the yardarm now, Venetia,' she says, glancing at the clock, 'so how about a small glass of something?'

'I've just got to finish these,' I whisper, waving a set of neon-pink toenails at her and keeping my voice down so as not to alert The Beauty, who has gone with Giles to make a larder raid. 'Help yourself.'

With the first sip of wine, a pleasant thought occurs to my mother, and she smirks, 'Don't let me forget to tell Peta that you are going to the Hunt Ball. She'll be horrified. Such a shame David isn't here to go with you. Although maybe he's anti-hunting. What do you think?'

'I must go and change.' I rush from the room, not wishing to speak of David the Rat. Would not have had to go to ancients' hairdresser or bother to paint toenails this early in the year if David hadn't rung at crack of dawn to say his plans have changed. He sounds distant, which is understandable, but distracted.

'I'm not going to be back home at the end of next month, I'm afraid, and I'm not sure when I will be able to come home. The thing is, I'm going to the Brazilian jungle to build sets for a massive new Tarzan film. I was incredibly lucky. The guy they originally hired to do it has got malaria and has had to be taken off the job at the last minute.'

'Doesn't sound to me as if you're lucky, it sounds to me as if you're about to get malaria,' I interrupt in Doom Queen mode. He scarcely hears me, though; he is finishing his spiel.

'I hate leaving you for so long, but it's fantastic money and a really great project. We'll all be able to live in clover when I come back.'

An expectant pause follows, which I am clearly supposed to fill with, 'How wonderful, clever old you.'

Instead I just say, 'God, I can't think of anywhere more horrible than the Brazilian jungle. If you don't get malaria you'll be bitten by a snake or a tiger. Can't you say no?'

David's voice is frosted glass as he replies, speaking very slowly as if to an alien, 'They don't have tigers in South America. Look Venetia, I'm not going to say no because I really want to do this. It's a chance to get into film work and I can't turn it down. It will be the right thing for all of us in the long run, I promise you. Please don't make a scene. After all, it won't be for more than a few months, and we can speak on the phone. We can get you hooked up on to email, too.' My jaw sets in Desperate Dan solidity, and I muster all my determination in order not to make a scene and not to cry.

'Fine. Good. Have a lovely time and we'll speak soon.' I am pretty pleased with this as a last line, and quickly slam the phone down. A few months in Brazil in the jungle. He must be mad. Or it's a ruse to disguise his new romance with a nubile film star. And is it surprising that he craves a new life when the height of my weekly achievements is a visit to the hairdresser? Having half decided not to go, I am now determined to attend the Hunt Ball for three reasons:

1 To show that I can.
2 To meet and flirt with men in red coats.
3 To be able to drop snippets about these fantasy flirtations and a long list of new male admirers airily into my next telephone conversation with David.

Have arrived at the hunt ball, where I am failing utterly to flirt with anyone in a red coat. They all have red faces to match, and are either bobbing about in vats of alcohol, or chasing the teenage girls who are selling raffle tickets around the room. Had not reckoned on anyone here looking fashionable, and am thus vastly put out to walk slap into Bronwyn Butterstone, a school mother whom I loathe, wearing the same dress as I am. Face to face at the bar, her prominent blue eyes bulge towards me in my long, pink-sequinned tube with purple fluff at hem and décolletage, and my own orbs bulge back at her.

'Oh, Venetia, it is you, isn't it? I'm never sure,' she shrieks, and I am irritated to note the flatness of her stomach, but remark some flab on the underarm to savour.

However, do not wish my own body to be scrutinised, so mutter, 'Gosh Bronwyn, great minds think alike,' before scuttling away behind my feather boa which I have positioned as if it is a fig leaf and I am Eve.

Find Vivienne talking to the Master of the Hunt, who has assumed the glassy, blissed-out look that all men, particularly those in positions of authority, get when they talk to Vivienne. She is suitably sympathetic, and dismisses the Master with smooth good manners before following me towards the door where I am skulking.

'Poor you, I'm sure Bronwyn feels awful too, and particularly as you look so great in it.'

'Not as great as her,' I wail, dragging Vivienne out into the dark and across to the ladies' Portaloo. 'Come on, we'll have to adapt it.'

I arrange myself expectantly, standing on the loo seat, looking down at Vivienne. She turns me round in a full circle, frowning, then dips into her handbag

39

to pull out a tiny pair of scissors. So brilliant, just like a Georgette Heyer character. I am charmed.

'Wow, a reticule full of useful things.'

Vivienne snaps the air with the scissors, giving an impression of utter competence at dress redesign in public lavatories.

'Let's cut it off above your knees, and tie your boa around your neck like a choker,' she suggests sadistically. Have no choice but to comply, but for me the evening never recovers, and my knees, which I was not expecting to have on show, become a preoccupation. The purple velvet boots from the charity shop which seemed beyond chic when peeping from beneath a long dress, now contribute to my Euro-vision Song Contest look and make me feel like a New Seeker.

As the dances slow, and the red coats lasso their now intoxicated prey into cheek-to-cheek shufflings on the dance floor, my eyelids begin to droop and I could weep if I had drunk more, so great is my long-ing for David to be there to take me home. I am deeply relieved when Vivienne and Simon at last approach, holding hands in a touching manner which only contributes to my big-kneed ugly-sister feeling. I should have brought a date. I shouldn't have come here alone. David should have been here.

Teeter out behind Simon and Vivienne, nursing self-pity as we thread through the long grass and cow pats. I am tired, sober and relieved to be leaving with-out having injured myself. The only glimmer on the horizon is that Bronwyn Butterstone has been removed in an ambulance, having fallen off the dance floor and into a pothole. I did not see this, being too mesmerised by the sight of the blacksmith, who is the size of three usual human beings, on the Bucking Bronco and then upside down with his legs wiggling like a vast beetle, on the giant mattress on the floor. Vivienne fills me in.

'She's sprained her ankle quite badly, and Brian, her husband, is furious because he'll have to look after the children on his own.' She pauses to negotiate a deep rut in the ground, then continues: 'He was even crosser when he realised she was so drunk she couldn't even feel any pain.'

'But she will after they've operated,' I point out, forcing my face out of its spreading smile with some difficulty.

'She is going to feel so foolish in the morning,' remarks Vivienne, and both of us shake our heads, revelling in our own sobriety. Wish I had a crocheted shawl around my shoulders to complete the effect of ascetic old harridan, or else a vast bottle of whisky to glug, to anaesthetise myself from the gruelling effects of rural debauchery.

Thumping music and the shrieks of those unwise enough to have a go on the electric Bucking Bronco accompany us out through crisp darkness to the car park, where orange licks the windscreens in small tongues of reflected light from guttering wax flares.

Simon is ahead of us, shouting back, 'There'll be a bit of a frost tonight, but not enough to worry the blossom. Now where's our damned car?' He suddenly stops, and exclaims to the ground 'Goodness. Who's there? Do you need a light?' Peering past him, I dimly detect a black hump moving about on the grass. Vivienne and I sweep up our skirts, or what is left of them, tilt our noses skywards and prepare to walk past this drunkard without a second glance. Simon can never resist a chance to boss someone around, and squats next to this hapless soul, intent on helping him find his feet. Much heavy sighing from me and Vivienne, shivering in our feather boas. I am particularly cold owing to the lack of knee coverage, and wish I had kept the extra length of stretchy fabric to wrap round my legs like a muff in the car, instead of throwing it into the bushes behind the Portaloo. We lean on the car bonnet, clucking and becoming more crabby and old ladyish by the minute.

'Why can't Simon just mind his own business,' sighs Vivienne. Sighing turns to catlike hissing when Simon approaches us with the man.

'This is Hedley Sale. Hedley, my wife Vivienne and our friend Venetia Summers.'

Can't see the point of shaking hands with someone so drunk they have been crawling about at my feet, so ignore the stranger and address Simon crossly. 'Come on Simon, we're freezing . . .' Tail off as Vivienne nudges me and nods her head towards the stranger, who is trying to shake hands with us. He starts to speak in tongues.

'Cum redeunt, titubant et sunt spectacula vulgi, et fortunato obvia turba vocat.'

The whites of his eyes gleam blue in the moonlight and I struggle to remember whether this is a sign of health or lunacy.

'What's going on, Venetia? Who is this man?' Vivienne whispers, interrupting Simon, who overrides her with his loud translation of the tongues.

'Ovid.' He scratches his head, presumably to stimulate his brain cells. 'Something about staggering home and a sight to behold,' he says reflectively. 'Funny, I haven't heard that for years, but recognised it instantly—' He is interrupted by the drunkard, who is doing English now.

'And the crowds that meet them call them privileged.' He turns to Simon. 'Yes, Ovid. It's the springtime orgy, which was held in mid-March. The point of it was to get very drunk, as the theory was that each drink prolonged your life.'

Simon has unlocked the car now, and I am halfway in, but can't resist muttering: 'Well, not much has changed, but I'd like to go home before I die of cold rather than lack of alcohol.' I sound about as glamorous and well read as the chief jam-maker of the Women's Institute, but am long past caring. Simon pushes me on to the back seat, then directs the sozzled loony to sit next to me. He settles down, and leaning back he closes his eyes and prepares for slumber.

Simon, avuncular to the last, pats my knee and whispers, 'He's lost his car keys in the grass, so I said we'd give him a lift home as he's practically your next-door neighbour, Venetia. In fact, I'm surprised you haven't met before.'

I am not surprised. I am not in the habit of hanging around speaking Latin on street corners, or rather in fields. Feel nervously out of my depth and wiggle as far from him as possible while trying to pull the shreds of dress down to knee level.

'Nice legs,' he says, in English, and I realise that his eyes are not shut at all, but that he has been watching me trying to organise myself, *and* that I have met him before. He is the car-crash man.

APRIL

April 3rd

Sensation of utter uselessness has enveloped me. Have noticed that I have started hanging around in doorways a lot, but never seem to make my way into any room to do any particular thing. The kitchen means cooking and clearing up, but any inspiration for cooking has long since departed, along with creative supermarket shopping. And anyway, Giles has entered a phase of fussiness and autocracy last demonstrated by him in toddlerhood, and will only eat steak, pasta or Grape Nuts. He is not offered steak, so his diet has been whittled down to Grape Nuts at either end of the day with pasta and Parmesan in between. With nothing green passing his lips, he will soon resemble a maggot or worse. Or perhaps he will become a millionaire and write a book called *The White Diet*. In fact, it could be quite balanced to eat only white food – after all, there's sliced bread, milk, pasta, cream cheese, fish, chicken, the occasional anaemic Chinese leaf, onions, white chocolate . . . It doesn't sound at all bad. I shall observe Giles closely for a month to see if it makes a difference. Can't help wishing Charles was the kind of ex-husband I could telephone to talk to about such matters. But my only attempt to do so, when Giles's start-of-holiday door-slamming became unbearable at Christmas, was met with a response so inadequate I cannot be bothered to try again. Charles may have been in a meeting on this occasion, but he is always in meetings, and half of them are with the sports channel on the radio. Anyway, he came on the line crackling with irritation that Minna, Desmond's then girlfriend, now fiancée, who works for him, had put me through to him.

'Make it brief, Venetia,' he said testily. I deliberately didn't.

'Hello Charles, how are you? Yes, I'm very well, thank you for asking. I just wanted to have a conversation with you about—'

He interrupted me, fuming. 'I simply haven't got time. I'll send the cheque,' and that was it. I know now that I am on my own in parenting, but at least I used to have David to support me.

It is late morning now, and I am still loitering in the hall, reluctant to go into my study or upstairs to make beds. From here, my view of the knot garden ripples in the old, stretched glass of the front door, then comes crisply into line through the abutting new pane, replaced when Giles was over-vigorous with a cricket ball. The ducks waddle past, leaving a trail of darker green through the grey sparkle of dew on the grass, and remind me that I have not fed them. It's too late now, though; they are off to the water meadows for the day, and will only return at dusk, following the same trajectory that they have just described. Leaning my forehead on the window pane to glimpse the last waggling tail as they stay in strict formation to scramble through the hedge, I am still rooted when the last of them has vanished between a cluster of primroses and sharp new iris leaves.

The Beauty started at nursery school today, and this rite of passage must have something to do with the cotton-wool-and-rag-doll version of life I am experiencing. I lingered when delivering her at nine o'clock, unused to the notion of a morning without her gnomic assistance with my daily tasks. Through hanging around, I was able to meet her classmates, including the redoubtable Timmy, a toddling cross-dresser. The Beauty was enchanted when Timmy arrived in her new classroom, executed a delightful curtsy and announced to the assembled children and the small mousy teacher, 'It's time for Timmy to dress up.'

He then applied himself to the dressing-up box, and was swiftly transformed into a middle-aged matron, complete with black patent shoes with bows and a floral nylon dress, perma-pleated and sporting a bigger pussy-cat bow at the neck. Thus clad, Timmy set about the nursery's toy kitchen, announcing gladly, 'I'll be Hannibal the Cannibal when I grow up, and eat everyone's *gizzards*.' Gruesome, but effective. The Beauty could hardly tear herself away to say goodbye to me, so keen was she to be crammed into the oven by darling Timmy. I crossed the road to the car, longing to have the potato-sack weight of The Beauty lagging behind, dragging me back by the hand when I try to leave school each morning after dropping off Giles and Felix.

It is difficult to keep up with the changing heart of motherhood, which yesterday morning had me bellowing, 'God, I wish you could go to boarding school,' at my precious tiny girl, who in a high-spirited moment had dabbed a few blobs of nail polish on the dog's paws and surrounding carpet.

Reach home full of good intentions as far as both work and domestic efficiency are concerned, and find the answerphone flashing with a message from Rose.

'Hello, Venetia, I'm sorry not to have rung before to thank you for the lovely Easter break, but life has been crazy. I just wanted to say that Theo's got hand, foot and mouth disease. I'm really sorry. It's extremely contagious, and there's nothing you can do except administer Calpol. I do hope none of yours gets it. Bye.'

Mental inventory of all the children's many physical blemishes yields the conviction that all of them are riddled with this vile-sounding plague. Am rather impressed by Rose's *sang-froid*, and long to emulate it, but a glance at the medical dictionary which David bought at a car boot sale is discouraging.

The child will develop blisters in the mouth, on the hands and the soles of the feet. These are likely to cause considerable pain. There is no cure.

Decide to go and see my mother, who will know what to do and may have some sort of witchy prescription for the poor little infectees.

The kitchen table at my mother's house has vanished beneath a landslide of envelopes and cardboard purple hearts. My mother and Desmond, both wearing spectacles and expressions of demented determination, are sitting side by side, confronting this mountain.

'I'm sure we've done Minna's aunt,' says my mother, smoothing her hand over a foothill of purple hearts with the effect of transforming it into a torrent which rushes on to the floor. My mother pays no attention to the cascade of invitations but muses, 'I did her envelope as well, I can remember her address.'

Desmond has a small address book on his knee and is referring to it, muttering under his breath, 'Bastard, bastard. Why do we have to have invitations? Can't we just put up a few flyers and have a guest list on the door?'

Leaning over his shoulder, I pick up a clutch of hearts. 'These are lovely invitations. What a brilliant idea to have purple hearts.'

'Yes, but I think people will get the wrong idea,' frowns my mother, pushing back her chair and lighting a cigarette which she retrieves from behind her ear. 'Purple hearts are downers, after all, and we don't want anyone thinking this is a depressing occasion.'

Desmond sees this as a signal for a break, and stands up to put the kettle on, his quiff of hair brushing the low ceiling of the cottage kitchen.

'I keep telling you,' he shouts, goaded by exasperation into making coffee for all of us instead of just himself, 'none of my generation was around in the sixties. We were innocent children playing with Action Man, while you were acting out your crazy fantasies. None of us took purple hearts. They just weren't for us. Neither was acid. It's just your gang of tripped-out old hippies we'll have to look out for. Or what's left of them, rather.' He turns to me, slopping milk into a mug with two spoonfuls of instant coffee, his raised eyebrow a command to listen, as he cranks himself further into righteous mode.

'You know, I reckon at least half of Mum's friends from the sixties have fried their brains with some substance or other. Look at The Gnome – what planet must he be on to want to go and live on a rock off the coast of Scotland? Apparently he's got a teepee instead of his caravan now.'

Mention of The Gnome brings mistiness to my mother's eyes, and she absently ignites another cigarette, forgetful of the one she already has smouldering in her bull-terrier-shaped ashtray.

'I like teepees,' she muses. 'They're better than Peta's yurt, at any rate. At least they're small.' She gazes into the middle distance, then jumps up. 'Oh, how I wish I still had The Gnome here. That woman Peta is driving me insane. She's put a healing arch up by the stream and she's decorating it with cottonwool blobs and red felt. She says it's going to be the centre-piece for a festival to celebrate the cat.' She pauses and drags on her cigarette with feeling. 'The *cat*, for heaven's sake. It would be different if it were the bull terrier, or even The Beauty, but *cats* – who cares? I wish she'd just stick to basket-weaving.'

'And I wish you'd stick to your job of sending invitations,' snaps Desmond. 'You know we've got to get the whole lot in the post tonight, before Minna gets here, and we're seeing the vicar in a minute.'

Anxious not to get back home to do any work, I offer to help and am given my own small pile of purple hearts. I do three in a quick burst of efficiency, then, exhausted, slow down to read the wording.

Yelp and drop my pile.

'Mum, Desmond, there's a mistake. Why has it got my address on it? I thought you were having the wedding here. What's going on? It must be a typing error.'

My mother sidles towards the dresser to find glasses and ashtrays for the vicar, should he require them. She smirks at me unapologetically, and directs a look of faux reproach at Desmond.

'Oh, Desmond, I thought you'd told Venetia.' Her pretence at anger is transparent. I drum my fingers on the table and wait to hear what she has to say. She blinks, piously, several times and says, 'We've decided it's best to have the party at your house because the garden is flatter than this one for the tent. We told Giles, when we came over to look and you were out somewhere. He must have forgotten to pass it on. It'll be such fun for you, darling, and it'll look so pretty.'

Desmond rushes over, hurling himself down on one knee, his eyes drooping meekly, hands clasping mine.

'Oh please, most wonderful sister, don't say no. I meant to ask you, I kept meaning to ask you, and suddenly it mattered too much, and I couldn't risk asking you in case you said no.'

I swat him away impatiently. 'Oh God, please don't touch me. I need to think. I can't believe you did this, you two, it's so unscrupulous.' My mother simpers, attempting a look of innocence and extreme scrupulousness and managing only to look cross-eyed. I am utterly pole-axed by the nerve of them, but also obscurely flattered. My own wedding, without the bother of being the bride. Cannot make out whether this is a good thing or not, but the bite and the fight have been knocked out of me.

'Oh, well, I suppose it's too late to do anything, so I haven't any choice. The invitations are all printed, and you've even sent some already, haven't you?' My mother nods, head on one side, doing her meek look. I shall get some form of reprisal. I must. I have achieved all the H surnames on the list, and am looking forward to I, which only contains one person, a mysterious-sounding 'Incie Wincie I-Boy', who lives 'c/o White City Greyhound Stadium', when there is a knock on the door and the Reverend Trevor Heel slithers in past a cacophony of barking, licking dogs. He, unlike any of the canines, is wearing a collar, and it peeps crisply above his grey flannel shirt.

'Good morning my dears, good morning,' he beams, patting dogs and sniffing as if to get his bearings in the noisy, smoky kitchen. He is a big fan of my mother, and has brought her a piece of the Wookey

Hole as a memento of his recent visit there. Of course my mother uses his arrival as an opportunity to get the sherry out, and the pair of them lean on the rail of the smoke-blackened Rayburn, chatting and dodging the extended limbs and tails of sleeping cats and drying washing festooned on the rack above.

'The new master of Crumbly has agreed to let the church hold the biannual car boot sale there this year,' says Reverend Heel, sipping his sherry as elegantly as a man can when it is presented in a half-pint beer mug. 'He's a chap called Sale, Hedley Sale. He was old Peter Crumb's nearest relation, some sort of nephew, I understand. You may have met him, Venetia, he's your neighbour more than ours, really, isn't he?' and Rev. Trev dimples at me and pats a wisp of his grey hair back down across his brow. He continues, 'I'm glad to see the place alive again, although no one seems to know if he'll be living here full-time or not. He may go back to America to continue teaching. It's a shame he can't do it here.'

'What does he teach?' asks my mother, more interested in whether there's any more sherry now that Desmond and I have helped ourselves, than in the man who owns all the fields and woodland we like to walk in.

'I think he teaches Latin and Greek at an American university,' said the vicar, 'I'm not sure which one. But certainly it's the classics. Your subject, Araminta, if I remember rightly.' He throws a twinkling glance towards my mother, positively roguish except that he waves an arm as well, and becomes entangled in a trailing and ragged towel from the rack above him, and somehow gets the end in his mouth. Desmond and I exchange a look. Araminta indeed. No one has called my mother anything so informal in years. She perks up no end upon hearing that Hedley Sale teaches classics.

'Oh, good. A classicist is just what we need around here,' she says, as if it were very useful to the community, like being a fireman or a childminder. 'I should like to meet him.'

I am about to say that I have met him, and to give a graphic description of both my encounters with this paragon, when Desmond interrupts, clicking the heel of his cowboy boot irritably, and snapping his fingers in a bid for attention.

'Look Mum, I think we need to get this playlist sorted out.' My mother and the vicar look at him blankly.

'He means the order of service,' I translate, moving towards the door. 'I've got to go, but will you remember that Minna's most favourite song in the world is "Jolene", by Dolly Parton, and try to incorporate it? Maybe it could be instead of the usual Wedding March at the beginning, or what about during the signing of the register? God, I wonder if Minna will wear a red wig? And are you dressing as Elvis, Desmond?' He grins, pushing me away, whispering, 'Let's get this bit over and we'll talk later.'

My mother, humming 'Abide with Me', sidles over to the sherry bottle. I close the door as she trills, 'More sherry, Trevor?'

April 7th

Everyone is talking about Hedley Sale. Even Mrs Organic Veg, who I always thought was above such things, arrives on her moped with my delivery of spring greens, cabbage, onions and potatoes. Always anxious for a diversion from work, I rush out to help her carry the precious, mud-caked items into the larder.

'Lovely day, isn't it?' I say, as I always do, even if it's raining, as it is some kind of social reflex with me and anyone who arrives to deliver something.

She wipes her hands on a big cloth she keeps in the box on the back of her moped and looks up at the sloppy sky.

'Could be worse,' she agrees cautiously. 'It was better yesterday, though. The sun came out just as we were meeting with the new Mr Sale. It went very well.' She pauses for effect, and I deliver the expected encouragement.

'Oh yes, what did he say?'

She continues, 'We were only talking about the land we rent, and he offered us the walled garden as well. It's just what we need.' Another pause.

'So what was he like?'

'He was a bit excitable, a bit prone to shout when he saw some boys walking round the lake. We had to remind him it's a public footpath, in fact. But he was nice enough to us.' Rags wiggles over to sit on her feet and she bends to pat her, adding, 'I've heard his wife ran off with another woman, but you'd never think it, would you? Unless she just couldn't bear his temper.'

I agree, without knowing what you wouldn't think, and return to my study to write a document on the way people spend their money in shopping malls. This is the most lucrative piece of work I have ever been offered, and also the most boring. It outstrips conference brochures by miles for tedium, and is responsible for my work-avoidance techniques becoming refined to the point of insanity. Standing in doorways leads to close examination of the backs of my hands, to be followed, when I am about to burst due to the build-up of disorganisation in my life, with a medley of unnecessary telephone calls to people's answerphones. If I accidentally telephone anyone who is in, I tend to put the phone down. They then employ 1471 and ring back, puzzled, a few moments later. I think there is another number you can dial to stop anyone knowing it is you who has rung, but I shrink from making use of this, as it is the stuff of perverts and maniacs.

April 10th

David has contributed most wonderfully to my work-avoidance programme, by organising access to the information superhighway. He and Giles have sorted it all out in a series of expensive phone calls, and they even got Charles to give me one of his old computers, which is little short of a miracle. It was delivered last week, and we have made great strides in getting it out of its box and up and running with some shooting and chasing games favoured by the boys.

I have to choose whether to have my email brought to me by Virgin or Demon, Sonnet or Silence. It all sounds so poetic, and romantic. David and I will communicate across the time zones in a highly modern and up-to-date fashion. We will be like the people you see in car and mobile phone advertisements on television, dressed in taupe and slate with lots of hair gel, smiling into green-screened computers as we download crucial documents and send them on. I'm not sure where to.

Finally select Angel as my delivery company, and persuade them to let me have 'heavenlybody@Angel. com' as my email address. I am delighted with my amusing and original idea, until I realise how silly I sound giving this address out to the various corporations I work for. David laughs when I ring him to tell him I have the technology and the address all ready to go.

'You'll get the hang of it very soon. And Giles and Felix will know what to do if you get in a muddle. But I think you should change your email address to something less provocative. You'll attract some very odd mail if you give it out indiscriminately.'

'But I can't. It took hours of nightmare on the telephone to the helpline to get that one, and I've given it to loads of people already. It'll just have to be fine. Or you'll have to come back and change it for me.'

He answers in the dead straight, very serious, smoky-voiced way I love, 'You know I would if I could.'

What is it about distance that brings resentment so powerfully to the forefront of a relationship? And is it just me, or is David also feeling resentful, but hiding it better?

Battle to keep truculence out of my voice as I ask, 'Well, are you coming back for Desmond and Minna's wedding?' But it is hard, as I am convinced that the answer will be no.

The line buzzes and snaps with distance and the strain of the connection, but through it he answers, 'Well, I was going to surprise you, but actually, I can't bear not to tell you. Yes, I am. I've got a week—' The line blips and dies. I haven't had a chance to tell him that the wedding is going to be here, but it doesn't matter. I'm sure he'll love it.

Dance around the kitchen singing hooray, hooray with The Beauty, who is taking after her grandmother as a reveller, and pronounces, 'Let's have a party.' She swiftly removes all her clothes and replaces them with an old nightie and a vest covered with pink sequins, bought at a recent jumble sale.

'Do dancing, Mummy,' she commands, bobbing about in circles like a shuttlecock in her ragged lacy nightdress, undeterred by the lack of music. I obey, doing just as she tells me, anxious to avoid confrontation and thus leave myself free to think.

The knot garden is waterlogged and swamplike, everywhere else is a mudbath, and there are no flowers anywhere to be seen. In the house squalor reigns, no one has made their bed or picked up any clothes since Easter. There are half-empty baked bean and tuna fish cans in the fridge, as well as certain items of sports equipment, and ants and hens (living, not oven-ready) in the larder, all testament to the slobsville level our domestic set-up has reached. Worst of all, neither Lowly nor The Beauty show any sign of becoming house- or potty-trained. The wedding is on May Day, in three weeks' time. David will be back in twenty days. We must make efforts to improve by then. Surely it is possible?

April 12th

Improvements are making everything a hundred times worse, and very much more expensive. Last week I had an ad hoc underwater garden and lots of nice places for the ducks. This week, although the rain has stopped, and the blue sky is like a clear conscience, the scene at ground level is frightful to behold. At the suggestion of Simon, who couldn't resist popping in for a bit of bossing on his way to a potato conference, I have hired a pump to suck all the unwanted water out of my garden. The pump arrives, a malevolent mound of grey metal and rubber reminding me powerfully of the rabbit intestines Lowly and Rags left in the kitchen this morning.

It is delivered on an unnecessarily large lorry, while I am trapped on the telephone, unable to suggest a fitting place for it to be dumped. The driver heads unerringly across the lawn, the only part of the garden looking remotely nice, and dumps the pump in a bush as far away from the flood as it is possible to be in this garden. He then reverses back to the gate, not covering his tracks, and drives off, leaving the lawn decorated with four bolts of herringbone-tweed indentation. Giles and I, assisted by The Beauty in her red mackintosh and bare feet, very excited because she thought the pump was the Teletubbies' Noo Noo, manage to work out how to turn the thing on, and wrestle with its stinking tubes, dragging them to reach a corner of the flooded knot garden. Flick the switch to start the suction programme and am suddenly in a mudbath.

Jump about shrieking.

'Oh my God. Oh damn. Giles, quick, it's the wrong way, it's pumping out, not in! Buggering hell, I'm filthy.' Am indeed coated with darkest gunge, but find it strangely liberating, so stop whingeing and get on with trying to angle the pump correctly. The Beauty capers about falling into mud and laughing while trilling her new set of swear words, 'Damn, damn and bugger, bugger. Oh my God.'

'Oh my *word*,' I correct her, automatically. She shoots me a filth-coated look and repeats, 'OHMIGOD' in a football chant over and over again. Giles is writhing about with the pipe, like Hercules with the Hydra, or was it Pericles? Just cannot remember anything any more. Never mind, it is something to ask Hedley Sale when we next bump into him.

Wonderful gurgling and squelching sounds indicate that Giles has vanquished the wrong flow, and the knot garden lake begins to subside. Giles and I, both resembling Fungus the Bogeyman in skin colour and scent, stand over the pump, fascinated, as it vacuums up the water.

'Is this what it would be like to work in a sewage plant?' asks Giles, and I nod.

'Yes, I suppose so, but without the smell.'

'Cool,' he says, and I wonder whether I should be encouraging him in a more white-collar direction.

Later

Felix zooms up to the window of my study where I have just written the first sentence of the day, extolling the joys and virtues of shopping malls.

'Mummy, quick, the pump is thirsty, it's run out of water. I think it's going to be sick.'

Jump up, delighted to have a valid reason to escape.

'Gosh, well done for noticing, Felix, I'd forgotten all about it. Let's go and have a look.' Follow him round to the knot garden, where a high-pitched whining accompanies a lot of smoke rising from the pump. Just as we reach the machine, the whining falters and drops rapidly in pitch to nought. An ominous silence ensues, broken by the bustling arrival of The Beauty and her pram.

'Look, Mummy, it's broken.' She points at the back of the pump, and a crack from which a treacle-dark ooze of water bleeds.

April 13th

Driving to the dentist on a glittering spring morning, we woosh through the puddles making the car even more disgustingly filthy than it already is, but delighting The Beauty, who drums her feet against my seat back and shrieks, 'Faster in the river, Mummy, faster right now.' We do 'faster right now' with disastrous consequences. The car splutters and dies in the middle of a dark and deep-looking puddle.

'You've flooded it, Mum,' says Giles, availing himself of the opportunity to sigh heavily and roll his eyes.

'We'll just have to wait until it dries out.' I am serene. The nine o'clock news has not yet come on to the radio, so we are in good time and can afford to loll around in puddles looking at the geese flocked in the wheat field next to us. The young corn shoots are vibrant green in the sun's path, but fade to grey where the cloud casts a deep shadow, causing some of the geese to appear celestial and the others to seem drab. Recall reading that it was ancient country practice for goose girls to take flocks behind the threshing machines and to steer them about through the harvested fields of yore, and would rather like to put myself forward for such a picturesque career now. The Beauty and I could work in tandem. Perhaps Simon will employ us this autumn? Musings brought to an untimely halt by horrible roaring in the back. Felix is writhing in agony, his hair twisted around The Beauty's fists and his chest drummed by her little feet.

'Ssshh. Let's see if we can will the car to start,' I say, in the manner of a playgroup leader. Giles glances witheringly at me, but Felix is silenced, and praise the Lord, the car coughs then hums into action, just as the news pips sound from the radio.

April 14th

Have still not found the opportunity to tell David that the wedding is to be held here. All our recent communications have been about communication, as I attempt to lose my email virginity by sending him a message. There are many bad things about trying to get online, but the worst is that as soon as you sit down with the computer, you know that hours and hours of precious time are about to be wasted, mostly on the telephone to the helpline. Have a phobia about reading instruction manuals which makes it impossible for me to understand anything written in them, so am very dependent on computer-literate friends (seem to have none) and the sodding helpline. David is now hardly reachable, as he is at last on set in the rainforest, and I have had email for days now without managing to send or receive anything at all except bad vibes.

David has become very important, no longer merely a carpenter as he was here and in Bermuda, but a big cheese with hundreds of telephone numbers, none of which have him on the end of them. Most just ring and ring. One or two have David's voice jumping down the line, impossibly near, but so far away, droning the usual voice-mail apologies. Finally find a number that is answered by a human, but still not David.

'Hi, this is David Lanyon's line. May I help you?' answers a purring Californian voice, belonging to a female, almost certainly with big lips and skin like cream.

'Ummmm, yes. I'd like to speak to David, umm, please,' I stutter, getting off to a feeble start against his Rottweiler secretary.

'He's busy, honey, call again sometime,' she says huskily. I cannot bear to tell her who I am, in case David has not mentioned us at all, and do not wish to reveal to her my email problems. Suddenly wish I had chosen a more appropriate email address than 'heavenlybody'. Perhaps 'harassedmother' or 'norfolkharridan' might have been better.

Manage, with great cunning, to get through to David himself by persuading Felix to ring for me. He has no truck with Big Lips, and tells her firmly, 'David always wants to speak to me. Why can't you take the phone to where he is? I want to ask him about the jungle and stuff, anyway.'

There is a silky silence, which I can hear as I have my head rammed against the receiver next to Felix's ear, and then Felix grins as David comes on to the line. Felix lounges in the swivel chair by my desk, gazing unseeing at the dancing cobwebs on the ceiling, which I too prefer not to notice, and laughs at something David has said, before barraging him with questions.

'Have you met Tarzan yet? Are there any monkeys in this film? How big are they? What are their names? Do they sleep in the caravans with all the crew? Has Tarzan got a bow and arrow? How many snakes have you seen? Can you send us something dangerous, like a scorpion or some snake's spit or something?'

Even though it is ten o'clock at night and Felix should be in bed, I let him talk on, trying not to think about the telephone bill, but about Felix, and how he misses David. This leads to a brief soul-search and the conclusion that I have got it all wrong, and should never have got involved with anyone, no matter how melting his voice or smiling his eyes, unless he could guarantee lifelong commitment to the whole family. Felix passes the telephone, saying, 'Mum, please can you try to sort out the email so I can send messages and stuff to David? It's really important. I need to show him the Necromancer stuff on the internet, and I want to download it on to an email. Isn't it time I was in bed, anyway?'

Am constantly bemused by the weird ways of children, and suddenly long for a cosy chat with David about all their activities today instead of the stilted conversation which follows.

I begin: 'How are you?'

'I'm fine, thanks, what have you been up to today?'

'Oh, nothing really, just getting on. What about you?'

'Well we're on set, and I've been trying to work out a way to get the bridge connected to the tree house, and none of the carpenters speak English. There was a huge storm here last night, and the electrics have been off all morning. They've only just got them back on. But I want to know about home.' He sighs, and pauses, then says, 'I miss you all so badly. Tell me what everyone's doing. Is Giles playing any cricket before he goes back to school? How's the flooded garden? How are the dogs? Have you set up your email yet?'

I begin to relax, and I stop hunching at my desk and move over to sit by the fire, thawed now into talking to him again.

'Not exactly, but everyone's fine, and missing you. The Beauty told her nursery school teacher that—' There is a click, and the line dies.

'Hello, hello. David, can you hear me?' I slam the receiver down. 'Bloody, sodding bastard phone. It does this every time I speak to him. God, it's primitive.'

Redouble attempts with the computer and the helpline, and am rewarded at midnight, with the ping of an email arriving for me. So thrilling. Excitement is undiminished by it being from Angel.com to welcome me as a new member, and not something more glamorous. After gazing at their message, and committing it to memory, I decide it is best to stop until tomorrow. Can scarcely summon the energy to crawl up to bed after this computer marathon, and cannot face getting it wrong again.

April 16th

Constant rain for the past week means that I need never have bothered pumping out the knot garden. It is back to its incarnation as a lake, and even has frogspawn lying like a pillow of tiny glass beads at one end. Should I keep trying to dry it out, or should I accept defeat and make it into a proper lake, or rather pond, and become a water gardener? Am gazing into the murky swamp, pondering this issue before collecting The Beauty from a morning with my mother, when Desmond and his marquee people arrive to check the space. I had been expecting a team of efficient country types with measuring tapes and theodolites and so forth, but instead Bass (as in bass guitar, he informs me) and his girlfriend Siren surge up the drive in an orange camper van with purple curtains and flames painted behind all four wheels. Despite the inclement weather, which has caused me to put on an old boiler suit of David's and two water-proof jackets in order to survey my flood, Bass, who has long ringlets like Charles II and a bulbous nose, is wearing just a waistcoat over his bare chest and a pair of tight and dirty jeans. Siren, clad more as the tooth fairy than an ancient Greek doom-seeker, alights from her side of the vehicle and pauses for a moment, blinking as if she has been asleep, brushing the creases from her short frill of a skirt with a tin whistle she holds in one hand like a wand. Music swells and rattles in the car and the windscreen wipers keep time. Siren shivers and reaches back into the cab for a bolt of gauzy paper which she wraps around her shoulders, pulling it without looking, so the other end falls off and tips on to the muddy gravel. Even though I am wearing a boiler suit, I feel as bourgeoise as a Tupperware picnic box.

'Man, this is a neat pad,' says Bass, moving over to me and standing too close, wafting the smell of beer and patchouli oil towards me. Siren homes in from the other side, tiptoeing in her Stars and Stripes platform shoes, and smiling to reveal a front tooth studded with a green stone which from any distance looks like stuck spinach.

'Your ducks are doing my head in,' she giggles. 'I'm mad about the one with the backcombed hair.' She points at Pom-pom, the smaller of our ducks, as he glides across the garden towards the pond.

Desmond extracts himself from the wriggling welcome of all the dogs and comes over. 'These guys have got the most fantastic tent,' he says, clapping Bass on the back with a firm hand. 'It's big enough for four hundred people, so we'll easily get everything in.'

I look round doubtfully. 'But my garden is very small. I don't think you could fit four hundred people in it anyway, even without the tent, and there's nowhere flat enough to put a structure that big.'

Bass walks over to the garden wall, and looks out across the water meadows.

'Hey man, let's just put the tent in this field. It's much better, and you can get all the parking on there as well.' Siren frisks over to look with him, flapping long, hennaed hair, and Desmond and I join them as the thin mist of rain continues to fall, clouding Siren's hair and blurring the view. Desmond also likes the field idea, and I can hardly bear to interrupt their excited discussions about generators, to say, 'But this field doesn't belong to me, it's farmland, wet farmland at that, and it belongs to the new man who lives at Crumbly.'

'Well it isn't any wetter than your garden,' Desmond points out. 'Let's find out if we can rent it.'

Siren and Bass, oblivious to the rain, have drifted off to the swing, where he pushes her and she skims to and fro, trilling with laughter, in between murmured sentences about amplifiers and sound systems. Start to envisage the wedding as a mini Glastonbury, and begin to feel very nervous indeed.

April 17th

Catch the train to London by running, bags flapping, down the platform shouting 'No, no,' in the manner of a spoof Anna Karenina. Really awful mistiming caused by the station having been entirely rebuilt since I last went to London, and this adds to my sensation of being an utter rustic, with hay almost sprouting from my ears. Am on my way to Minna's hen night, and will have time beforehand to go shopping for the children's wedding clothes and also to attend an exhibition. Realise just how long it is since I have been here when walking down the King's Road. The thronging, weaving people on the pavement and the jerking traffic move fast and purposefully; my pace and my intent are hesitant, and I am bumped and jostled until I alter my stride and move swiftly, like them. Legs begin to ache and I veer over into the slow lane, right next to the shop windows, where I and other pedestrian out-of-towners meander, gasping to catch our breath and staring blankly at windows bursting with colour – neon-blue dresses with pink roses sprigged across the skirt, lilac cardigans with sea-green beading, all the same and all trumpeting their individuality. Every shopfront has three or four mannequins in uniform of slithery dress, cardigan and tiny handbag, and every shop window has a flutter of words daubed above or beneath the clothes, a marketing message to the subconscious, a version of *Stand out in a crowd, be yourself.*

How can they all be such sheep? Even though I have been looking forward to this stolen day of indulgence with secret, guilty longing, I find my interest in making a purchase confounded, and decide that the National Portrait Gallery will raise the tone and put me in a more celestial frame of mind. However, I arrive in Trafalgar Square, to find a queue chicaning impenetrably towards a far distant ticket booth. Much of the queue is made up of elderly couples; women with crisply set grey hair, men restless, with the *Telegraph* folded under an arm and highly polished brown brogues.

'It'll be another hour before we're even inside the building,' sighs a matron with a quilted jacket and a scarf emblazoned with Scottie dogs. 'It's because the exhibition closes tomorrow. We'll have to stay, but I'm afraid we'll never make it to Peter Jones at this rate.'

Her husband sighs, thwacking his newspaper against his hand.

'Well you did insist on coming, Marjorie. I said it was madness.'

Marjorie pulls her lips tightly in around her teeth in a disgruntled sigh, and adjusts her position so she is looking away from her husband. They are a picture of crossness.

I stand around for a few minutes, pretending to be in a welter of indecision and even put myself at the back of the queue to see what it feels like. It feels terrible: maddening and achingly boring. I have no intention of joining it. I never have had. Wander off, sideways like a crab, hardly able to admit to myself that my first attempt to see art for several years has been so easily thwarted. Once I reach a safe distance, I scuttle away, disliking to admit a degree of relief, even though I really wanted to see the exhibition, and wondering if many people are as shallow as I am.

However, simply cannot bear to have such a total absence of moral or cultural fibre, and turn back once more to hurl myself in through the main doors of the National Gallery, bypassing the special exhibitions, for an hour with Piero della Francesca and his contemporaries. The relief of being among these paintings is as powerful to me as a session in the confessional would be to a Catholic, and I return to the street renewed, walking on air and determined to know more about art.

Reach Rose's flat at seven o'clock, and find her grinding carrots and beetroot into a health-giving drink. 'Don't let's talk about it,' she shudders. 'Tristan gave me a total detox programme as a birthday present. I think he must have a mistress who has put him up to it, or else he's developed a really vile and worrying streak of sadism. I'm on day three. I have to go and be colonically irrigated every afternoon for a week, and the irrigation man is really good-looking, which makes it double-embarrassing, and we can see the gunk as it comes out and we talk about it. The story of my life is being revealed through poo, it's just awful.'

Rose cannot come to the hen night because of the demands of the detox programme. 'I'd love to,' she says longingly, looking at her timetable, 'but I can't. I've got to have a shower at nine o'clock, followed by a body brush and another lot of disgusting powders at ten-fifteen. I've also got to drink two gallons of distilled water between now and bedtime and fill in my progress chart, and I haven't even taken the powders before the last ones yet.'

'Well, you look fantastic, it must be worth it,' I say, admiring her glowing clear skin and shining eyes.

'Do you think so? I hope you're right. I've had to put Theo with a childminder and take a week's holi-day from work to give myself time for all this. It's insanely stressful trying to keep up with it,' she says, rushing to turn off the kitchen timer she had set to remind herself to take her early-evening powders. 'It just shows that all these treatments are aimed at fantastically rich women who do nothing all day but paint their nails. You can't possibly look after children or work, there just isn't time.'

Put on my make-up and get dressed, slightly crest-fallen not to have Rose to giggle and swap things with, and half longing to have the detox treatment given to me as a present – such a luxury to think only of oneself and one's bodily functions for a whole week. Just like being a toddler again. On second thoughts, the implied criticism of a husband giving a wife an expensive and enslaving beauty treatment is grim. Better to buy it oneself, or, given that it costs a fortune, best just to sip a drop of camomile tea before bed and stay off the booze.

Minna's hen night has been organised by Incie Wincie Inglethorpe, who isn't a boy at all, and who does not live at White City Greyhound Stadium where I clearly remember sending the wedding invitation. In fact, the stadium turns out to be the venue for the hen night. Incie is a corruption of Celia, and Wincie is a reference to her stature. Incie Wincie is about half my height and has a mop of black curls and dark eyes. She also has a girlfriend, Sophie, with a swanlike neck and for ever legs, with whom she is holding hands.

'They're lesbians,' I whisper to Minna. 'Look, they're holding hands.'

'Yes, they're chefs, and they're making the wedding cake. It's going to be Elvis in his white trouser suit with sugar sequins and a guitar, but don't tell Desmond. It's a surprise.'

I have not seen Minna before in a crowd of her own friends. She has always either been at work at Heavenly Petting, where she is chief receptionist, or she has been with Desmond. Had quite forgotten the mesmerising effect she has, with her Dolly Parton proportions and coiffed, candyfloss hair. Manage to become paranoid and clumsy instantly, as cannot help noticing that *all* Minna's friends have the same pocket-Venus bodies. The only people at our table who are over five foot four and have a bra-cup size less than double-D, are me and Sophie the lesbian. We sit next to each other and we talk about one-day eventing (her pet subject) and children (mine). Realise as she begins to set up little jumps with matchbooks and cigarettes to illustrate what is fast becoming a lecture, that I have no passions whatsoever, and my social skills have diminished to two conversations: one about football scores, and the other a debate on supermarkets versus delivery rounds for the best deals on organic foods.

I blame this restricted field of knowledge on the children. They are the only people I see, and I only know what they tell me these days, thus I know much more about *The Simpsons* than *EastEnders*. Stop listening at all to Sophie the lesbian, who is cantering a pony keyring around her plate, reminding me of Felix and his 'life is a game of Warhammer' philosophy, and start trying to list my own interests and areas of expertise. After ten minutes, during which time I have bet and lost on the first dog race without being aware of it happening, I have established my areas of expertise as being:

1 Nit control.
2 Opening bottles of wine when I have lost the corkscrew.
3 Making and losing lists.

My interests are rather more limited. In fact, I can't think of any at all, which is disgraceful. I must get some immediately. What can they be, and where will I find them? Gambling is not likely to be among them. By the end of the evening I have bet on seven races and lost every time, except for the one when I was in the loo, so Sophie placed my bet for me.

April 18th

Leave Rose measuring powders and puréeing apples, grapefruit and lemons for a tart mid-morning drink, and catch the slow Sunday train home. Driving back from the station towards the house I open all the car windows and sing along to Don MacLean's 'Bye Bye Miss American Pie'.

It is a beautiful wistful day, the air soft and mild and gentle when I get off the train, the quiet stillness save for a church bell contrasting with London's Sunday-morning busyness.

I follow the straggle of Norwich's suburbs out into the countryside, past grey pavements and streets pearled pink with blossom. Under gates, petals drift and shore up like soap flakes, and there is an almond scent of warm optimism on the air. I am perfectly, serenely happy, in a way that is only possible with the not-a-care-in-the-world sensation that comes with a slight hangover.

The sun is shining and as I park my car at home and turn the engine off, I hear my first cuckoo of the year in the silence that follows, and breathe deeply to inhale scented springtime. No one is in the house, but the trail of dolls, guns and odd shoes that follows Felix and The Beauty, and to a lesser extent Giles, wherever they go, leads to the garden. I head the same way, anxious to be reunited with my loved ones and to thank my mother for coming to stay with them last night. Voices lead me to the flooded knot garden.

There, leaning over from the field, is Hedley Sale, smoking with my mother, who is on our side of the wall watching the children frolicking in the wet grass of Hedley Sale's field. The Beauty runs back towards the wall when she sees me, looking like a member of the Home Guard in an old army helmet with goose grass all over her face and hair.

'Mummy, come and play hiding in the field,' she yells, and my mother and her companion turn to greet me, my mother beaming delightedly, 'Venetia, do come and meet Hedley Sale. He's your new neighbour, and we've been talking about the field and the party and things.' Her expression tells me she has achieved whatever it may have been that she wanted, and I smile and shake hands with Hedley, trying to decide whether or not I shall admit to having met him before.

He decides for me and says, 'Ah, yes,' before setting off in a rather showing-off fashion, gabbling away in Latin.

'He does this a lot,' I whisper to my mother, and she gives me a sharp look.

'Do you know what he's quoting?' she hisses back at me, and I shake my head. 'Well I do, and it's most unsuitable. He may imagine he's the only one around here who can recite Catullus. He'll have to think again.'

My hangover begins to buzz in my brain. The man stops talking Latin, lowers his monobrow to its customary position grazing his nose and says, in a special voice for simpletons, 'I hear you were attending a hen night and visiting an art gallery.'

I nod. He continues, 'I don't know if you had a chance to catch the Mantegna exhibition while it was in Europe? No, I thought not. I saw it in Amsterdam. Marvellous, quite breathtaking. What did you see yesterday? Oh, it must have been the Goya. What did you make of it?'

He is machine-gunning me against the wall, never drawing breath for me to answer, and suddenly the boys make an assault of their own from the right flank.

'What did you bring from London? Did you get us anything? I don't want to wear stupid satin shorts for Desmond's wedding. He said combat trousers were cool, it's just stupid Minna—'

'Minna is *not* stupid, and you are not to be rude.' Roused from my deadhead state, and as the haranguing words leave my mouth, I have a sudden clear picture of myself as a mother who ignores her children ninety per cent of the time and only connects with them to tell them off. Hateful. Dole out the yo-yos and felt-tip pens I have come to view as the form of taxation I pay for going to London, and hear my mother inviting Hedley Sale to lunch. In my house. Today. How could she? She and the children must have had lunch hours ago. And there's no food. There hasn't been for days – we've been eating noodles, broccoli and stock for the past week. It is the only dish everyone likes, so I have not seen the point in trying to cook anything else.

To my relief, he refuses. 'I would have loved to have come, but my stepdaughter is coming to stay and I need to get back for her.' He pauses, narrowing his eyes, or rather clamping down his eyebrow, intent on Giles, who is attempting to make his bicycle rear like a Lipizzaner on the lawn.

'Would your son like to come over this afternoon? Tamsin and he must be the same age, and it would be good for her to get outside with someone her own age.'

Knowing Giles's views on girls, I open my mouth to refuse, but not quickly enough. My mother pounces on the opportunity to infiltrate the Sale head-quarters.

'Oh, what a kind offer. Giles would love that. We'll come and collect him later, shall we?'

Try to override her, but to no avail. 'I think we should ask Giles himself if he wants to go,' I suggest feebly, convinced that he will refuse. Oddly, he says yes. Am convinced that he has not heard properly, and repeat to him as we head for the house to gather a few belongings, 'This is definitely a girl, you know.'

Giles looks at me patiently. 'I know, Mum, step-daughters usually are girls. Can you pass me my trainers, please.'

He drives off with Hedley Sale. Cannot rid myself of the conviction that he is an early Christian martyr being fed to the lions, but my mother says this is pathetic, and due to my hangover.

We retreat to the kitchen, noses tipped red with cold from too long in the shadows and weak sunshine of the afternoon.

'I must say, that man may not throw Giles to the lions, but he certainly is very hard work,' sighs my mother from the armchair, where she has slumped with a warming cigarette. 'I wouldn't want to be too neighbourly with him, Venetia, oh, no.' She shakes her head, brooding on the nastiness of Hedley Sale. Am incensed by this.

'Well why did you force poor old Giles to go?' I snap.

'I didn't force him, he wanted to go. And Sale is letting us use the field, so it would be churlish to refuse him a simple request of one small boy for a day.'

'That makes him sound even more sacrificial,' I point out, then change the subject. 'So what did you all have for lunch today?'

My mother is defiant. 'Oh, goodness! I'm afraid we haven't had time for lunch today, what with one thing and another. But I think there's some cheese some-where. You'll manage. I must go. I have things to do.'

Her hair is flailing madly now it has escaped the confines of her hat, and three rings glow witchily on her right hand. She looks as if she may whip a crystal ball out from inside her cardigan at any minute and start seeing the future. Can't think where she gets the energy for all her plots and intrigues.

She departs, leaving me with the customary back-from-away sensation of irritability and exasperation. No matter how short the absence or how devoted the child carer, I always find that I am punished for going to London. When I return, the whole house has an air of reproach about it. The Beauty generally contracts an unattractive ailment; anything from conjunctivitis to eczema, or a nasty cut that will serve to agitate me and bring on a guilt attack. Then there is the pile of dirty washing, mournful and neglected in the laundry basket, and, if I steel myself to address the school bags, there is a shoal of letters from school requiring home clothes, money for outings and homework by the tome, all of which I have missed the last possible date for. Term has only just begun, but today I find a frosty missive from Giles's form master, requesting that: *Giles must remember to wear proper uniform for the school photograph, or forgo the opportunity to be in it or any of the team photographs for which he is eligible.*

There is no chance that Giles will have remembered his blazer for the crucial day, which has passed. We will doubtless be sent the photographs and will thus have the permanent reminder of a blank space in the team to say that I slacked from my duties as children's factotum and secretary, and went to London on a mission of fun and frivolity. Pull myself together from this festering state of mind, and try to make a cup of tea. The fridge holds more annoyance, there is no milk and the wrapping for the cheese my mother had earmarked for lunch is empty in Lowly's basket, along with Lowly.

Decide to go and find The Beauty and Felix. They are not, as I expected, playing on the swing in the garden, but are sitting in the dark in the playroom, noses close to the television screen, watching cartoons. Grab them and hoist them, protesting, into daylight and the hall to find outer garments.

'Come on you two, let's go to the sea and have a walk, and then chips and an ice cream for tea. We can collect Giles on our way home.'

Felix wriggles and refuses to look for his shoes.

'Aw Mum, do we have to? I've been outside today. I don't need to go more than once a day or I'll get too much exercise. Please can we stay here and watch something?'

'Mummy, you're a filthy girl. Don't do it in the house,' scolds The Beauty, pointing at my wellingtons, with their tidemark of brown slime from pumping the garden. Cannot believe they are so reluctant to do something that I, as a child, considered the most wonderful treat possible. Despair rises as I try to avoid looking into their cross little faces and pile them into the car.

Why am I doing this? What is the point of trying to impose my own childhood upon them? They don't want it, and I feel let down by them not wanting it. Ghastly vicious circle making everything more difficult than it need be. But what are the alternatives? Ask Felix what his idea of a perfect day is, and find he has schizophrenically changed his tune: 'To go to the seaside and have chips, then throw stones into the sea and sticks for Rags,' is the entirely satisfactory answer.

Cannot help feeling blessed in Cromer, where we sit on the pier with chips and watch the glittering sea rise and fall through the boards beneath our feet, and Felix regales us with his new joke repertoire, the best of which is: 'What do you call a quarrelsome composer? Answer: "De-Bate Hoven".' Dusk meets the sea as the early-spring sun wanes, and we almost forget to collect Giles, so engrossed are we trying to get skimming stones to bounce three times.

Crumbly House, with the 'b' silent, has gates with stone gryphons and a potholed drive. The front door is shut, and when I knock on it, the sound of my knuckles is swallowed by the density of the oak. Leave the children in the car listening to the Top Forty, and wander round to the back of the looming brick building. Warm yellow light spills from a window and the door next to it is open. I knock and go in, unable to rid myself of pulsing nervousness. The big kitchen I have entered is empty, but plates on the table and a dog stretched in front of the hearth suggest that people are nearby. I call out 'Hello,' in a relatively normal-sounding voice, then jump and scream as a hand touches my elbow.

'Oh, for God's sake,' says Hedley Sale behind me, and I turn to see Giles deadpan with embarrassment at my reaction, following Hedley and preceding a girl of his age who is wearing jodhpurs. Giles and the girl are carrying riding hats and have clear eyes and flushed cheeks.

'We've been riding Arrow in the woods,' says the girl, flashing a friendly smile, aimed to put me at ease. 'Shall I go and get your other children out of the car, so you can have a cup of tea?'

Nod feebly, aware that this child is Giles's age, and yet has more poise than I will ever have, even if I live until I'm ninety. She and Giles step outside and are swallowed by the purple night. Hedley puts the kettle on and pulls out a chair for me. He perches on the table edge nearby, and wipes his face with a large red handkerchief, blowing his nose loudly.

'Thank you for letting us have Giles. Tamsin has loved it, and she's had a difficult time.' He pauses, clearly wanting some response beyond a nod.

'What sort of difficult time?'

He clears his throat before replying. 'She's my step-daughter, she is the product of my wife's first marriage. And my wife has recently left me for her personal trainer.' He pauses again, and gets up to fill the teapot from the boiling kettle as he adds, 'Her female personal trainer.'

Am not sure I know how to respond to these intimate revelations from someone I hardly know, and have to bite my tongue hard to stop myself saying, 'Oh yes, Mrs Organic Veg told me that.' Fortunately the children reappear in a rush of voices and slithering-off of boots and coats. Tamsin offers crumpets with Marmite and sits them all down at the other end of the table in a chattering group, which The Beauty particularly adores being part of.

'What a nice girl,' I say, wonderingly, watching Tamsin as she ties a napkin around The Beauty's neck and pours her a cup of milk. Hedley smiles, looking incredibly pleased, and I realise that in my several encounters with him he has always been glowering. For no reason I can work out, I suddenly say, 'My boyfriend is working on a film in South America. He won't be back for months.'

This has not come out as it should have. Hedley's one brow rises, making him look years younger, and he says, 'Really?' getting about a thousand intonations and suggestions out of the one word.

A hot flush of embarrassment covers me and I get up to depart, hurrying the children so they leave their crumpets unfinished on their plates.

April 21st

The Beauty and her brothers are to be bridesmaid and pageboys for Desmond's wedding. After my abortive trip shopping in London for clothes for them to wear as normal guests, had decided that the boys could just wear coats over normal clothes. But their new role in the spotlight calls for more. Minna says she told me weeks ago that this was to be their role, but I have no recollection of it. I have ten days to find or make something for two fussy sons and a very opinionated daughter. Nonetheless, panic aside, am hugely proud. Have bolt from the blue brainwave while watching Giles play in a cricket match during a hailstorm, and have decided that the boys must wear cricket whites. The Beauty's outfit is more of a challenge. Veer madly between wanting to make her into a sequinned pearly queen from the East End and an angel from a Titian painting.

Plumping temporarily for the former, I purchase many yards of pink and electric-green net from a market stall and then spend a time-warped morning in a haberdasher's shop where the array of dyed feathers, trims of marabou and lace and yards of sequins derange me utterly. Under the pretence that I am a deft needlewoman, I buy three hundred pipe cleaners and twenty squares of felt, plus two bulging bags of kapok while I am in there. Vivienne, whom I meet in a café for lunch, does not attempt to disguise her amusement.

'You can't sew, Venetia. You're suffering from delusions. You even have to glue your children's name tapes on with Super Glue.' She smiles the smug smirk of one who can effortlessly thread a sewing machine and run up a pair of curtains. 'You'll never do anything with all that stuff.' I grunt a protest, my mouth full of bread, and she tones things down a little. 'All right, all right, you can sew on name tapes, but I did once find you gluing them on, and you tried to bribe me to do it for you.'

Defend my purchases stoutly. 'Well, I thought the children would like them. Anyway, they're bound to be useful, that sort of thing always is.' We stare for a moment at a bunch of candy-striped red and white pipe cleaners wrapped around a tinsel feather. 'Mmm, very useful,' says Vivienne.

April 23rd

Awake to find a thin stratum of snow covering the garden and decide that The Beauty's bridesmaid outfit, more carnival queen than chaste bridesmaid, will not do. Her little arms would freeze, and anyway, she must not upstage Minna, and the trailing train of net, pipe cleaners and feathers as customised by me and the children, is a show-stopper. Have so enjoyed this sewing experience that I have also customised several of my own garments, and am especially pleased with the ice-blue cardigan (a run-in-the-wash casualty) hemmed with white pipe cleaners twisted into heart shapes. May well be appropriate colours for the winter wedding which seems to be approaching. Howling wind accompanying the blizzard of snow outside is pierced by the telephone and a tinny, echoing grunt which I make out as David. He mumbles away, interrupted by shrieks of 'What?' and 'I can't hear you' from me.

'I'm supposed to be catching a plane next Thursday, I'll be home on Friday night,' he yells, suddenly deafening me as the line clears for a moment.

My reaction is instinctive. 'All right, no need to shout.'

There is an offended pause before David, now muffled again, says crossly, 'You could try to sound pleased,' and puts the phone down.

Wonder why he didn't just send an email, now my preferred form of communication with just about anyone I can discover to have an email address. Am now on fondest terms with the chimney sweep, whose email address is sooty@sweep.co.uk, and would like to expand my pen-pal repertoire.

The Beauty and Felix are out in the garden gathering snowflakes and what appear to be hailstones in a bucket. They have donned protective clothing, and I am aghast to see my precious pink straw hat shielding Felix from the weather. Bought it on the pipe-cleaner day, during a mysterious and so far unrepeated mini heatwave, unperturbed by the knowledge that I have nothing that even slightly goes with it. The hat, and related summer outfits, are an irrelevance today. The Beauty is leading the way sartorially; her beloved army man's tin hat and a pair of very large wellingtons are for once spot on rather than eccentric. She and Felix rush into the house when called, bringing a cloud of chilled air and their ice collection. Each hailstone and drip of melted snow is placed in its own space in an ice-cube tray and secreted in the freezer until needed.

'We're going to collect a lot more and make an ice sculpture for the wedding,' announces Felix, pausing to discard my hat in favour of an orange one with a bobble on top.

'Gnomic,' he gloats, flashing a cartoon, daft smile at his faint reflection in the kitchen window before slamming out into the storm. I shuffle upstairs beneath a pile of laundry and try not to think about hypothermia. Remember that this sort of weather in April is known as the Lambing Snow, and probably Vivienne and Simon are up to their elbows in maternity work. We have this and the Blackthorn Winter before we are safely through to spring.

Start rethinking The Beauty's outfit around a small rabbit-skin cape I used to have when I was little, and wonder if Desmond and Minna's London friends will think she is a refugee Eskimo and send an SOS to Unicef. Reach the children's rooms and am astonished and somehow deeply irritated to discover Giles still in bed and asleep. Nonetheless, decide not to wake him as cannot face dealing with his extreme truculence. School, as is so often the case, is closed for a day, I can't remember why, but it's a good thing, because we can concentrate on the wedding outfits.

Unearth spare cricket trousers from a box smelling of mould and worse in the attic, and find that they have all got green knees and are wilted and defeated-looking, not at all the crisp white flannel Rupert Brooke garments of my dreams. School regulation ones are now made of drip-dry nylon, so even though these are pleasingly clean and folded in Giles's drawer, I cannot bear to use them. There is nothing for it but to set to at the sink with the proper flannels. Am employing methods used by ancient peasant women, and pummelling the knees with stones, when my mother and Rev. Trev arrive in a transit van. Pleased to be caught at such a domestic moment, I dally at the sink waiting for them to come in. This takes a great deal of time, and they finally stagger into the house heralded by Felix and The Beauty, swaying beneath a large hunk of painted wood.

'Do look, Trevor has lent us this marvellous altar-piece,' puffs my mother.

'What for?'

She glares, not liking my tone of blank unenthusiasm.

'Well, we can put it behind the drinks table – it'll look marvellous, won't it?' I know better than to ignore the menacing frown accompanying this question.

'Yes, yes, it'll look marvellous, but where are you going to put it right now?'

'I thought the best thing would be to have it in the sitting room, propped on the mantelpiece so it's out of the way,' she says brightly, and the harassed Trevor Heel nods enthusiastically.

'Yes, the church would be so much happier about lending it if they thought it was in your charming parlour,' he pleads, and compassion for his predicament thaws my mounting outrage. Clearly my mother has been taking advantage of his devotion to her.

'All right then, but you'll have to fix it to the wall with something or it could slip and collapse on The Beauty.'

Rev. Trev's haunted expression intensifies, and he lurches forward with his end of the altarpiece, muttering, 'Oh, we couldn't have that, oh no, no, no.'

'It won't, it's got hooks. Come on, let's finish this and have a drink to celebrate.' My mother, with the strength of six ordinary grandmothers, heaves her end of the slab up, and pulling poor Trevor behind her, totters through to the sitting room.

'Did you steal it from the church, Granny?' asks Felix admiringly. Rev. Trev shuffles uncomfortably, but Granny is serene as she flops back on the sofa, undoes the buttons of her scarlet felt jacket and fishes in her pockets for her cigarettes.

'Ahh, such dreadful weather, but apparently there's going to be a heatwave next weekend, so we needn't worry. What did you say, Felix darling? Oh, no, we would never steal anything. That is not our way. We've just borrowed it while the church doesn't need it, haven't we, Trevor? Now what about getting me a small drink, Felix love? Just a drop of gin and tonic would do the trick, and I'm sure Trevor would love one too.' She reaches for her glasses, keen to watch the dispensing of the drinks. 'No, no, a bit more than that, please. Always think of it as Ribena, darling.'

Felix does, with intoxicating results.

April 25th

A small wooden crate containing two cases of butter-flies (dried and pinned) and one of beetles, less dried and seeming to crawl about a bit, unless it's just the jolting of the packaging, is delivered to the door just as we are leaving for school. David has attached a card saying, *All local to the Tarzan set. Working on lizards to bring by hand. See you next week*.

We are all overjoyed. Or not. I hate the crawling ones, which were evidently sedated, not dead, and are now ricocheting about in their see-through plastic box. It is only a matter of time before the children let them out and terrible germ warfare begins with bot flies and weebles (or is it weevils?) burrowing into everything, especially skin. Share these fears with the children on the way to school. Giles claps his hands over his eyes.

'Yeah right, Mum. Honestly, you are cracking up.' How right he is. But David will be home in just a few days, and the wedding will have happened. Find myself openly praying to God that none of us are eaten by South American insects, and also that Minna does not change her mind.

April 26th

Hysteria is mounting. Minna and Desmond have arrived to stay with my mother in order to finalise preparations, and we discover that very little has in fact been organised. Terrible lists mount up by my telephone and by my mother's, all beginning crisply with our five organised items. These are: *Cake, Car, Hymns, Drink and Glasses*, and each one merits a big tick as well as being crossed through with a red line to denote doneness. Everything else sprawls on torn bits of paper, bobbing in a sea of question marks and doodles and causing Minna to burst into tears if she accidentally comes across any of these litanies of incompetence. Having quarrelled with Desmond and my mother about the correct moment for the bridal couple to depart from the reception on their honeymoon, Minna appears on the doorstep at lunchtime, with just four days to go, her suitcase in one hand and her wedding dress in a navy-blue body bag over the other arm.

'I can't stay with them,' she sobs, 'they're ganging up on me.'

'Poor Minna, no need to cry,' says The Beauty, taking control of the situation and leading Minna inside, holding her hand very gently as if she is made of glass. Must agree with The Beauty that Minna is looking fragile. Even her forehead has lost weight, and she is now almost transparent in ethereal blondeness, with perfect shining nails, coiffed hair and a faint tint of sunbed on her limbs. Putting my arm around her as she sits forlornly on the sofa, I cannot fail to notice the contrast between her twig shoulders and featherweight limbs and my own, which are solidly rounded like duck-down cushions. Time for some disciplined exercise, I fear, but no point thinking about it until after the wedding. Damn, should have got it together months ago. Will now be sack-of-potatoes mother of bridesmaid in all the photos. Wonder if I can employ a stand-in mother for the formal ones. They must have supermodel types at the local agency. Or perhaps Minna knows someone glamorous in London who wouldn't mind the job.

Suggest it, and Minna looks at me as if I am mad. 'Don't be so ridiculous,' she says crisply, subsiding on the sofa and dropping her head into her hands. The Beauty busies herself making Minna comfortable, flourishing a flannel and advancing to clean her face before selecting a pink crocheted blanket from her dolls' pram.

'Like Barbie,' says The Beauty approvingly, placing the blanket around Minna's tiny frame before moving off to the playroom to find more dolls to mollycoddle.

'It's all going wrong,' Minna sobs as soon as we are alone together. 'Desmond has turned against me. We'll have to cancel the wedding and my aunts are coming and one of them lives in the Hebrides, so she's probably set off already, and I'm so miserable.' Her voice has been rising on a crescendo, but she now casts herself face first into the sofa to wail unreservedly. The Beauty returns cradling a mutant baby in her arms. From the splodges on its cloth body, I recognise it as Mouldy Baby, one of The Beauty's favourites. The name is all too accurate, the splodges being mildew, brought about by Lowly mistakenly thinking the doll was his toy and recently taking it out into the garden for a few weeks. Mouldy Baby, The Beauty and I regard Minna with curiosity and sympathy.

'I thought it was women who were meant to become like their mothers,' moans Minna from deep within the sofa, 'but Desmond has started drinking and smoking as much as your mother, and now he's taken to wearing that horrible velvet cape of hers. Nothing has been done about loos or chairs or even a floor for the tent for Saturday, and whenever I ask them they just cackle and pour more gin and say, "Don't worry, we'll take care of it." But they won't! I know they won't.' Minna pauses to slam her hands down by her sides and then to blow her nose.

The Beauty shakes her head and her eyes fill with tears. 'No, they will not. They will not take care,' she agrees sorrowfully, sending Minna into a further paroxysm of gloom.

'And that awful Peta woman is threatening to come and turn the tent into a red womb. She says she's going to do a performance of a Roman birthing ceremony at the party in the evening. How can we stop her?'

I am fascinated by this prospect. 'What can she mean? Is she bringing someone in labour, do you think?'

Minna wails. 'Oh, God, don't even suggest it.' I quickly change the subject.

'All right, let's have some lunch.' Try to suppress my own mounting panic that Minna might decide to bolt and leave Desmond on our hands, and employ soothing tactics.

'We'll make a list over lunch. After all, we've still got four days, and we can get through a lot with the right sort of list.' The Beauty brings a box of tissues and we begin.

April 27th

List now sixteen pages long and Minna has drunk three bottles of Rescue Remedy and taken up smoking for the first time in her life. She and Desmond are not speaking to one another and it snowed again in the night. I have gone off weddings, but am very keen on outfits. Managed to persuade Minna to let me alter her wedding dress slightly, and she agrees that the addition of white angora pom-poms around the hem lends an air of insouciance. Making the pom-poms, with doughnut-shaped pieces of card and hours of winding white angora, was as calming for her as a huge hit of Mogadon. Am thinking of marketing pom-poms as executive stress toy. Perhaps with a launch campaign on the front of *Brides* magazine. Must ask Charles what he thinks.

April 28th

The loathsome Bass and Siren have been here for seven hours erecting the tent, and have so far only achieved one end of it. Despite there still being snow on the ground, Bass has taken his shirt off and replaced it with a fur waistcoat over his pimply naked torso, a sight designed to put me off my rabbit-skin cape idea for The Beauty. Their camper van is parked bang up against the wall of the house and I can feel as well as hear the thud of relentless techno music from their car stereo. Can only be thankful that Minna has gone to spend a day at a beauty sanctuary near Norwich and knows nothing of the new depths of incompetence being mined back here at the house. Felix and Giles are dropped off after school, and wander about at the periphery of the tent, hands in pockets, looking supercilious.

'Come on guys, give us a hand with this,' urges Bass, his arms full of festooning tent wall, and within moments the boys are stuck in, heaving on guy ropes and becoming plastered in soggy bits of grass. For as the tent rises, it becomes clear that this is not the meringue-white marquee of our dreams, nor does it have a satisfying striped lining to lend an air of celebration. This structure is more akin to Wellington's campaign tents in 1815, with its streaks of mud and black stain, its primitive lacings and its mossy skin of dried grass cuttings.

'Why is it so dirty?' Giles asks Siren.

'Oh, they're always like that,' she says authoritatively.

'But don't you clean it?' he persists.

She tosses her purple hennaed hair back, twining it up into a bun secured by a butter knife from my kitchen, before she answers, 'We do, but you can't dry something this size, so it's always like this. All big tents have grass and stuff on them.'

Complete tosh. I think back to the gleaming, huge tent hired by the village for a charity dance a couple of months earlier, to the spotless Hunt Ball tent, and to the bright white tent Vivienne hired for her sister's wedding last summer. Not a mark on it, and it was twice as large as this one. I bite my lip and move to talk to Desmond. He is ecstatic with the work Bass and Siren have achieved, and I start to feel like the Bad Fairy in this pantomime.

'It's brilliant that the guys have done all this today,' enthuses Desmond. 'And Siren's got some great backdrops to hang because their lining got stolen, and the floor will be here on Friday night—'

Bad Fairy puffs of green smoke are about to pour out of me. 'Friday *night*, but Desmond, your wedding is on Saturday, and we've got to set up the tables and lay them and put chairs at them and decorate the tent . . .'

I am cordially at one with Minna now; Desmond is as absurd and annoying as Bass and Siren. Persuade him to get the floor here on Friday morning, and turn to face the next challenge. Siren enters the tent carrying a Day-Glo green and black tiger-striped strip of fabric with PULSE written on it in giant pink script.

'I've got loads of these backdrops to hang instead of a lining, and I'm making one especially for Minna. I'm going to sew it up tonight, so it's all nearly sorted, isn't it?' she says, beaming moronically. I have to do three deep breaths ending with an exhalation, as learned in my active birth classes before The Beauty, to stop myself removing the butter knife from her hair and stabbing her with it.

Harness every ounce of diplomacy to say confidingly, 'The thing is, Minna's in a real state and she's refusing to listen to any of us. She says the tent has got to have apple blossom and nothing else in it, and she especially asked not to have anything with writing on it or any colour except white, or anything big.' Shrug my shoulders, hoping to signify that I think Minna is crazy not to want her wedding tent full of filthy old bits of acid rave paraphernalia. Can see Siren's tiny brain trying to remember what else she has brought, and pray that I have covered all of it in asking for only white and apple blossom.

To my relief, Siren is bemused but biddable, just nodding and murmuring, 'Yeah, right. So you don't want any of these?'

'Well it's not me, it's Minna, and it's her day. I think we've got to let her decide.' I hardly dare to breathe as the backdrops are rolled up and returned to the truck, and Siren passes again, still nodding, and agreeing, 'Right, so she wants a really natural look for this gig. She's on a weird rustic trip, right?'

'It's not a gig, it's a wedding,' pipes Felix, and shuddering I retreat into the house to inspect the monstrous list of undone duties.

April 30th

Ravishing day with warm sun, chirruping birds and the scent of spring clinging to every leaf and flower. Have to take my vest off to avoid unpleasant hot flush sensation ruining my morning. Morning not entirely salvaged by this manoeuvre; the prospect of David's imminent arrival is all I can cling to as madness and disorder swirl about me. Minna has become cata-tonic, which is a marked improvement on her former hysteria. Her oldest friend Cascade, who lives in California, has come to support her for her last few days of single girldom, and despite having a name nearly as stupid as the vile tent people's, she is an asset. Giles is fascinated by her gadgets, which are so many and so varied her whole body seems to beep and whirr as if she is a robot. Her clothes are all made of cutting-edge nylon and come in every shade of bruise, from magenta to evil fungal yellow. Even with these sartorial disadvantages, she is enchantingly pretty, with an elfin face and long straight pale hair.

Giles finds her the coolest being on earth, and to Minna she represents steadfastness.

She has even effected a rapprochement between the bridal couple and took Minna to the rehearsal yesterday. Felix, Giles and The Beauty failed to attend as I was involved in a fierce altercation with Bass the Moron over the flooring for the tent. His promises that it would be here this morning are now visibly empty, as I knew they would be, and I have taken the law into my own hands and ordered a floor from another company which will arrive in half an hour.

I want to kill Siren and Bass, and in fact all of Desmond and Minna's friends. People keep turning up saying they want to help. They clomp through the house in search of Desmond or Minna, then, having found them toiling with apple blossom and wire in the tent, these helpers throw themselves on to the grass, open cans of beer and proceed to soak up the sun which has schizophrenically taken the place of the blizzards we had earlier in the week.

Despite the attendance of Bass and Siren plus henchmen until eleven every evening, the tent still looks more like a low-grade shelter for also-ran cattle at an agricultural show than a celestial wedding venue. Siren has a roll of white crêpe paper which she is attempting to suspend from a high wire, but otherwise she and Bass have given up all pretence of working and are intent on getting stoned and turning my garden into a happening event. A sound system has been set up, and mellow music pulses out, but not loudly enough to stop the hens moving in and contributing their mite. So far three eggs have been found next to the stage, and Bass has a blob of chicken shit between his naked shoulder blades, a memento of one of his many siestas under the awning. Siren has brought her child, Tree, with her today, and he is teaching Felix and Giles how to juggle, using three of the plates delivered this morning. The so-called helpers have a flurry of activity at one o'clock which results in a picnic on my doorstep of smoked salmon bagels. I am absurdly touched when they offer me one, then immediately furious to find myself such a pushover. I skulk in the house, darting out like a spider now and again to issue an order, but fearful of moving too far from the phone and missing David's call. Finally forced outside when an articulated lorry surges up the drive and disgorges an ant-like army of men with furniture. The scene shifts in mood from an early seventies rock festival to an old Charlie Chaplin movie where everything is speeded up. In double-quick time the lorry doors are clanking shut and the ant men are departing waving cheery ant waves.

The tent is transformed. A wand has been waved, and apart from the small blot of Siren standing on tiptoe tying crêpe paper into a stupid bow, the interior is a glow of dazzling and efficient prettiness with tables, cloths, napkins, chairs, floor and even a cake stand. Burst into tears of relief, and am about to take my car and camp at the airport because I cannot bear another moment without David being here, when a phone is brought to me.

'Hi, sweetheart. It's David. What's the matter?'

Am wailing now. 'Oh, thank God. Where are you? I need your help. There's something I haven't told you—'

'And there's something I haven't told you.' His voice is a caress, but not close enough.

I stop crying and say suspiciously, 'Where are you? Why aren't you here?'

'That's what I was trying to tell you. They've stopped everyone's vacations. The project is running into debt already and there's another twelve weeks to shoot. People are getting ill.'

He stops, and then he seems to whisper, 'Venetia, I don't know how to say this. I can't come back, because if I do, I'll lose my job. I'm sorry, honey.'

For a few moments I have no reaction except irritation that he is calling me 'honey'. Then it sinks in. Shaking, whisper, 'How could you?' and without waiting for any more self-justifying rubbish, I jab the off button on the phone and escape back into the house in search of peace. Downstairs, it is impossible to find. Every room is occupied by little groups, beavering away at something or other like workaholic gnomes.

Find sanctuary in my bedroom, and also The Beauty, who greets me with a smile and tells me, 'I know a little girl called Generous. She's got brothers and a polar bear.' Nod weakly and subside on the bed for a bout of frenzied weeping. Heart begins to harden like quick-dry cement, and I struggle to remember that David does not know that the wedding is here, in his house, or my house that he lives in, at any rate.

This cannot mitigate his behaviour, however. To ring up the day before the wedding is too much. Just too much. Does this signify the end for us? Will we ever—

'Mummy, look. Generous is holding hands with Mouldy Baby.'

Thinking time is up after a matter of seconds. The Beauty has plumped her dolls on the bed next to my head and is demanding participation. The chaos she has created on my dressing table is crying out to be untangled, and voices from downstairs are becoming increasingly high-pitched.

'Venetia, we need to know where you want this. Where are you, anyway?' is followed by a strident 'Coooeee.'

'Oh, no,' I groan at The Beauty, 'it's Peta. Come on, we'd better go down and get on with life.' Cannot help adding, 'Bastard, sodding bloody bastard,' under my breath, but The Beauty's radar-sensor ears catch what I said easily. She follows me down the stairs, chanting, 'Soddin' bluddy bastard' with relish.

Peta the basket-weaver has leaned her bicycle against the gate and is untying a vast bundle bound by rope.

'I've got the performance planned, but we do need a projector,' she beams, 'and if there were a few loud speakers I know the womb sound effects could make this an unforgettable happening.'

Desmond, who should have gone off somewhere to chill out by now, ambles over, the picture of affability, and asks how she proposes creating the 'happening', and Peta, brightening at the prospect of a bridegroom to convert to cat worship and basket-weaving, polishes her crystal on her skirt, holds it up between her face and Desmond's, and starts to chant something.

I interrupt before the first verse is over, trying to muster an expression of sorrowful helplessness.

'I'm so sorry, Peta, but Minna is in a real state and her latest decision is that the whole wedding must be really simple. We've had to cancel almost everything.' Pause and cough, which is often my reaction to telling a big lie, hoping Peta does not notice the microphones and podium for the identikit Elvis Minna has booked. 'Anyway, I'm afraid I'm going to have to stop you right there and send you home before Minna sees you. We mustn't have her getting in a state again before her big day.'

Desmond is goggling at me in blatant disbelief, but luckily Peta misses this. She looks at the trusses of cloth regretfully, but begins to pile them back into their bundle, silent for a moment as she digests my words.

It is one o'clock in the morning when we finally finish laying the tables, placing the chairs and twining apple blossom round the tent poles. Everything is ready, and if it wasn't for the fact that Bass and Siren are still here, 'kipping in the rig' as they put it, and the unbearable absence of David, all would be perfect. Have decided not to allow David's vile behaviour to affect the wedding at all, and have joked airily and trilled with ready laughter when anyone has asked what time he is coming, as if nothing could be further from my thoughts than David. After all, what could be nicer than hosting a wedding for God knows how many people for my brother without so much as a boyfriend, let alone a husband of my own, to share the responsibility? Tra la la. So glad we tested the wedding champagne at supper. Had to make sure it was a good one.

MAY

May 1st

Absence of domestic harmony due to breadhead mother (me) having failed to get any milk for breakfast, and having left cricket whites on the washing line all night so they are now sopping wet thanks to heavy dewfall. Put them on the Aga to dry, and rush to take Minna a cup of calming vervain tea, hoping to make a virtue out of the no-milk crisis. No time to make the children breakfast, they must do their own; nuptial activity is all. The hairdresser arrived two hours ago, as did the flower girl. Both are upstairs with Minna in her bedroom discussing the construction of her headgear, which is part-tiara, part-flower garland. The Beauty is also there, transparent and pink-eyed with exhaustion, but spellbound by this reconstruction of Minna from beloved family member to High Queen of Barbiedom.

Entering the bedroom to prise her away, I am instantly mesmerised by the scene which has so captivated The

Beauty. We are in a fragrant bower of springtime loveliness. Minna, wearing a floral dressing gown and an expression of celestial calm or vacant terror, depending on how you interpret it, is sitting in front of the mirror with Cascade bowed over her feet like Mary Magdalen, anointing her toes with shimmering pink polish. Cascade's wedding-day outfit of silver pac-a-mac and matching thigh-high boots is less biblical. Her mobile phone lies on Minna's dressing table, and I note, covetously, that it too is wearing a special silver outfit. Scent, rosewater, puffs of Evian and hairspray mingle to form a diaphanous cloud above the heads of Minna's ministering angels who hover, murmuring blandishments in dove-soft voices. The Beauty, rapt, passes a cotton-wool bud to the hairdresser and turns back to her unblinking contemplation of Minna's reflection in the mirror. Minna's head quivers, and out of it rise bean-sprout tendrils of ice-blonde hair, slicked with unguents: the hairdresser must be giving it some sort of fabulous lengthy treatment therapy. I glance at my watch and realise that we are running out of time.

'Minna, when will they get started on doing your hair?' I say, alarmed that we will be late. She turns wide, half made-up eyes towards me.

'They've done it, it's finished,' she says.

Oh, what a fool I am. When will I learn to keep my mouth shut? Gabble wildly, trying to improve the situation.

'Oh yes, I see the tiara in there now, I just thought they hadn't done that bit yet.'

★　　★　　★

Back on the landing, the door closed on the fragrant temple, I find aroma of burned toast indicating that the children have had their breakfast. Begin the absurdly difficult task of finding them all and posting them into their clean clothes. The house has gone native; piles of garments are strewn everywhere, crumpled and thrown aside like unwanted jumble-sale items. Somewhere among them are the things I ironed for the wedding.

No washing-up has been done for two days, and Lowly has smashed three plates in the kitchen jumping up to steal the chicken carcass from the night before. Don't suppose it matters much, as the wedding is being catered for by a caravan of dreadlocked reggae freaks who took one look at my cooking arrangements and made a plateful of bacon sandwiches for my house guests when they arrived to set up this morning. Their caravan has a side window, like a fish and chip van, and through it I see them swaying to the beat of music I can only just hear because there are so many other sounds competing with their ghetto blaster. Chief among them is the strumming of Peta the basket-weaver's lute, and some foul coughing from behind the orange camper van to indicate that Bass has risen and is ready to face the day.

Somehow find myself outside, still searching for white plimsolls and my hairbrush. Wonderful bird-song and truly fresh May-time smell of blossom and the warming earth distract me for a moment from the mini Glastonbury that my garden has indeed become. Bass has found it necessary to park his camper van in the middle of the lawn, where it sets the tone and is the focus of interest for all the hens and the ducks, who are scratching and clucking around it, in happy anticipation of breakfast. Peta, her boyfriend and a tandem occupy the next pitch on the lawn. The boyfriend has laid his gold suit out flat on the grass, and is doing a head stand, lost in topsy-turvy contemplation of the garden. Peta, still clinging to her yards of red felt and white muslin, has made a kind of nest or pyre for herself to sit on, and is plaiting her hair with beads and strumming the lute. She is wearing a long pink dress with trailing sleeves and, apart from her glasses and the tandem, looks as if she has just stepped out of a medieval tapestry.

Thankfully, none of the happy campers is in the tent, when I unlace the entrance and peer in. All the jam jars of bluebells and pink campion have released a wonderful scent, and the air seems hallowed and expectant. I unlace several panes to let the breeze in, and my spirits soar as light fills the space. Despite all Siren's attempts to ruin it, the tent is a triumph.

Felix appears at my side, hair on end, mud spread liberally across his cricket flannels, a button already missing from his white shirt and a guilty flush mounting. He holds out a tennis ball, flat on his palm as if I am a donkey and he is presenting me with an apple. We both look at the ball.

'It's a ball,' I say intelligently.

'There must have been something wrong with the window, Mum, the ball only bounced really softly. But the glass went everywhere. I tried to clear it up but there's still a bit of glass in the hall. And those people with the boy who can juggle are here again, in fact I think they slept under a table in the backyard because there are loads of duvets and stuff everywhere. And anyway they say they need to set up the PA again because they missed a bit yesterday. They just want to move a few tables out of the way.'

Wish Desmond and Minna had got married in Las Vegas and just shown us the photographs afterwards. Deal with Bass in a frosty fashion he is oblivious to, and rush back to the house. Not a hope of lavishing time and bath oil and hair care upon myself. Grab a handful of festive-looking pink clothing from my wardrobe, recently improved by the addition of sequins, pink glass beads and some tiny crystallised fruit I found in a sweetshop in Cromer. Discard the clothes again and scurry in pursuit of The Beauty, who has put on a bath hat and some surf sandals from last summer and is hurtling along the corridor, running into bedrooms and through the queue for the bathroom, squeaking, 'Peekaboo, it's my birthday,' at the seemingly millions of strange people changing in every corner of the house. She finds a captive audience in Cascade and Giles, who are playing a game of Worm on Cascade's mobile telephone.

'Mum, look, I've scored forty-seven this go,' says Giles, unable to look up from the bleeping green-lit screen. The Beauty claps her hands together three times.

'Come on now, sing Happy Birthday to Me,' she commands them, but breaks into a vile roar when I scoop her up and peel off the sandals, vest and bath hat and start trying to cram her into her angel outfit. Leave her sobbing and drumming her heels and scramble into my clothes, rejecting the electric-pink T-shirt saying *Try it, you'll like it* in favour of a knitted vest which I think the height of chic until Cascade looks up from Worm and says in a voice which isn't meant to be patronising, 'Oh, boy. A camisole, that's such a great retro look. It makes me think of land girls and stockings and the Second World War . . .' While she rhapsodises, I remove the camisole, but can hardly get it over my vast land-girl arms. Chastened, late and irritated, I put on the suggestive T-shirt and hasten, with half-dressed children, to church.

May 2nd

Email to David – jolly nice of me under the circumstances:

Still have confetti in my hair and marabou trim on my mind post-wedding. Also, can feel a new career burgeoning, as about ten people asked me where did I get my cardigan and five of them have commissioned me to make them one as soon as possible. Am I perhaps dreaming or still drunk? Somehow, the tangled muddles and tensions of yesterday morning dissolved, and Desmond and Minna's wedding was a most moving, joyous, glamorous occasion. Minna was the ultimate Jane Austen heroine for the twenty-first century, radiant and ethereal (and humorous with the pom-poms) while Desmond was twice as large as life and wildly excited, punching the air as Rev. Trev said, 'I now declare you man and wife.'

Many tears shed by Granny and self as the darling little bridesmaid tripped down the aisle with her brothers, her tiny ballet shoes twinkling with sequins, her dress an angelic ivory with the strawberry marabou around the hem, and her virtuous expression defying anyone to chastise her for hurling her bouquet into the font as she passed it. Granny's sniffing intensified at the touching sight of Egor following the bridal procession, a blue satin bow around his neck and his little pink eyes matching the apple blossom tucked into his collar. Coming out of church, he took charge and led the procession down the village, only stopping to pee once on a parked car.

Cannot bear to think how the party might have then sagged and collapsed due to an inaugural free-form dance performed by Peta and two of her side-kicks in the middle of the tent. Minna, in her new role as wife, took a firm line and hissed at an astonished Desmond, 'Get that freak show out of my party,' before turning on her heel and walking out to stand beneath the drifting confetti-pink petals of the cherry tree. Atmosphere not helped by the unconscious form of Bass, the creep who put the tent up, rolling out from under a table as revellers sat down to lunch. Managed to deal him a swift and savage kick while pretending to pick up a napkin. Placement not all it should be, as I was next to two empty spaces, one which should have been filled by you, and the other by Hedley Sale, the guy who let us use the field. As neither of you showed up, I looked very unpopular until my mother beckoned me over to where she and Rev. Trev were quaffing wine and toasting everything in sight.

Speeches were made. Desmond's best man, thanks again to your absence, was his drummer in Hung Like Elvis. He bounced on to the stage in his chalk-thick pinstripe suit and black shirt with dark glasses on and a cigar in his mouth. He made a perfect, short and funny speech, bowed, but thought better of leaving the stage at the end and bellowed into the microphone, 'Thanks guys, and here's one for the toast to the happy couple:

'Hooray, hooray, the first of May
Outdoor fucking begins today.'

As you can imagine, it didn't go down that well with everyone. Rev. Trev said he must remember to add it to his sermon notes and there was a lot of fidgeting and muttering, during which the sound system whined and expired. Then Siren, the girl version of Bass the tent creep, wafted up to the stage in a long yellow paper toga which looked like lavatory paper, and stared expectantly at a loud-speaker. Terrible moans and squawks filled the tent as Peta and her friends, who turned out not to have been expelled by Desmond earlier, leaped to fill the sensory void with their fiddles.

All appeared lost, and even the sun departed to be replaced by drizzle, when there was a clopping noise outside, and Hedley Sale, the landowner, arrived in a pony trap with his stepdaughter Tamsin. It was just what was needed; Tamsin leaped out, bowed to Minna and Desmond and lowered the tiny step to the little brass-decorated door. Minna was thrilled and got into the trap, with Desmond looking acutely embarrassed, and they did a lap of honour round the outside of the tent, observed by all because I had taken the panels off earlier when it was hot.

Someone did something to the sound system and it boomed back to life, and the whole party became more relaxed. Two of Minna's friends from the hen party came and admired my cardigan. They couldn't believe I'd made it myself, or rather decorated it myself, and one of them said she thought it came from that shop Rose loves called The Blessing. I was, as you can imagine, thrilled, as even though I have never been there, and never will, as you have to be a member of their club to get in, it is the height of chic.

And as if by divine intervention, the weather changed, the drizzle spluttered, paused, then coughed and became a deluge, accompanied by timpani thunder and much flashy lightning.

'Splendid good luck to have this happen,' agreed the redoubtables from the older generation who had wanted to leave moments before.

The party really got going, and then didn't stop. Have to admit, I got pretty exhausted and retreated to the playroom with The Beauty where we watched *Grease*. Music still pounded from the tent as darkness fell, and a few people like my mother and Rev. Trev and Hedley Sale came into the house to eat boiled eggs. The Beauty fell asleep on the sofa with her posy clutched close to her, and Giles and Felix, now changed into their usual sludge-grey clothes with logos, vanished out into the party. At midnight, I decided I had had enough, and carried The Beauty up to my room. Horrified to discover the door locked and whispering and giggling going on in there. Yelled, 'Will you please open my door,' and was ignored. The Beauty woke up and began to yell, and I was about to give up and go and sleep in her room with her, when Hedley (Sale) who was drinking brandy with my mother and the vicar in the kitchen, came bellowing up the stairs like a bull and started hurling himself at the door, bawling, 'Get out of her room, scum.'

Very impressive. The door was opened in seconds and two very young and embarrassed tousled blondes came out, the boy one covered in lovebites. Felt about a thousand years old as I nodded in graceful acceptance of their apologies, and Hedley frogmarched them away. Rather wanted to change my sheets, but was prevented by the sight of Minna's friend Cascade asleep in the airing cupboard. God knows what had happened to her bedroom.

Anyway, today was spent picking up glasses and

finding things in strange places. One of my shoes was on the village signpost, looking so depraved this morning, and I discovered a table lamp in the freezer when burrowing for ice cubes for Bloody Marys.

Wish you hadn't been in the wrong place,

Love Venetia xxxxx

May 4th

Email from Minna and Desmond, saying could I fax their wedding certificate, as they need it for the second hotel they are going to in order to secure the honeymoon suite. Cannot find it, but use it as an opportunity to get the boys out of bed and usefully occupied in searching the church, the tent, the house and then the dustbins for it. Gout has recurred. Most depressing to be hobbling with a stick, but pain too great to soldier on. I limp around the kitchen trying to clear up, thankful that everyone has left and none are there to see me fall victim to antique disease. Couldn't face the school run, so have given the children the day off, and am washing up in a daze, half the time seared with pain and the other half floating as if I am a meringue, fluffy on the outside and gooey in the middle on a cloud of fatigue brought about by three sleepless nights with The Beauty in my bed.

She, however, is buoyant, and has been getting married to her imaginary friend Generous since first light. Watch her parading around with a tea towel on her head, singing 'Twinkle, Twinkle'.

Searching again for the wedding certificate, this

time in The Beauty's sock drawer, I have a strong sensation of having missed my chance. This pursuit of someone else's marriage contract is as near as I will get to being married now. The Beauty is moving inexorably to the centre of the stage, and I must accept that from sister-in-law of the bride, my next move can only be downhill. How many years before I am mother of the bride? As for me being the bride for a change, fat chance. Shake off mawkish thoughts, and attribute them to gout. Giles finds the certificate in a packet of Shreddies he is trying to eat, and we fax it immediately. Sense of achievement this brings is colossal.

May 5th

Gout is receding now, thanks to a foul diet of vinegar and potatoes. Decided to try this torture after reading that it was popular with Byron. Am not sure that he had gout, but feel confident that he must have, and am in any case desperate. Will try anything I can think of, and no one more contemporary seems to find gout a problem. Cannot even find it on the internet. Am therefore planning to become an internet millionaire with a site called gout.com. Have not yet convinced anyone that this is a good idea.

May 6th

Have not had an email or telephone call from David since before the wedding. Am coldly furious with him.

May 7th

A pea-green knitted hat and shoulder bag set I mail-ordered weeks ago have arrived, but do not give me the dash of hippie chic I had hoped for. Their inadequacy encourages me to believe that there is a market for my designs. No matter how I position my head and arrange my expression, the hat looks like a hot-water bottle, while the bag must surely have been a pyjama case in a previous incarnation. Even my new-found enthusiasm for trimming things founders on these depressing items. They must go.

Spend three-quarters of an hour rewrapping them and trying to find the address to return them to. Hang endlessly on the telephone listening to Vivaldi's *Four Seasons* in an attempt to speak to the mail order company. No one answers, although the music is occasionally interrupted by an electronic voice promising, 'An operator will be available shortly.' Spend almost forty minutes waiting for said operator, tethered by the spiral wire to the telephone. Finally give up because my ear overheats, I am on the brink of tears, and it is time to collect The Beauty from nursery school.

Take horrid hat and bag and post them on the way to the nursery, addressed to an unconvincing PO Box number. In sending them back, I experience happy sensation of having unspent, and therefore saved money. This quickly changes to a belief that I have in fact made a profit by returning the goods. I am therefore quite justified in not working too hard on my cider brochure today. Just as well, as The Beauty's return from nursery tends to limit creative flair on my part.

Wander into the garden to inhale balmy scent of spring and to seek inspiration for my cardigan commissions. Am instead assailed by dreadful old sock and sick aroma. The tent is, of course, still here. Bass and Siren have not been seen since they were piled into a motorbike sidecar and driven at speed from the wedding party. Their camper van is also here, and has become a new second home to The Beauty and her coterie of dolls and dogs.

It does not take more than thirty seconds of suspicious sniffing to realise that the tent is the source of the disgusting smell. Why or how I do not care, I just want it to go. Even though the tent is in the field and not technically my responsibility, I cannot wait for someone else to get round to removing it, the smell is too bad. Open the gate to the field and half-heartedly tug at a guy rope for a moment before deciding that I must call a team of demolition men to do the job for me. Go inside to consult the Yellow Pages, but am diverted by the telephone ringing.

It is Hedley Sale. Having the same thought about the tent.

'Venetia, hello, I wondered if you'd got rid of that tent yet on my field, mmm?' He sounds a little irritable, but I decide to try being blithe.

'Well, put it this way, Hedley, I don't suppose you know how to take a tent down, do you?'

He laughs. 'Well, it shouldn't be too difficult, although those people of yours who brought it should really take it down. It's their property on my property, you see. I'll come by later and have a look.' He gives a little yip of laughter and rings off.

The Beauty and I are engaged in some very engrossing role-playing when Hedley arrives. I have been tucked up in the camper van bed, and am being given my medicine as I am, according to her diagnosis, 'Streemly ill.'

Hedley's blaring voice reaches us in our van from the other side of the house. 'For Christ's sake, Venetia, what the hell are you and those hippies playing at? This tent is ancient. And rotten. It probably dates from the Crimean War, for Christ's sake. It'll take a crane to get those poles down, or at least a tractor. That long-haired fellow must have been as strong as an ox to get this lot up. I haven't got time to deal with it now, but you should get rid of it fast. The grass is rotting underneath it and apart from the smell, I want to put my bloody sheep back on this field.'

The Beauty and I cower in our bed, not liking to interrupt the lava flow of fury. The Beauty begins to whimper, and presses her hands over her ears, and I remember from the end of my marriage to Charles how much children loathe shouting voices.

'What the hell are you doing in there?' Hedley is peering in through the door of the camper van at us. 'Honestly Venetia, you are an ass. Why didn't you tell me you were having trouble with the guy who owns it? I can sort him out.'

Don't really like the familiar way he calls me 'Venetia', although I don't know how else I want him to address me. 'Duchess', perhaps, or if that's too bovine, 'Ma'am' would do.

'I didn't think of getting in touch with you. Why would I?' I mutter, but he is not listening. Beckoning crossly, he marches us over to the field. The Beauty lags, pausing to crouch over a snail. This increases his pent-up rage. Suddenly lose patience with him and snap, 'Look, I don't see why you need to be so angry, you don't have to live with the smell.' His brow shoots up to meet his hairline and he shuts up for a moment, then sighs and stomps away around the tent, occasionally slowing to kick a flap of canvas. He returns, monobrow now diving down between nose and forehead.

'Where are the imbeciles who put it up anyway?' he demands. 'They must come and take it down. It's too bad, it really is.'

'I can't get hold of them, so I thought I'd leave it on the side of the road for them when it's deflated,' I reply, trying to soothe him. 'I'm sure they'll collect it at some point, they'll need it for another party soon. But someone said they've gone in a convoy to Madagascar for the summer, so it's possible it could stay here for months.'

An expression of pain crosses his face; he seems to be taking the tent's continuing presence as a personal slight. Wish I had not asked him to help, but now that our initial shock has passed, The Beauty and I are able to ignore his tantrums, allowing the catalogue of complaints and irritations to flow over us. The Beauty wanders off to play, and I lean on the wall, inhaling the first heady wafts of this summer's honeysuckle on the afternoon air. After another flurry of clucking, brought on when he realises the camper van belongs to the hippies too, Hedley jumps into his truck and zooms away, only to reverse at full rev back up to the house because he has forgotten his dog.

Whistling and swearing conjures a nasty-looking lowlife mongrel from behind the wall where the dustbins live. I refrain from commenting on the yogurt pot the cur is carrying and wave him off.

May 10th

Cannot get out of the garden gate on the school run because a large tractor and trailer are parked there, and a doughy man is sitting at the wheel eating sandwiches. He waves one at me.

'Elevenses,' he mumbles.

'How can you have elevenses at seven forty-five?' muses Giles, before shouting out of the window, 'You mean sevenses.'

All this knife-edge wit does not get us to school, and the man appears to be in no hurry to move his tractor. Giles gets out to look, but is back in moments, his face lit with amusement.

'The tractor is completely stuck, Mum. We can't get out. That guy says someone's coming in a minute with a pulley thing.' Indeed, closer scrutiny reveals that the trailer is wedged across the gateway.

Claustrophobia in me combines with great sympathy for the tractor driver. I achieved the same position in a multi-storey car park a few weeks ago, and the door panels of my car are still a buckled testament to my attempts to free myself. Giles and Felix dance about in front of the tractor chanting, 'We can't go to school, we're prisoners in the garden.'

I mentally run through the list of things I was going to do once they were safely at school and The Beauty ensconced at nursery. Am just writing today off as a dead loss and planning a hike over the tractor and on to the village green, when blaring car horn on the other side of the mechanical barricade announces salvation. It is Hedley. Of course, this must be his tractor. He has sent someone to take the tent down. Cannot feel grateful, as it has all gone wrong already. They should have driven straight into the field from the road rather than trying to fit through my garden gate. Hedley starts steaming away about incompetence from behind the trailer, then goes strangely silent. Giles and Felix throw down their school bags and scramble up on to the tractor and over towards the road.

'Don't vanish, boys, we may be on our way any minute.' I remain in hopeful anticipation of a biblical moment, with the mountain of tractor being moved by a simple act of faith. Odd grunting and sighing, and Hedley emerges in front of me having crawled under the tractor and trailer to get to me. He hands me the keys to his car, huffing and brushing gravel and leaves from his jersey.

'Here you are, you can take the kids to school in my car. You just have to go under the tractor.'

'No fear.' Gracelessness at his chivalrous instinct is unavoidable; nothing would induce me to crawl under a vast agricultural vehicle, particularly now I have come to terms with skiving today. In fact, am looking forward simply to hanging out with my family, and not bothering to do any of the weekday things I should be doing. Naturally, do not tell Hedley any of this.

'We'll wait until you get it out, thank you. Giles and Felix can help you as long as they don't get run over.'

I mount a retreat into the house with The Beauty, promising cups of tea which I have no intention of delivering. Something tells me that Hedley is not qualified for the mathematical and spatial concepts involved in unjamming my gateway, and I do not wish to stand around watching and being maddened by him. The whole point of not being married is not having to deal with moments like this.

May 12th

Have not seen my mother since the wedding, so greet her with huge pleasure when she appears for tea wearing a big straw hat to protect her pallor from the perfect May sunshine. The Beauty is wallowing in her paddling pool, so we have tea outside, but spend several minutes carrying the table and two chairs around the garden to find the best spot. Finally settle in the lee of a south-facing wall where the view of yellow, slimy field beyond is uninterrupted, but the breeze is kept off. My mother puts on her glasses and squints at the vast rectangle of rotted grass. 'Goodness, what's happened over there?

Is it genetic engineering, or GM crops, or have they had a chemical accident? It might be poisonous, you know. We should wear masks.' She pulls the collar of her coat up over her mouth, gasping dramatically.

'It's the tent.'

Cannot believe that she has already forgotten its existence. She is standing now, giving what promises to be a long speech. 'I am against the use of chemicals. Apart from washing-up liquid, which is extremely useful—' She suddenly interrupts herself. 'The tent? What do you mean, the tent? Oh, the *tent.*' She nods in satisfaction, then looks suspiciously round the garden. 'Where is it, then?'

Is there any point in explaining to her?

'It's been taken down, but it has rotted the grass.' I kneel beside The Beauty, assisting her as she performs some mermaid manoeuvres along the bottom of her paddling pool and comes up grinning and blowing bubbles. My mother is most impressed.

'Gosh, isn't she aquatic,' she says admiringly. 'Mind you, I suppose you might have been the same at her age, but I can't remember. You did spend a lot of time sitting outside in saucepans of water, though. So did Desmond.' Her face takes on a faraway, arrested expression. 'I still can't believe Minna actually married him,' she says. 'It's a miracle. When do they get back from their honeymoon?'

'Next week, I think.'

She darts a beady look at me. 'You never said what happened to David. Why didn't he come to the wedding? He was supposed to be best man, and if he

124

had been, we wouldn't have had to have that absurd friend of Desmond's.'

Find her aggrieved tone a bit much. I am the one suffering from David's absence, not her. Say so. A mistake. My mother is able to deliver a smart retort.

'Well, I think it's high time you settled down like your brother and Minna. I am in favour of marriage,' she says, then abruptly changes the subject before I have a chance to say, so am I.

May 15th

Spring is racing ahead and has almost become summer without my getting to grips with anything. Particularly the garden. Cannot possibly go to the Chelsea Flower Show this year, as the excursion would only highlight the fact that I have achieved almost nothing since last year. I still have numerous packets of sample seeds in a tin in the barn, awaiting the ideal time for sowing, and along with them, a whole notebook full of scribbled ideas, none of which have been carried out.

Telephone Rose to tell her I will not be joining her, even though she has got tickets for the VIP day, and she is resigned.

'I knew you wouldn't come. You don't ever come to London now,' she says, irritating me, as I like to think of myself as someone who nips to London on a whim and fits in immediately, becoming cultured and stylish.

'Nonsense, I'm always coming to London. I was there when you were on that awful regime of yours.'

Rose hoots with laughter. 'That was ages ago. What a mistake. I'm doing Pilates now. It's the most brilliant form of exercise – but I meant to say to you, I bumped into someone who came to your brother's wedding the other day, a girl called Sophie who makes wedding cakes. Anyway, she said she'd commissioned you to make a cardigan. Is this true?'

Nettled by the amused astonishment in her voice, I decide to be nonchalant rather than thrilled.

'Oh yes, didn't I tell you? I thought it might be amusing as a sideline.'

'You know you could do really well if you organised yourself,' says Rose. 'Send me some things you've done and I'll see if I can get this shop I know interested. They do a lot of one-offs. It would be so brilliant if it worked.'

Catch her enthusiasm. 'I know, no more brochures. A new life as a fashion designer. I can't wait.'

Rose is first down to earth, as always.

'Well, you had better get on with making the garments then.'

Decide that I must seize the moment, and spurred on by the thought of the brochure I should be writing to sell advertising on Heavenly Petting's deaddog?.com website, I decide to start right away with Sophie's order. Experience not a qualm as I raid my own wardrobe for the basic garment, and select an old pink cardigan I have never worn as the sleeves were much too short.

'Sophie will think it the height of chic,' I tell myself, and set to embellishing it with some tiny silver coins I found in the playroom in a toy treasure chest of Felix's. Fold up cardigan, having christened it 'Treasure Trove', and attach hefty invoice. This after yet another conversation with Rose.

'Come on, you're trying to start a business here. In London that sort of thing goes for hundreds of pounds. She'll think it's a bargain, I promise you. And don't you dare do it for less. I'll check up on you.'

Dispatch my first attempt at becoming a rag-trader, having wrapped it in pink tissue paper and cravenly added a lavender bag made by Giles as a kind of bribe to force Sophie to accept the invoice. Determined not to think about it again for a week. Put notes on the fridge, by the telephone and on the calendar to this effect.

May 16th

The white froth of may blossom on the hedgerows has turned pink, and new life is everywhere, sprouting and budding like mad. However, I am reassured to see that some farmers, like me, are a bit behind. It is the sugar beet that seems to have missed the boat. There are whole fields in which ranked rows of two-leaf or at best three-leaf plants do their best to look large in the midst of vast weed-free stretches of earth. Must ask Simon when I next see him how they keep four-hundred-acre fields weedless when I have just a quarter of an acre and it is bursting with them.

May 19th

Glorious morning, and having dropped the boys at school, The Beauty and I go in search of elderflower cordial ingredients. These are not difficult to assemble, although the tartaric acid can cause remarks in the chemist, as some pharmacists suspect mother and toddler duos of being drug dealers wishing to buy this innocuous powder to mix with other noxious ones. I avoid questioning this year, though, and we are about to depart to a hedgerow near home for the flowers when I notice a vigorous elder tree in the supermarket car park. Warmed by the sun on the south-facing brick wall behind it, this is a prize specimen with flower heads as big as plates. Most pleasing. The Beauty stands on the bonnet of the car and I pass her the creamy blooms, breathing deep the sweet heavy scent as tiny petals scatter from the thousands of mini flowers clustered on each head. We pile them all into her car seat gently as if they are glass, and drive home swimming in the smell of summer.

May 20th

Half-term begins at lunchtime, and by 3 p.m. no one is speaking to anyone and we have all been sent to our rooms. Being nominally in charge, I do not really have to go to my room, but it is a good place in which to sulk and consider my failings as a mother. Unfortunately, The Beauty is also in my room, so sulking has to be put to one side. She has an oven glove, and is collecting small change in it.

'Mummy, can I have ten pounds?' she demands breathily, clinking her ill-gotten gains. Luckily her idea of ten pounds is any coin from any country, so slip a one-hundred lire coin into her collection pouch, while regretting that her recent trip to church seems to have inspired her as a consumer rather than a believer. Must speak to Rev. Trev about The Beauty's faith. In fact, he might be able to sort out all the children and set them on a path of righteousness once again. Telephone him to book a spiritual guidance meeting as soon as possible.

After an hour in our rooms, which I spend wracked with guilt at having screamed, 'You sodding little philistine swine,' while throwing half their Nintendo into the fire, we reconvene. Giles still poker-faced and not looking at me when speaking, Felix now happy and chatting, even though it was at him that I screamed, 'You are driving me insane', to which he replied, 'But you've always been like this, Mummy.'

How can I expect them to behave when my own performance is on this level?

Am wondering whether to take everyone to Le Moon, our favourite Chinese restaurant for conciliatory supper, when mad terrier barking announces Hedley Sale. Open the front door, quaking inwardly, wondering what we have done wrong this time. However, he is looking bashful on the gravel.

'I'm off to listen to the nightingales on the heath,' he announces, his voice carrying on and on and echoing through the garden as if he is proclaiming classes at a gymkhana.

'I wondered if you would all like to come with me. I've got Tamsin in the car too.'

Am rather impressed by this, and should love to listen to nightingales. The boys, chastened by the earlier battle, agree meekly that they too would love to hear nightingales, and we pile into Hedley's purple and yellow truck.

As we bowl along, crammed in, with Hedley and Giles discussing the merits of ferreting over shooting as an effective method for disposing of rabbits, I try to imagine what a nightingale can possibly sound like. Do not wish to reveal ignorance of something I am sure everyone should know, so anxiety mounts as we approach the heath. Cannot help fearing that I may have heard the liquid voice of the nightingale before, and been too insensitive and tone deaf to realise. After all, it is a common English bird. Or is it? Irritatingly, the children, who can usually be relied on to make animal noises and to be fountains of information on any subject at virtually no provocation, do not attempt to make nightingale noises or to discuss them at all. Instead they all sing along to a song on the radio which seems to be called 'A Little Bit of Erica'. Surely that can't be right? No one is called Erica – it is a truly dreadful name.

The heath is golden in the late afternoon light, criss-crossed by small grey roads like ribbons and undulating for miles. We cut the car engine and wind down the windows to listen. There is a hint of woodsmoke in the air and the distant buzz of a tractor engine floats over the still gorses and scrubby plants.

The children scramble to get out but Hedley makes them wait.

'Now listen, you lot,' he says in a voice full of quiet menace, 'if you burst out of the car screeching and shouting, that'll be it, we'll hear nothing. But if you manage to keep quiet, we've got a good chance of hearing the nightingales. Are you ready?'

Delivering a speaking look in response to the threat in Hedley's voice, Giles then Felix tiptoe from the car, led by Tamsin who has The Beauty by the hand and is guiding her across the road and into a clearing in the gorse to listen. Am tempted to shout at Hedley and ask him to refrain from bullying my children, but do not want to break the silent spell. I follow, silent, ears straining for something I half expect to sound like the opening of one of Mozart's flute concertos. And then a flutter of something disturbs the tree next to us and the evening is filled with a silver sound; highly wrought, plangent and at the same time joyful and vigorous. Even The Beauty is silenced, and gazes in wonder up at the tree. I have the creeping sensation caused by all my hairs standing on end, and tears prick my eyes. Am weepy with emotion, and have to wipe my nose on my sleeve three times in the opening aria. The nightingale serenades us for several magical minutes, and gradually, out of the gorse and scrub, figures emerge and join us until there is a crowd of people listening beneath the tree.

'Who are all those people?' Felix hisses.

'They're twitchers,' I hiss back. A tall one, wearing a green cagoule and dangling a new and expensive pair of binoculars, glances at us, and frowning, shakes his head.

'How do you know?' Felix tugs my jacket, pulling me down to whisper in his ear.

'Because there are always twitchers on the heath, looking for rare birds. That's why they've got binoculars.' Am silently congratulating myself for not pouring scorn on twitcher outfits and pack behaviour when Giles steps back and links arms companionably with me.

'Mum,' he says after a moment, 'I wish David was here, don't you?'

Hug Giles back very hard, sniffing again as I realise that I haven't even thought of David for an age. Last conjured him into my mind when searching for a hammer in the woodshed two days ago. My thoughts were not fond, but were concerned more with the chaos and teetering danger of the logs and planks, and whether he would ever come back to sodding well do something about it.

But now, on this schmaltzy evening with the children behaving beautifully and Hedley not shouting for once but being a perfectly pleasant companion, I suddenly suffer a heart-stopping pang of loneliness. Why has David not been in touch since the wedding? What can have happened? I must make a proper attempt to speak to him when we get home. The awful truth is that I have become accustomed to his absence. Shiver, and hug Giles more tightly, rubbing my chin on top of his coconut-matting hair, my arms going almost twice round his narrow ribcage. Look up and notice with irritation that Hedley, who was watching The Beauty, has turned and is gazing at me and Giles with a peculiar arrested expression. Anxious to change the mood, I make a face at Felix, who has zoomed up to me. He roars with laughter and shouts, 'Come on. Let's go home, I'm starving.'

Hedley drops us off without getting out, or turning off his engine, and I am so relieved that I agree to his suggestion that we all come to lunch in half-term without hesitation. After all, anything could happen between now and then. Maybe David will be home.

May 21st

The hen Concubine, willing consort to every despotic cockerel we have had here for the past five years, is unwell. Administer Rescue Remedy when I find her staring blankly at a wall, but it is no use. By teatime she has taken to her bed in a disused bicycle basket under the washing line, and has closed her eyes, something hens don't do very often. The other hens ignore the need for solemnity, and spend the afternoon scratching around her sickroom, groaning and clucking. Dastardly, the cockerel, son of Mustard and Custard, who have gone to live in the village as wild, free birds, is a typical male, and having peered nervously into the bicycle basket to offer help, is now giving vent to his feelings with some crowing practice on top of the hen house. The scene is far from tranquil, and becomes busier still when Giles and Felix return from cricket practice in the village and start patting a basketball around the yard. It has been a treat of a spring day, the sky high and truly blue beyond the whispering soft green buds and unfurled leaves brought visibly forward into full bloom by the warmth of the air. Winding down the zigzag path to the pond I inhale the rich blossomy perfume of the balsam poplar but am interrupted from halcyon thoughts by the squeaking bounce of pram wheels and heavy breathing which herald The Beauty. She is wearing purple sunglasses and a floral apron and has three dolls in her pram and also a cap gun. She is ready for anything.

'Time to bath Tiny Baby,' she says breathily, and hurls the smallest of the three dolls into the pond without ceremony. Wonder if her rough approach to baby care is instinctive, or if I have somehow imbued it in her. Perhaps by being on the telephone too much? Or by my constant shouting and swearing at the dogs? Am now praising Rags to the heavens, as she has shown her own motherly instincts to be finely honed and has dived into the pond to rescue Tiny Baby. The Beauty receives her child with much fuss. 'Oooh Bay-bee, Oooh Baybee. Get dry now,' she urges, busily kissing Baby's slimy head while keeping a beady eye on me for approval.

Giles advances across the garden bearing a shoebox. He presents the stiff corpse of Concubine.

'Look, Mum. She must have been dead for hours because she's got rigor mortis.' Felix joins us, carrying a spade.

'We've got to bury her, Mum, and we'll have to make the hole really deep or Lowly will dig her up again.'

Am moved by their responsible and mature approach to death, and by their desire to give a dignified burial to this little hen.

'Let's put some flowers in her coffin,' says Felix, stroking the soft neck feathers. He and Giles perch the shoebox in a tree out of dog reach and go off to pick flowers. They are back within moments.

'Mummy, why aren't there any flowers in the garden?'

'Oh dear, are there really none out yet?' Clearly should have gone to Chelsea, if just to purchase samples on the last day and stick them with cut stems into my garden to give the illusion of glamorous planting for a few hours.

'Go and have a look in the wood then, there's plenty of wild ones.'

A suitable bunch of cow parsley and pink campion is collected from the outer regions of the garden, while I survey the borders, which are empty of colour but choked with thistles and tufts of grass. Must buy some bedding plants or at least do some weeding so my few perennials have a chance to see daylight this summer. But when? Roused from reverie by Concubine, now cosy beneath a blanket of cow parsley, wobbling pastily in her coffin as Giles and Felix process to the burial ground. Scooping up The Beauty from her baby bathing, I follow them down into the wood.

'Where shall we bury her?' I ask Felix, who is bashing nettles with his spade to make a path for me and The Beauty. He considers for a second, then says, 'Let's put her next to the rat.'

'No way,' says Giles, disgusted. 'We should do it where we've got other graves, not next to vermin.'

'Well, we haven't got any other graves, and we had to bury that rat to stop Rags bringing it back into the kitchen,' Felix points out. 'We usually just throw dead animals over the hedge, don't we, Mum? You always say it's a family reaction to Heavenly Petting.'

Realise that my approach to pet death has been much too cavalier, and that, contrary to my beliefs, the children were paying attention when the three goldfish went over the wall into the potato field. Recall my mother's reaction on hearing of my disposal methods on this occasion.

'It's a kind of heavenly fish and chips. It seems right. It seems good,' she mused when I told her.

Dig a fine hole, and make it double the depth I think it should be, remembering from childhood when grave-digging was a regular chore, that the corpse is always bigger than one expects. Giles lowers Concubine in and we all peer at her for a moment before scattering earth and stamping it in. The Beauty is very taken with the whole ceremony, and capers about on top of the grave saying, 'In the hole, in the hole, down, down, down.' Then, chillingly, as we are all standing around, 'Come on boys, let's pretend to cry.' Is this how psychopaths begin their career?

*   *   *

Spend the evening alternately in mourning and on the telephone trying to arrange the purchase of new bantams. My mother, summoned by Felix who is trying to persuade her to help him write a Greek tragedy for his Warhammer figures, appears just as I have persuaded The Beauty that it is bedtime and indeed dark, by hanging a black towel across her window.

'I know you liked that hen, but I think black curtains is going a little too far,' remarks my mother, sliding into a chair at the kitchen table and reaching into her bag for her vital paraphernalia. Ever since I can remember, she has needed two packets of cigarettes, a lighter and a notebook and pen on the table in front of her to be able to enjoy herself. And if there's a bottle and a glass, so much the better. She has recently added a portable ashtray to her permanent accessories, a gift from Giles last Christmas, and this now rests next to the glass Felix is filling for her.

'I've read that you can get lap chickens,' she says. 'I don't know what kind they are, but there are some hens that love to sit on your knee and watch television with you. A couple of those would be nice.' She puffs enthusiastically at her cigarette and pours us both another drink. Noticing that she has little use for it at present, Felix appropriates her notebook, opens it at a blank page and pulls a chair up close to hers.

'Granny, can we have the Argonauts killing a troop of Bloodthirster elves? And can we set it in the future, like *Star Wars*?'

Can clearly see the whites of Granny's eyes as she rolls them heavenwards and sets to work.

May 22nd

Oops. Forgot to go to lunch with Hedley yesterday. He rang to ask us just as Concubine began to fail, and the drama wiped it from my mind. Wonder why he didn't ring to remind us? A short tussle with the answerphone reveals that he did. And, not surprisingly, he sounds cross. I think I'll send a postcard to apologise.

May 23rd

Email David a businesslike message.

> Did you get my email about the wedding? Why didn't you reply? Please ring me. There are things we must discuss.
>   Yours, Venetia

Cannot understand why there has been no communication from him, and can only assume that I was right all along and he has gone to live in the treetops with a bikini-wearing beauty. Am not sure when I should accept this as a fact. Certainly not today.

May 25th

The postman has broken down in our garden. He is sitting in his van right outside my study window, making work in there impossible. How can people in offices close deals, make phone calls and generally get on, with other people sitting right next to them? I find that even if there is a window and a car between me and someone else, I am utterly distracted by their presence. Suppose it is the novelty. Having given him a cup of tea and a newspaper (last Sunday's broadsheet, which he does not look pleased with), and agreed that it is a lovely day, I retreat into the house, wondering where I can go. Am faced with staying in the kitchen or skulking in doorways off the hall until his mechanic arrives from miles away. The sitting room and my study are too exposed. Feel it would be rude to shut the windows now, but can hear every breath he draws, which means he can hear my telephone conversations. Ring Hedley anyway, to thank him for the very civil card the postman has brought asking us to lunch again in a couple of weeks. Again I accept, but have every hope of remembering this time. Tell him so, and see the postman smirk disbelievingly.

Too much. I poke my head out of the front door and ask with great courtesy, 'How long will your mechanic be, do you think?'

The postman is lolling with sunglasses on, and starts when I speak, tapping his mobile phone to simulate impatience.

'Oh, not more than an hour and a half,' he says.

Retreat into the house again and sit at my desk, mentally running through the list of two-person chores I keep in my head for opportunities such as this. Reject the putting-up of the hammock as it might suggest to him that he could spend the rest of the day in it, but linger on moving The Beauty's sandpit round to a shadier part of the garden. Just as I am mustering the courage to go and ask him, his mobile telephone warbles, and after a short conversation, he puts on his jacket, takes off his shades and trudges off down to the road with a bundle of letters. I should have offered him my bike.

May 28th

Well within the allotted time, a cheque from Sophie the Lesbian arrives. For the full amount! I am a top businesswoman and will soon take over the world like Ralph Lauren. Hooray, hooray! Wonderful, balmy morning with hens clucking like mad and eating grass with zeal as if they are equines. Or bovines. Had forgotten the lovely, peaceful summer ritual of a dozen young cows arriving on the water meadows beyond the garden. And had forgotten how much I love springtime and what energy comes with it. Suddenly the landscape has become Turneresque, and what was formerly just an emerald backdrop for the swooping barn owl, has become the rural idyll personified. Can vaguely remember some stuff about Rousseau and getting back to nature, so decide that now is the moment for the children to make a vegetable garden and generally start living off the fat of the land. The Beauty and I have beetroot with chives for lunch to celebrate, from my present ragged vegetable patch, and I become very excited about an earthy, natural existence, but with reservations about sandals.

After lunch, while The Beauty sleeps, I weed the potential new vegetable garden and am suddenly struck with a design for a shirt with a wiggle of string weaving in between the buttons. During the evening, having persuaded the children that they would like roast chicken with bread and mayonnaise for supper, I have time to make this garment using my pale blue linen shirt and a ball of twine. Despatch to Rose with two cardigans (my last, where can I find some more?) and a feather-trimmed skirt, as she says she has girl-friend clamouring for my garments after I sent her the ice-blue pipe-cleaner one which I called 'Ice Cold in Alice'.

Am enjoying making up names as much as designing the garment itself, and have employed the children at fifty pence an item to make individual labels for them.

May 31st

Am devastated. A parrot arrived this morning. From David, for the children. Another animal to be cared for by me no doubt, is my first Bad Fairy thought upon opening the door to a harassed courier and the acid-green monster. Would have sent it back to the depot, but most unfortunately the children heard it issue a ripe wolf whistle at me, and came running.

'I'm Gertie,' squawked the parrot. 'Dirty Gertie, dirty Gertie. Have you got pants on, Missus?' All three of them roll on the hall floor, paralysed with mirth as I grimly sign for it. Am sure it should go into quarantine. In fact, I think it *must* go into quarantine. No need to ring the Foreign Office and disturb them with little daft questions, I'll just book Gertie in. Right now. Why has David done this to me?

JUNE

June 1st

I am, according to the children, Hannibal Lecter and Attila the Hun and every other ruthless swine to have walked on earth. Gertie is installed at Golden Graham's Pet Haven, a parrot hotel near Cambridge which Charles told me about. I was drawn to it by his saying, 'Actually, they're among our best clients. Parrots seem to be very difficult to keep alive.'

'Don't tell the children,' I hiss, 'but I am very much hoping that Gertie lives out her days there.'

'I wouldn't be too complacent,' Charles responds, and I can tell that he is enjoying this conversation and especially relishing my desperation. 'You know they can live to be eighty years old if they're tough, and those green ones are among the toughest. Nice for the children, though. He's a decent chap, that fellow David.' He rings off before I can make a decent retort. I grind my teeth and stand on one leg, arms above the head and other leg folded against inner thigh. However, yogic magic is not strong enough to overcome my outrage. Topple off balance and reach again for the phone, dialling the numbers I have for David over and over, and listening in despair to the clicks and long tones, but never to his voice on the other end saying 'Hello'.

June 3rd

The vegetable garden is coming on apace. Sort of. I am interested in it, so is The Beauty, but this morning, when I asked Felix to go and fetch the spade from it, he said, 'What vegetable garden?' thus giving the game away, and revealing himself to be entirely lacking in spirit of Rousseau.

Rather discouraging to read the seed packets and find that we are two months behind with planting, and have little hope of catching up, so will be eating lettuce in the winter and tomatoes next spring if we plant them now and madly mollycoddle them. The Beauty is keen to do this, and I find a stash of seeds in her pocket when changing her to go out to lunch with Hedley.

Cannot decide what to wear, and cannot remember when any consideration beyond sartorial last occupied my mind for more than three minutes consecutively. Is it, I wonder, a ploy of my brains to prove that my future is as a mover and shaker in fashion, or is it that I am an airhead? Find the latter possibility much more likely than the former, but am distracted by the more immediate puzzle concerning the whereabouts of my other shoe. Arrive late for lunch, thanks to prolonged, fruitless shoe search. Have had to wear purple high-heeled boots, much to the chagrin of Giles.

'You're really weird, Mum. You should try to act more like a grown-up,' he says witheringly on the way, deaf to my protestations that there is nothing I would like more than to be serene and adult in every aspect of behaviour and appearance. Still brooding on what exactly being grown-up looks like to disdain-ful eleven-year-olds, when we reach Crumbly. Hedley is nowhere to be seen, so after ringing the bell, we retreat to lean on the car while Giles aims small stones at an old paint pot by the front door.

Summer is in full frill and flourish. Hedley's house has woods to one side, and untamed vegetation which runs down a small valley before swooping up to a flint church standing on the next mound of high ground. According to Rev. Trev, the gardens at Crumbly were famous in three counties a few years ago, but now nothing but wild flowers remain, and the gnarled shapes of ancient azaleas and rhododendrons which flank a wide ride down towards the common. At the end of this ride, three beehives form a picturesque boundary, and Giles leads us towards them, stating, 'Tamsin said that Hedley was always mucking about with the bees. He's bound to be down here.'

And as the words leave his mouth, a startling figure leaps in front of us, swaddled to the hilt in white, his movement curtailed by padded clothes, his face obscured by a broad-brimmed, black-veiled hat. The Beauty is horrified. She shrinks back against me weeping, 'Mummy, it's a mummy, it's a horrid mummy, not a proper mummy like you,' conjuring the image from the Tintin book I was reading the boys in bed this morning. Her sobs turn to shrieks as the mummy squats down in front of her, and having moved too hastily, loses its balance and tips over to lie, legs and arms wiggling like an upside-down beetle.

'I hate that thing,' she wails, and yanking my hand, begins to pull me back towards the car. Giles and Felix have run on ahead, but hearing The Beauty's cries, they come back to save her. However, one look at the wriggling figure on the ground and they collapse into unstoppable giggles. The Beauty can never maintain an angst-ridden pose for long, and her tears dry the instant she sees her brothers are unafraid. The mummy's head falls off, as I have been expecting it to for some minutes, and, also as expected, Hedley's reddish face and his black caterpillar eyebrow are revealed.

'I was just sorting the hives out a bit,' he says, ignoring the mirth of our whole party and concentrating his gaze on Lowly, whom we accidentally brought with us because he was asleep in the car and no one noticed him until it was too late.

'Let's go and have a drink now, shall we, and after lunch we'll come and see if we can get some honey. I've got more suits somewhere.'

'How kind,' I hear myself saying, not meaning it at all, as I am allergic to honey and swell up like a balloon if I so much as lick a drop. 'The children would love to do that, wouldn't you?'

Glare furiously at Felix, panting and sniggering behind us, and aim a kick at Giles when he mumbles, 'Not really, I don't like bees,' just out of Hedley's hearing.

'It's such a beautiful day,' I witter as we approach the front door. 'We've been so lucky with the weather this spring, haven't we?'

Am always quite amazed when I hear platitudes and clichés such as these emerging in an effortless string from my mouth. They are so at odds with image of self as a free spirit and higher thinker. Soothing second thought that the weather is vital as social currency, and it doesn't matter what you talk about as long as you keep talking, enables me to babble on drearily as we enter the house. Hedley departs through a series of doors off the shadowy wainscoted hall to change out of his bee-keeper's outfit. Felix is spell-bound in front of a suit of armour. 'Look, Mummy, it's real. I love it,' he whispers. 'How do you get into it?'

'Don't be silly, you can't just get into armour. You aren't even medieval,' says Giles scornfully. Look round expectantly for signs of other guests and find the dining table laid for eight, which is a big relief. Find Hedley pretty hard work on my own, and cannot depend on the boys at all at the moment as they prefer not to speak to me or indeed anyone, in words of more than one syllable and sentences of more than one word. Doorbell and voices announce the arrival of fellow lunchers. Am delighted to recognise Simon's booming tones.

'Well, what have we here? The Knight of the Round Table, is it? I say, careful there, old chap. I SAID CAREFUL—' Almighty crash follows and then much wailing. Felix has clearly become closely involved with the armour. He appears wearing the helmet, through one door into the dining room, where The Beauty and I are delicately sipping fruit juice, and Hedley simultaneously enters through the other. Both of them recoil in horror at the sight of the other.

Cannot decide whom to apologise to or for, and beam with extra joy as Vivienne and Simon come in to support us all through the difficult moments of removing Hedley's precious helmet from the head of an hysterical Felix. Tornado of chaos erupts. The helmet will not budge. The only bit we can open is the visor, which rises and falls obligingly, while the catch at the back which unhooks the neckpiece is stuck fast. WD40 found and applied to no avail, and Felix starts shrieking that he is the Man in the Iron Mask and will never escape, never. The Beauty sobs in sympathy, Vivienne tries to comfort her and earns a black mark from me for giving her a sip from a glass of Coke. The Beauty, canny even in deepest distress, grabs the glass from Vivienne's unsuspecting and therefore limp grasp, and swigs the lot before giving a throaty burp and demanding, 'More.' Glimpse this displeasing scene out of the corner of my eye as Simon and Hedley yank at poor Felix as though he is a rugby ball, and Giles photographs the drama and makes irritating remarks.

'Mummy, why did they phase out armour?' Can he not see for himself?

Finally, just as everyone is losing interest and I have picked up the telephone to make the numbingly embarrassing call to the fire brigade, there is a pop like a champagne cork and Felix is free, tear-stained but beaming with relief. 'It just suddenly came undone,' he says, holding up the helmet.

Ice well and truly broken by this start to lunch and Vivienne has The Beauty on her lap and is dealing with the wild reprobate fork-flinging and demented expression that the quantities of Coke have caused. I am therefore able to converse freely with anyone I choose to, and to drink several glasses of red wine.

On the way home, driving with flair and vigour, I say to the children, 'I think Hedley's quite nice really, don't you?'

Felix stiffens next to me. 'No, he's really grumpy,' he says, adding, 'I'd rather have gone to the parrot hotel to visit Gertie than go to Hedley-stupid-Sale's for lunch.'

Giles leans over from the back and grins, 'Guess what!' He pauses for effect. 'Tamsin says he's got false teeth.'

June 5th

Rose telephones.

'I didn't tell you because I didn't want to get your hopes up, but I took those things you sent to The Blessing, and they loved them. They want to order ten more. Can you make ten?'

149

Am overwhelmed. Immediate reaction is to say 'No way,' but conquer it.

'What did they say? How much did you say the clothes were? Have they sold any yet? Oh, Rose, do you think I can give up the Vanden Plaz brochure contract now?'

Rose is cautious. 'No, I think that would be a mistake, but you should be able to if your stuff goes down well. I charged them one hundred and fifty pounds per garment. I know you only said one hundred, but really Venetia, you've got to be able to make something out of this, and don't forget, you have to make the garments.'

Extraordinary. Can Rose honestly think I knitted those cardigans, or cut out and sewed that skirt? Just shows how little idea she has about sewing or clothing manufacture. I think the skirt even had an old label in it from the chain store I bought it in years ago. Still, if that's what she thinks, who am I to disabuse her?

She is still talking, but my mind has wandered. Staring out of the kitchen window, I spot The Beauty flitting behind the washing line, an egg in each hand and three of the most scraggy-looking hens following her. Her voice carries in on the balmy spring air.

'Come on hens, let's have a boiled egg and soldiers now.'

Suddenly do not want to think about work, so cut Rose short.

'Sorry, I've got to go. I'll send you them as soon as they're made, shall I? Bye.' Slap telephone back in its cradle and it immediately rings again. I ignore it and walk out into the yard, growing visibly taller, as taught in my yoga class, by breathing deeply and exhaling and thus experiencing total serenity. For a millisecond. Ghastly wailing indicates that The Beauty's boiled-egg breakfast with the hens has not gone well. Follow the sound round to her sandpit and meet a circus-ring scene. The three hens are lying in a row in The Beauty's sandpit, evidently enjoying a dust-bath. The eggs are neatly placed in the sand in front of them, and The Beauty is prancing about waving a magician's wand and glaring.

That's not right,' she scolds. 'Don't sit down. Make toast.' Scoop her up and we return to the house where the anwerphone flashes. Play back the message and I almost pass out with the enormity of what I have just missed.

'Hi there, Venetia. It's David here. How's the parrot? By the way, I ordered it from a pet shop in Norwich, so it doesn't need to go into quarantine, you know. I suddenly realised you would think it came from the jungle. Look, we really need to talk. All our lines are down, but I'm in the nearest town for a couple of days, so I'll call you again.'

How can I have thought I was reconciled to being on my own again? My heart is thudding and rushing madly. The message finishes too soon, leaving the house horribly empty and far too quiet. I play it again. Kick the hall door, disappointment at missing him spreading like nausea. The Beauty eyes me severely. 'That's quite enough now, Mummy,' she says. 'Never do it ever again.'

June 6th

Minna and Desmond appear, dovetailing with us as we turn in through the gate, hot and thirsty after school. The children run to them, kicking a tiny dust cloud in the yard, and are enveloped in Minna's fragrant embrace. She swings The Beauty up into her arms, and approaches me with Desmond. They are like a couple from *Hello!* magazine, bronzed and blonde with the children lolloping around them and huge sparkly smiles decorating their faces. The only element missing is the snow-white towelling bath-robe. I have never seen such a display of coupledom.

Heart sinks rather as a huge tower-block stack of photographs is placed on the kitchen table.

'We thought you would be longing to see the pictures of the wedding and the honeymoon,' says Minna. We flick through, and apart from noticing that I have not seen the shoes I am wearing in the pictures since the wedding, I remain silent until a picture of me aiming a covert kick at Bass the hippy is reached.

'Do you know, we've still got their camper van,' I remark to Desmond. He claps his hand to his fore-head and then reaches across me to clasp Minna's hand.

'You are always right, angel,' he says, smiling into her eyes in an idiotic fashion. 'You said I'd forget to tell Venetia about the van, and I did.' He sits back again, contrition writ large. 'Bass sent me a postcard from Madagascar weeks ago, right after our honeymoon. They're joining a commune there, and they want you to have the camper van as a present. They think it will help you reach a level of karmic consciousness where you will be able to see Bass without kicking him in future.'

Godsake! as The Beauty would say. Anyway, jolly nice to be given a camper van. Shall now have it towed to the garage to have the battery charged.

Desmond and Minna, murmuring and fluttering at one another like a pair of doves in spring, stay to supper and leave after dark, driving off into the still silver landscape illuminated by the low disc of a rice-paper moon. Find that I am wide awake and my senses are jangling, so wander around the garden, enjoying the whispered rush of the grass beneath my feet and the odd creaks and shrills of night creatures. For once I am outside on the right night to appreciate the ghostly blooms of the white rose, Wedding Day, and the night-scented stocks I planted with this moment in mind. Except this moment is flawed. I was not supposed to be alone in my garden on a moonlit summer night. I lean over the wall looking away down the water meadow, over the stream which glints pewter light. And with desolating clarity I suddenly realise that I want to be married. Am immediately ashamed of this desire. I have after all got children, a home and a career. This should be more than enough for the emancipated modern woman. Surely it is greedy, and belittling, to want to be married as well. It is not feminist, not emancipated, certainly not necessary, and sadly, not likely.

Nonetheless, acknowledging my shameful desire is curiously uplifting. I continue my stroll, and find myself singing Van Morrison. Pause to do a spot of moon-dancing, but have to stop immediately as it makes the dogs anxious.

June 7th

David rings this evening, as I am about to go to bed. It is another perfect night. I stand in the doorway, watching bats flit in the half-light and house martins swoop towards me, humming more Van Morrison and indulging in total fantasy. He is proposing that we marry immediately and have a honeymoon in the Tuscan Hills with every cliché in attendance. I am accepting gracefully, with tears sparkling in my eyes.

'VENETIA. CAN YOU HEAR ME? I SAID THE PARROT MUST HAVE DISTILLED WATER.'

Oh, for heaven's sake. Why is everyone so animal obsessed? I would like to give them all to Pet Rescue myself. Somehow manage not to convey this to David, and skirt around the parrot's present whereabouts, not wishing to admit that it is, as we speak, running up a room service bill for sunflower seeds and sundries in David's name at its hotel in St Neots. Am brisk and irritated when I can get a word in, but on the whole, this is David's one-way conversation.

'I'm sorry I haven't been in touch, it's just been such an engrossing project and there is never a moment when someone doesn't want you for something . . .' He bangs on about jungle life and I become increasingly petulant. He seems to take it for granted that I am delighted to be stuck at home on my own, with no messages from him and no indication that he is anything to do with us any more.

Suddenly, as if from a great distance, I hear a voice which I recognise as mine saying, 'I'm sorry, David. We can't go on like this. I think we both know it's over, so let's not pretend otherwise. When you return to England you can collect Digger and Lowly and the parrot. I'm sorry.'

My ear is throbbing and red hot, I can't believe I've said these mad, no-going-back words. There is a silence, then David speaks, his voice flat and sad. 'I suppose this was bound to happen. What can I say?'

I can think of plenty that he could say. How about, 'Will you marry me?' How about, 'I will love you for ever. I would do anything to win you back.' Or, 'I'm catching the next plane home, darling.'

But I don't make these suggestions. I just say good-bye and hang up.

June 9th

Make a tank top adorned with miniature rosettes found in a charity shop in a Julip horse set. Get bored of sewing each tiny rosette on by hand, but remember that my mother always used Copydex to hem curtains and attach our school name tapes. Find a pot in the playroom and have the job done in moments. The end result is most pleasing. I christen it 'Gymkhana', and am about to post it off to Rose when I remember that there is a pair of ancient jodhpurs in the dressing-up box. Can I get away with selling them too? I have enough rosettes left to decorate the front pockets and the opening at the bottom of the leg. Finish this job and wrap the whole ensemble in tissue paper, adding a small plastic horse from The Beauty's farm as a treat. Cannot believe that this is all considered work, and that I am being paid for it. Have decided not to tell anyone David and I have split up until I can say it to myself in the mirror without crying.

June 12th

Felix asks to send an email to David. Flailing and panicking, I decide it is best that he just does it. After all, there is no reason why the children can't continue to have a very good relationship with him. They are in charge of the parrot or will be if I ever let it return from the hotel, and they're supposed to be looking after Lowly the Weirdo. Felix spends hours on his email, and prints it out to show me.

Dear David
Today a police officer called PC Baxter came to our school. He is the liaison officer of Norfolk. There are 1400 policemen and policewomen in Norfolk. First he talked to us about what you get if you call 999 and what you get is the police, the fire brigade and the ambulance. Actually, we know this isn't true because when The Beauty calls 999

sometimes when Mummy is in the bath the police just ring back and say DON'T. You can also get the coastguard on 999. Then he talked about his code name. It was Foxtrot Romeo One Zero. After that he talked about different kinds of handcuffs. We are going to the parrot hotel to see Gertie next time we stay with Dad.

Love Felix

Cannot help glowing with pride as I read this interesting and informative email, then shriek in horror as I reach the last line.

'Oh *no*, you haven't sent it, have you? Quick, get it back.'

Felix gives me a pitying look. 'Don't be stupid, Mum, you can't. Can I go to the Dancing Hamsters?'

Wonder for a moment if this is a new skateboard hang-out in the village, but realise swiftly that it is a website. Felix crashes the computer three times while looking for it, but I am so alarmed by the possibility of confrontation with David over the parrot hotel that I don't care.

Felix then redeems himself utterly by finding a site called freakytoys.com and we manage to buy five hundred plastic trolls for three pounds. Very excited as they will trim several cardigans, and maybe even a travel rug. I like the idea of moving into Lifestyle, and also enjoy the modern sensation of being in the middle of the countryside and effortlessly buying things off the internet. Of course, cannot even begin to find my way around without Felix and Giles, but as they are almost nerds in their computer knowledge, I am poised on the cutting edge.

June 15th

A taxi pulls up just as I am about to collect The Beauty from nursery. It contains Gertie, her cage and a bill from the parrot hotel for seventy-eight pounds plus the forty-seven-pound taxi fare.

'Hello darling,' chirps Gertie, swaying rhythmically in the passenger seat. 'I love this one,' she adds as the vintage-tunes channel on the taxi radio delivers the opening bars of Andy Williams singing 'Music To Watch Girls By'.

Without hesitation I adopt a gormless expression and a thick Scandinavian accent. The driver, scratching his head and reading his directions, is no match for my Norwegian trawlerman voice, and is alarmed by my expression as I approach his side of the car, leering horribly.

'I dunno what they're playing at, sending parrots all around the countryside,' he says, hopeless acceptance writ large on his countenance. 'And this one hasn't shut up since we left St Neots. It's got quite a vocabulary too. I reckon it's spent time in the nick or somewhere else pretty rough.' He sighs then says, 'Course, you don't know what I'm saying, do you, love? I think I'll take it back to the pet hotel. They've got an account with us, so there won't be a problem with the fare that way.'

Spirits soar for the first time since I dumped David as I watch Gertie accelerate off down the road again in her taxi, still chatting away. The last thing I hear as they round the bend out of sight is her fruity wolf whistle, and her appreciative squawk to the taxi driver, 'Nice pants darling.'

While I am gloating over my quick-witted escape, Charles rings to say he would like the children next weekend.

'I'm surprised you can remember what they look like,' I remark sourly.

In the gap that follows I hear him buttoning his lip before replying, 'Don't turn into an old cat, Venetia, you can't afford to.' Am gobsmacked by this, but unable to think of a riposte because he is so right. Relationships going wrong on all levels now. Have fallen out with everyone except The Beauty, and if the boys find out that the parrot doesn't need to be in quarantine, and worse still, I have turned her from the door, they will never speak to me again. Must now get on, as The Beauty awaits. Macaroni cheese does not make itself and the boys will be back from school in half an hour.

June 17th

Children depart, leaving me wretched. Had forgotten how awful it is when they go away with Charles, as they have not been for months. The Beauty appears not to know who he is, and when he invites her to climb into his immaculate people carrier, she shrinks and clings to my legs.

'I will not go, no, I will not,' she says stoutly, but is won over by Giles who rustles a packet of sweets from the other side of her car seat. Charles slams the doors and rubs his hands together, smirking like a slave trader with his cargo.

'I expect you'll be putting your feet up and relaxing for the next couple of days,' he says to me, managing to make it sound like a gross act of self-gratification, akin to eating forty doughnuts. Manage to smile and make jolly thumbs-up signs as they glide down the drive and away, but when I walk back into the kitchen, the clock ticks loud and slow.

June 18th

Get through the day by cleaning out two garden sheds and making a bonfire. Am as manic as Rumpelstiltskin about my business and only stop at teatime because the dogs have joined me in the garden and are taking it in turns to trip me up in order to remind me to feed them. Go into house to do so, and become afraid of the yawning evening ahead. Cannot face doing internal spring cleaning, so hover for a while, reading cereal packets on the kitchen table and eating biscuits from the tuck shop the children have created in a turret of Lowly's castle. Time crawls, and am finally forced to watch television.

Enjoy *Baywatch* hugely. There are mad-looking plastic crocodiles wrestling with butch men, and girls with bosoms that jut like cliffs. Everyone is the colour of maple syrup with proper blonde hair, not former blonde hair like mine. Make a mental note to buy colour-enhancing shampoo next time I am out, as it will be much cheaper than highlights at the hairdresser, and there is no occasion to merit a big spend on hair at present. *Baywatch* ends while I am thinking about my hair, so I never discover what happened to the crocodile in the lifeguard's bath. Speculate fruitlessly for ten minutes but give up, and am disappointed to find that the evening has still hardly begun. Telephone my mother to moan, but she is not there. Peta the basket-weaver answers the telephone, and offers me a place in her all-female drumming circle.

'We start at eight with meditation for half an hour. Do come, but leave your ego at home,' she titters. 'And do be sure to wear hemp or hessian, we try to be reasonably medieval at all times.'

How does my mother put up with her? She must be hypnotised, as I seem to be.

'Let me just see if there's anything on the calendar,' I mutter, dropping the telephone and charging into the kitchen, brain whirring uselessly. Stare at the wall for a while experiencing ebb and flow of adrenalin but still no excuses, before finally turning to the calendar in a vague hope of escape being offered through its pages. Today's date leers out at me, and I gaze at it with horror. I am already going out. Hedley has asked me to supper. How can I have forgotten? Should I try to get out of it? I can't. Anyway, I need something to do. He said he would be on his way back from some-where and would pick me up at seven-thirty. He is presumably hosting a *soigné* dinner party. It is seven now and I have crescents of filth under my nails and cobwebs in my hair from the barn-clearing. Must get *soignée* right now. It is only when I am in the bath that I remember Peta, and the dangling telephone.

Hedley's car heater is whirring as I step in, even though the rain of this afternoon has evaporated into milky mist and the air outside is warm.

'It's stuck on,' Hedley yells above the roar of the heater. 'You'll have to keep your window open.' Am glad to do so, as a very natural aroma is seeping towards me from Hedley, and a dead rabbit lolls next to me on the seat. Hedley reaches to remove it and it thuds to the floor, disappearing beneath mounds of newspaper and old crisp packets.

'I've been doing silage,' he yells, noticing my shrinking away. 'The dog caught that just before we came in. I'm going to give it to the owl-sanctuary man in the village.'

'Make sure you don't forget, or your car will become a midden,' is my only contribution to the conversation. It doesn't matter, though; Hedley is in high spirits, and hums a bit of *La Traviata* as we go, drumming his fingers on the steering wheel in time. The journey to his house from mine involves a thread of the smallest lanes, high-banked with corkscrew bends and a small unbridged ford. Wood pigeons clap a retreat from the road outside Crumbly as we slow to turn up the drive; they flutter through low-lying mist to vanish into the dusk creeping in from the distant fringe of woodland.

Hedley unlocks the house and vanishes to change,

and I wander through into the hall and on to the sitting room. The house smells of beeswax and lilac and order; making my way slowly around the books and pictures, I try to imagine what it would be like to lead an existence in such a rarefied atmosphere. Am sure I could become accustomed to it. Peer into the dining room to see how many people are coming tonight, but the room is pitch-black with shutters and curtains barring every chink of light. Clearly this evening is one of those kitchen suppers I always wear the wrong clothes for. Pause to inhale a fragrant bunch on the dresser, and admire the taste of the Constance Spry disciple who has put pale mauve lupins in a jug with flaming orange roses and red-throated honeysuckle. The smell is intoxicating, and I float on it into the kitchen in search of a drink – nectar will probably be available, or some other ambrosial juice. Cloud nine musings suffer a setback in the kitchen, and Hedley following me into the room hears my exclamation.

'What's the matter?' he asks nervously, wiping the front of his shirt as if afraid jelly or gravy has planted itself there. Tear my eyes away from the kitchen table which has been laid with candles, more roses and honeysuckle and two places.

'Just us?' I say brightly, and Hedley's one brow, groomed upstairs to a fine satin-black sheen, flattens like a Plimsoll line, belying his nonchalant answer.

'Oh yes, I just wanted to talk to you about Tamsin, and see if we could organise a pony for Giles to use a bit more.'

'Well that's very nice, but I have to be home for my babysitter by eleven, she's got toothache,' I say, with no planning and no blushing at all. Breathtakingly successful lie. I could have used similar on the basket-weaver and would like to write it down so as to practise the crisp yet regretful tone. Hedley accepts this non sequitur without comment. Hugely relieved, I slug back my first glass of wine and become very overexcited. Half of me is shocked and nervous to be having dinner alone with a man in his house, and half of me is enjoying the fantasy of moving in and becoming chatelaine of Crumbly and never having to write another corporate brochure or plunge the sink myself again. Hah! That would show David. Hah! More wine and malevolence and revenge begin to occupy my whole mind. It would serve David right if he came back to collect his things and we were all living here in the lap of luxury. The fourth glass of wine has me tittering and smirking, talking non-stop, secure in my alcohol-fuelled belief that I am marvellously clever and very attractive. Hedley's eyebrow begins to slant towards the ceiling as coffee succeeds food and wine continues to flow. Fortunately for self-preservation, the beeper on my watch, which I set in sobriety earlier, goes off at half past ten. Leap up from my seat as if I have been scalded, as does Hedley, who starts running around the kitchen flapping a tea towel.

'It must be a smoke alarm. We must have caused a fire somewhere. Quick, open the window. No, on second thoughts don't. Keep it shut, and shut all the doors.'

Like a clockwork toy he whirrs manically about the room, bouncing off doors and walls, gradually losing impetus until he comes to a halt in front of me, an arrested expression on his face.

'You made that noise,' he says accusingly.

'Yes. I did. I've got to go home now.'

'Ahh yes, the babysitter. Come on then.' Frowning and over-revving the car, he drives me home in silence. Luckily left a few lights on at my house, and am out of the car almost before Hedley has stopped at the gate, so desperate am I that he should not realise that there is no babysitter and no children. Cannot rid myself of the notion that my situation, with family away, is more provocative than that of a woman who lives alone all the time. Why is this?

June 19th

A Sunday morning of unsurpassed loveliness, making lounging in the hammock imperative, after which I shall of course set about accomplishing some of the goals I set myself for the weekend. Have actually not got around to doing anything at all and it is already midday. Minna and Desmond, still rose-tinted and holding hands all the time, have just been over. Sticky moment when Desmond said, 'So is David ever coming back, or has he succumbed to a jungle girl?'

But managed to answer in similarly light vein, 'Oh, I dare say he'll turn up to collect his dog if nothing else.' And we all laughed. Surely that counts as having told them? And I didn't cry.

165

Spend the afternoon nurturing small seedlings and planting them in rows in my vegetable patch. Straight lines astonishingly difficult to achieve, but vital to the zigzag pattern I am planning for my parsley edging. End up making most satisfying implement with two balls of string on sticks. It looks charming, like a couple of toffee apples with a thread of toffee linking them, and has the extra merit of being free, whereas the one in Horty Hortus costs forty-nine pounds.

Wind billows warm yet persistent from about three o'clock, and by mid-afternoon rain is pelting down on my bedraggled seedlings. Put my only plastic cloche over the zinnias, having reasoned that as I have only one row of them, they need to be saved, and retire to bed to watch the clock until the children return.

June 20th

Blazing heatwave causes ill temper all round. Felix excavates an old stick of chewing gum from the floor of the car on the way to school, and finding it disgusting, attempts to spit it out of the window. Of course, he misses.

'It's gone down the side, Mum,' he yells.

'Well get it out.'

'I can't.' Shrill crescendo is muffled as he dives between the seats, thwacking my ear on the way. Wish I had a car with a glass partition to protect me from abuse and noise pollution of my children. Bad mood exacerbated by arrival at school, late, and the sight of a group of mothers who have miraculously already acquired suntans and uncrumpled summer dresses and the right shoes. Cannot face going over to them, and doubt that I would make it anyway, as my summer skirt has lost all its buttons and is staying up thanks to The Beauty's dressing-gown cord. My shoes are last summer's plimsolls, which I thought were fine when I put them on this morning, but now a horrible smell emanates from them and if I move my toes, their environment is revealed to be squelchy. Make do with a cheery wave and zoom away, hoping I look as though I am very busy. Notice in the rear-view mirror that the one in strawberry pink with freckles sprinkled prettily across her nose is gesturing madly at me, but with iron discipline persuade myself not to be paranoid. Much later, after visiting the village shop and the post office and having a lengthy discussion about strawberries with Mrs Organic Veg delivery, I go to the loo and discover that paranoia was spot on. Felix's chewing gum is lodged on my shoulder like a small but deformed cousin of the parrot Gertie and no one has told me.

June 23rd

Should not be complacent, but am beginning to relax about Gertie. The children enjoyed their visit to her at the weekend, and Charles, who can do no end of selling at the parrot hotel, is delighted to take them there whenever they want. But the boys are perplexed.

'Why does she keep saying, "Call a taxi and take me home"?' asks Felix. 'Does she mean here, or does she mean the jungle?'

'The jungle,' I say emphatically. 'Was she coughing?'

'No, why?'

'Oh, they cough in the later stages of quarantine,' I lie glibly.

June 25th

Summer morning of spectacular loveliness and we have breakfast in the garden in straw hats. It is Saturday, and my mother is staying. She and I are reading the papers while Giles and Felix are squashed into the same chair reading an email from David. I suppose I can't stop him sending them, but I have stopped using the computer myself to avoid the anguish of reading his missives. Giles and Felix do it all on their own now. The Beauty has absorbed the scholarly mood of the morning and has found an old copy of *Vogue* in the log basket. This she hugs to her chest while dragging her small orange chair over to sit next to the boys.

'Is it good news?' she asks politely as she settles herself with her magazine open but upside down and sliding off her lap. Giles glances at her and grimaces.

'Mum, can't you do something about The Beauty? She's getting worse and worse. Look at her.'

I look. She puts her chin up and turns deliberately away.

'Don't look at me,' she orders. 'I won't have it.' She has been very keen on headgear since Desmond and Minna's wedding, and today she has chosen a lime-green tutu, upside down and pushed back like a hairband on her head. This is worn with flower-shaped sunglasses and a swimming costume.

'Very Busby Berkeley,' says my mother, lowering her newspaper to look, 'but I don't see what's wrong with her, Giles; she looks odd, I agree, but she always looks odd.'

Find this a bit rich myself, coming from the High Priestess of Odd, who today is sporting an orange turban underneath her straw hat, and a long purple velvet skirt, even though it is baking hot. Am about to say so when am engulfed from behind by Felix, who puts his hands over my eyes for a fragment of a second, then dances off shouting, 'I've got a joke, David's sent me a new joke. It's totally cool.' He rushes back and slumps on the grass at my feet, and shoots a mischievous glance to see if Granny is listening. 'Mum, Mum, why does Tarzan wear plastic pants?'

'I don't know, maybe to save on laundry?'

Withering look accompanies the answer: 'No, silly. He wears them to keep his nuts jungle-fresh.'

'Felix!' Of course Granny was listening, and manages a scandalised expression which no one pays any attention to, as we are all giggling stupidly.

'I like nuts,' coos The Beauty.

Pick up the printed-out email from David as it flurries across the grass towards my newly weeded rose bed. He has drawn a cartoon of Tarzan flitting from tree to tree in his plastic pants with an arrow pointing to the trapezes.

I make these, he has written. *I will send you one. Gertie will love to swing on it with you.*

Scrumple the paper up and hurl it on to the breakfast table where it rolls into the butter dish. Has David stopped to think how I will hang his stupid trapeze vine? Or is he secretly mailing a Tarzan, complete with rubber knickers, to do it for me? Doubt somehow that he has thought that far ahead, and comfort myself with the near-certain knowledge that he will never get round to it.

The hens approach the table, groaning thoughtfully, and fix us with the unwavering gaze of the gormless. Wonder what gormful would look like as I retreat into the cool of the house and await the post. This promises to be most satisfying, as am expecting some new ribbon samples.

June 27th

Ribbon, ordered by old-fashioned telephone method, arrives three days late and is all wrong. Am despairing of ever getting my new career off the ground, and have nothing at all left to wear, as all my clothes have been trimmed and sold. Enjoy futuristic fantasy of self aged eighty with gnarled fingers trying to stitch a toothpaste trim on to a neoprene cardigan. Am about to give up on work for the day to follow my instincts into the garden for carrot and radish work and a little rose-tying, when toothpaste notion grabs me again. It could be great. So could neoprene. Especially for surfers. Draw some hopeless pictures, look at them. Realise they are hopeless and so go and get out The Beauty's Fashion Fuzzy Felts.

In no time, have created beautiful sample of cardigan and Copydexed it to a piece of white card to be sent to Rose. Post it on the way to nursery to collect The Beauty and experience utterly fulfilling moment of having cake and eating it. I am a working mother, and today it's going according to plan. Hooray.

Float into the nursery school on a cloud of conceit, scarcely stopping to glance at the lesser mortals around me. Cloud evaporates, though, when The Beauty shows me her morning's work, and she appears to have made a very similar garment to the one I have just posted, only hers has pink appliqué flowers on it. I shall capitalise on this undermining of my talents as a designer and call my company Child's Play. Am rather pleased with this notion and try it out on Hedley when I see him driving past, as The Beauty and I are footling about near the road on our way back from the nursery. I wave and he stops and reverses back to me and The Beauty, who has climbed on to the garden wall for a better view. With her bunches and dungarees, she looks exactly like one of the Waltons.

'Hello man,' she greets Hedley.

'Hello child,' he replies with a very real attempt at a winning smile. He points at The Beauty's jacket picture which I still have in my hand, and taking off his glasses, leaving a red mark on either side of his nose, he attempts neighbourly pleasantries.

'I'm pleased to see you're hard at work,' he says. 'That one looks rather good, doesn't it. Most useful. Sort of thing my ex-wife wears.'

Rather touched by his enthusiasm, but can't face telling him that this one is not my design but is a play-group daub done by The Beauty, and conceit falls another notch as a result of his mistake. Maybe I should employ The Beauty as chief designer and just concentrate on marketing as I have such good ideas, particularly the name of the business.

'I thought I'd call it Child's Play,' I mention, casually tucking the picture behind my back before he sees The Beauty's name across the corner. Hedley is still in his car, and at this he revs the engine and crashes into gear.

'You can't call it "Child's Play"! You may as well call it "The Emperor's New Clothes" and be done with it. Don't for God's sake let them start thinking it's easy, or they'll just make their own. Have you no sense?' he yells, and departs in a cloud of disapproval. Very lowering.

June 29th

Children at school, The Beauty asleep and I am sewing individual lavender heads on to my pink cooking apron. Rose telephones, delighted with the neoprene drawing.

'It's great. Get it made up as soon as possible. I wonder if you can find something that will seal real toothpaste so you can use it. The colours are so tingly, so minty.' She coughs. 'Anyway, sorry, mustn't get carried away,' and her tone changes. 'I'm afraid you've got to look for better manufacturers,' she says regretfully. 'The garments you are trimming just aren't up to it. Also, you'll never be able to keep up with demand.'

Rumbled. Actually, I had wondered how long it would be before she noticed that these are my clothes. Amazing that she still hasn't cottoned on to this detail. 'Don't worry Rose, I've got some great contacts,' I say, running my eye down the jumble sale and car boot column in the local paper. 'I'm in negotiation with them now. We should have new clothes to trim by Monday.'

June 30th

Horrible wolf-whistling outside the house at first light indicates the return of Gertie. How she travelled eighty miles from St Neots is shrouded in mystery, but she is there on the gravel, on her perch, a brown envelope dangling beneath her. This time the bill is for three hundred and sixty-two pounds including carrier. Having opened the bill, I leave her outside the front door, singing 'Old MacDonald' at the top of her voice, and pray she will not wake the children until I have composed a pithy email to David.

I shall have to call the RSPCA if you don't stop forcing that parrot to travel across country through

173

the blazing summer. She will remain at the parrot hotel until you collect her, as I would rather not take responsibility for the life of such a valuable creature which does not belong to me.

JULY

July 1st

Email from David to the children, completely ignoring me, and reiterating the fact that Gertie does not need to be in quarantine, and that he has paid her hotel bill. Reluctantly realise that I am outmanoeuvred, and allow Gertie to come with me to school to tell the children the good news. I park in good time, and becoming rather carried away by being in the camper van, turn up the Andy Williams tape that Gertie inspired me to buy in a charity shop the other day.

The door is suddenly wrenched open, and a hatchet-faced Giles glares in.

'Mum, why did you come in this awful car? And can you please turn the music off and *don't swing*.' The final instruction comes as I sway in time to 'I Love You Baby' and clap a bit to keep up with The Beauty, who has made the back of the van into a tented nightclub with spangly scarves and a couple of those Day-Glo sticks you get for camping.

'I thought you'd like me to bring Gertie.'

'I'd like you to be quiet,' he says, reminding me horribly of his father for the first time in ages.

Felix appears, rolls his eyes and says, 'Mum, let's face it, you're just too weird.'

So much for cries of joy and upturned, happy little faces.

July 3rd

Wake the children early, even though it is Saturday, as am anxious to beat the stampede at the car boot sale. The boys are cross and taciturn on the way in the camper van, and grunt as I explain our tactics.

'I've got to try to find clothes, so you must look after The Beauty. I'll give you each a pound so you can buy anything you fancy.'

Deep sigh from Giles. 'Mum, you're really sad. Where have you been? You can't buy anything for a pound any more.'

'Oh, can't you? I was hoping all the clothes would be fifty pence each. Do you think I'm wrong?'

'Of course you're wrong,' he hisses, before subsiding again into silence. The car boot pitch is on a giant field sloping towards the cliffs. The sea glitters and heaves beyond, melting into sky as the sun rises, and intense blue floods the horizon. By the time I have extracted The Beauty from her car seat, the boys have also melted away, having helped themselves to fistfuls of coins from the jam jar of change I collected from the bank yesterday. The bank girl looked a little pitying as she watched me slide all the pounds into my jar, but did not offer one of those nice Sheriff-of-Nottingham-style pouches, even though I rattled my jar in a most tragic fashion. Anyway, can only hope that a purchase will act as mood-altering therapy on the boys and send them back to be helpful. Trap The Beauty in her buggy where she writhes and screams as if in an electric chair, rubbing the palms of her hands woefully against her eyes.

Reach the rows of stallholders considerably harassed, and fed up with the glances of sympathy The Beauty is receiving from total strangers who sneer at me before passing on. Even though it is not quite eight in the morning, the field swarms with people in a state of tranced-out dementia. All are seeking the ultimate bargain, and their hands move ceaselessly over the items on the tables while their eyes are craning to see what canny stallholders are keeping back. The Beauty and I swiftly adopt the same methods, and within moments I have found three cashmere golfing sweaters, and with ruthless bargaining, secured them for a song. Golf appears to be a theme, and the pushchair begins to sag beneath harlequin socks, waistcoats, yet more jerseys and one vast pair of plus fours, which I think may be big enough to turn into two skirts if I just cut off the bits I don't need and add some elastic. By the end of the first aisle, I have spent all my money and have a fine haul of clothes and ephemera.

Giles and Felix are in high spirits now that they are doing something, and have adopted the gypsy-jackdaw mentality, eschewing Warhammers and other bargain plastic toys to haggle for sequins and glass beads. Giles rushes up to show me a tin of marcasite buttons, sparkling like fish scales as he runs his hands through them like a trader in a souk.

'Look Mum, these are really old buttons. We got them for a quid. Felix has agreed that we'll sell them to you for a fiver.'

Souk trading at its most obvious. I protest, 'No fear. I gave you that pound in the first place. You keep them if you want them, and I'll keep this.' Tuck my arms around a plastic bag splitting with the weight of a dozen Tintin books. Giles is no match for this lure, and thrusts the buttons at me, throwing in a Barbie-doll pink jeep he had been planning to keep for The Beauty's birthday.

'Cool. Thanks, Mum.'

Felix chips in. 'Yes, thanks, Mum. We'll take The Beauty now, she can play with us.' And, leading her to the edge of the field, they spread their Tintin books on the grass and settle down to read, hardly noticing as The Beauty brooms her pink jeep up and down their backs and legs.

July 4th

Giles is revising for exams and insists I test him.

'Come on, Mum, ask me about turning fractions into decimals. Just make up a sum with fractions and I'll do it and you can see if I've got it right.'

Fat chance. I have no idea how to do such a thing, and am sure fractions were abolished when Britain went decimal. Thought that was what the decimal point was for, in fact. Shall I confess to being a total dimbo, or shall I affect an air of comprehension and try to bluff my way through? Either way will not help him with his revision. But who can? It is pointless to depend on their father, as he is increasingly distancing himself from them as Helena expects him to be a New Man-type of father to the twins. Am amazed that she wants this, and more that she achieves it, as in our marriage, Charles never once changed a nappy or spoon-fed a baby. It just was not appropriate, and anyway, he was too chilly and thin-lipped to cope with the jolly roundness and gurgling laughter of babies. He has mellowed now, of course, but we never see him.

David would be a much better bet for revision tips; and for the thousandth time I wish I had never had that fateful conversation. Suddenly have a good idea. Giles and Felix have a robust email relationship with him. All is not lost, and I will not after all have to confess to dimness.

'Darling, I'm really sorry, fractions aren't my thing. Why don't we do a whole page and email it to David? That way it'll seem more like an exam, and I can help you revise something else.'

Giles sighs but agrees, and vanishes into my study to write this mysterious, coded email. The Beauty and Felix are engrossed in a game which involves Felix lying on the lawn like Gulliver, with many small teddies strewn about him and a plastic teapot, cup and saucer balanced on his chest. Gertie is marching around him, head on one side, observing proceedings and looking like a member of the royal family with her hands, or rather wings, clasped behind her back. I take advantage, and escape outside to the water butt to set up my new sprinkler system. Erect a series of hosepipes linking sprinklers around the garden, with much tourniquet work at the joins. Moment of truth comes when I turn on the outside tap. There is a brief pause, then most satisfactory jets of water sparkle in every direction, including all over the washing, almost dry, on the line. Rush to remove it and fail to notice the wheelbarrow blocking my path. I fall over, screaming and swearing.

'Sodding hell. Why does no one ever put anything away in this godforsaken dump?' Felix and The Beauty pop their heads round the wall to have a look.

'She's all right,' I hear The Beauty informing Felix. 'She's just had a little bump. Stop fussing about, Mummy, you're fine.'

'You're fine. Put your pants on. Put your pants on,' cackles Gertie. That parrot is a bad influence.

The beautiful fountain splutters, gurgles and dies, and an ominous swelling appears in one of the hoses. Also, have grazed my shin on the wheelbarrow and will now have foul scabs instead of glossy suntanned legs for the rest of the summer. Decide to let nature, or rather gravity in the form of water pressure, take its course with the hose, and return to Giles and his revision, disconsolate, brooding on the pointlessness of my existence. Only a few months ago, I was forced to hire a water pump to deal with the quagmire that was then my garden if I did not want to lose every plant to root rot. Now I have desert in the place of swamp, and having started watering, will be chained to this chore until the weather breaks.

'We're doing biology now, and we need to start with photosynthesis,' Giles announces, revealing another gap in my education. He plonks his textbook on my knee and I try to look relaxed and alert as well as knowledgeable.

'Oh, yes. Chlorophyll and things. I remember,' I lie, comforting myself with the thought that none of it looks any use to anyone except biology teachers anyway. I would much rather Giles learned a few practical things like wiring plugs, washing up properly and ironing his shirts. In fact, a decent watering system for my garden would be a fine project to kick off with, and that should surely count as biology, or at least biology supplement.

Giles sees straight through me.

'Mum, there's no point in doing this if you don't understand it,' he says patiently, making me feel about four years old. 'I think I'll go over to Byron Butterstone's to revise.'

Am incredulous and outraged at once. 'Does his mother understand all this? I bet she jolly well doesn't.'

'No, but we can test each other, and he's got a really cool computer which can talk.'

'Shall I drive you there?'

'No thanks, I'll go on my bike. See you later, Mum.'

Hugely relieved not to have to do any revision, but heartstrings are twanged as Giles spins away on his bicycle with Lowly trotting by his side. He is independent now, and I will soon be redundant in all areas, not just prep. Worse, though, than being redundant is being passed over. Giles has frequently mentioned the superiority of the Butterstone household with regard to parents (two, and apparently amusing and good-natured at all times), food (ice cream and pizza and a tap on the side of the fridge dispensing Coke all day and night) and siblings (just one silent sister). And since the camper van got going, he has been eloquent on the subject of the Butterstones' cars (one Jaguar, a Mercedes and a new Land Rover). Can do very little to reach these standards in our household, so will doubtless suffer the ignominy of Giles moving out to live in the next village with them soon.

Telephone rings as I contemplate this prospect. It is Bronwyn Butterstone, perfect mother and number one seed in the local lawn tennis club.

'Oh, Venetia. I thought you would want me to let you know Giles has arrived safely. I know how difficult it is to stop yourself ringing when they cycle off, just to check they're safe. Anyway, we're going water-skiing later on and we'd love to take Giles, so shall we drop him home this evening?'

'Yes of course. Thank you. I was just about to ring, I've been mentally following his progress,' I lie smoothly, determined she shall think me caring, although it has never occurred to me to check up on Giles, who is much more grown-up and safety-conscious than I am. Put the phone down and try to think of something to do with Felix and The Beauty that could be considered on a par with water-skiing. The options include painting some shelves for Felix's room, planting out some very overgrown hollyhock seedlings and picking strawberries to get ahead with jam-making. Ask Felix to choose.

He picks himself up from the teddy chaos on the lawn and says, 'Those are all really chod, Mum. Why can't we go out somewhere?'

'OK then, where would you like to go?'

Expect hours of indecision, but Felix answers instantly, 'Let's go to the Badlington Tank Collection. It's my favourite place. And can I have some money to buy an Airfix, please?'

The Beauty also adores the tank collection, and a happy afternoon is spent among the trappings of war until The Beauty climbs up a ladder into a cappuccino-coloured tank, a relic of the Gulf War, and therefore camouflaged for dust and desert rather than mud and rural fields like the Second World War ones, and vanishes. Felix and I, inspecting a glass case in which the Charge of the Light Brigade is taking place, complete with puffs of smoke and sound effects, do not notice her absence until an elderly blazer-wearing man taps me on the shoulder.

'I think the noises in that tank are less than authentic,' he says, winking. We turn to hear Miss Bossy Boots, her voice booming as if from the bottom of a well: 'I need to do the driving. It's my car and we're going to London.'

Felix collapses in a heap of horror. 'God, Mum, why did we have to bring her? She'll break it and we'll have to pay for it.'

Am distracted by this. 'I wonder how much a tank costs?' I muse.

Thudding sounds from within the tank suggest that The Beauty is now charging up and down and we are about to find out the price of one Gulf War relic, until recently in perfect condition.

'Wheee! I'm bouncing about. It's like a boat, isn't it!' confirms this, and Felix begins to resemble one of the wounded soldiers in the Light Brigade, rolling on the ground groaning.

'She's ruining it, she's ruining it.'

I am pretty sure that even The Beauty's demolition skills are no match for a tank, but am as keen as Felix to get her out before anyone official sees her. As I begin to climb what I hope are the main steps, she appears in a gun turret, a tiny frontierswoman in her Liberty-print apron and smocked dress, selected as Sunday best by me this morning. Am about to coax her down, when someone behind me causes her to cackle a mad 'ha ha' and disappear again like a puppet.

'She is the original for *Annie Get Your Gun*, isn't she?' Hedley, wearing a khaki windcheater with a suspicion of dandruff on his shoulders, appears from behind a giant cannon. His hands are behind his back, but I catch a glimpse of a helmet which he is trying to conceal beneath his jacket. Am less astonished than I should be to see him here; this is his sort of place. Wonder what his excuse is, though.

'What are you doing here?'

Hedley looks at the sky, looks at the ground and looks at the tank. 'Ummm,' he says.

'Come on, Sale, we've got a platoon to command.' Another voice issues from beyond the cannon, followed closely by a snowy handlebar moustache decorating a large bluff face. 'Ahh! That's where you've got to.' There is a smart clicking of heels, and the moustache and I turn expectantly to Hedley, awaiting introduction. Social grace is not Hedley's thing. Instead of introducing us, he scuttles up the tank steps muttering, 'That child should not be in there.'

He opens a lid and, reaching in, pulls The Beauty out like a prize in a lucky dip. She is outraged, and immediately spouts tears, while roaring and drumming her heels against Hedley.

The moustache is appalled, taking a swift step back as Hedley, holding The weeping Beauty at arm's length, descends the steps. 'Christ, Sale, I thought you were well out of all that juvenile stuff. Come on now, we've got to get back to the war.' He doffs an imaginary hat to me, and turns on his heels, anxious to put a decent distance between himself and The Beauty.

Both Felix and I are engulfed by giggles. Hedley thrusts The Beauty into my arms and attempts to follow his friend, but Felix grabs him in a rugby tackle to the legs. 'You're playing war games, aren't you? Please can I come and do it with you? I love war games, I've always wanted to play it. What's your friend called? Can you ask him for me? Please, *please.*'

Hedley is turning redder and redder; I can tell that he would love to deliver a swift kick to disentangle himself from Felix, but luckily doesn't dare to.

He manages a twisted smile and says to Felix, 'Look, we can't do it now, but I'll make a date for you and Giles. Now be a good chap and let go.'

Felix has radar sensitivity to adult intonations, and recognising both finality and desperation in Hedley's, he allows him to depart to his game, shouting after him, 'All right then, but I'll hold you to it,' before turning to me and whispering, 'He's left his helmet.'

July 5th

Rose has no idea of the pressures of single motherhood. She has left me a bossy message saying I am too slack, and she thinks I should give up the business and get a job as a supermarket checkout woman as I clearly have no ambition and no entrepreneurial drive. Irritated, I unpack the over-the-head charlady aprons I had previously discarded as too depressing and decorate them with tinsel and fun fur. Send them to Rose with a label saying 'Production Line', and take The Beauty to the sea for an afternoon of sand-castles and ice cream.

July 7th

Extraordinary. Rose *loves* the aprons. She has left a mad message saying, 'Please let's do more pregnancy wear. I think we should call the whole label Production Line. Clever you. I've sold them to The Blessing for one hundred and twenty pounds each. They're heaven. Can't wait for whatever comes next.'

Ego only slightly punctured by attempts to harvest a bowlful of peas from my recently rather neglected vegetable garden. Thought there would be enough to freeze superior spares in the manner of Captain Birdseye, but in fact a whole Production Line apron pocketful of picked pods yields only a saucer's worth of peas. Thank God for Mrs Organic Veg, as the purpose of the pea harvest was to show off when Vivienne comes to supper tonight. Ha ha, can still do so.

Give Vivienne delicious pea and mint soup and home-made bread, also made this afternoon espe-cially to impress her. It does. Unfortunately, we are both still hungry, and as I neglected to plan further than this course, we leave our elegant table under the lime tree and head for the fridge, where we find some frankfurters. 'Oh look, is this one of the aprons?' Vivienne asks, picking a garment up from the vast laundry pile.

'Oh yes, I managed to find a whole box of them in a charity shop.'

Vivienne has been grilling me on my business, and through her own fascination, revealing that I know shockingly little about how to run anything properly. Am quite embarrassed, and would much rather talk about Guy Clarke, my new favourite country singer, discovered in the same charity shop as the aprons.

'It's amazing how attractive a cowboy hat can make men look,' I say to stop her banging on, and I start to hum 'Desperadoes Waiting For A Train'. She looks at me very severely.

'I've been meaning to talk to you about this, Venetia,' she says, sitting down at the kitchen table to eat her frankfurter. Clearly, the stylish part of our evening is over, and I am quite sure she is not about to start listing her favourite cowboys.

'Simon and I are very concerned about you being on your own. You've got to grow up and stop living in a romantic fantasy, you know. Just because David is good-looking, and yes, all right, he's good with the children, and great company—'

Am astonished at this sudden list of his attributes, as had always thought Vivienne didn't much like David, but find the shock of hearing him talked about is breathtaking.

Vivienne continues, enunciating carefully, as people do when they are determined to say something that they feel has to be said but they know will go down very badly, 'And what it really all comes down to is this, Venetia. Do you really think he is still going to come back?'

So unfair to ask me that, just as I am pulling myself together and taking my first mouthful of hot dog. Go off it completely and put it down.

'We've split up,' I say bleakly. Vivienne, poised for her own second mouthful, stops, her hot dog oozing unnoticed ketchup in dollops on to the table.

'You haven't!' she says in amazement, and then, as my efforts at putting on a brave face crumple and slide, she comes round to where I am standing, leaning on the Aga, and hugs me. 'Oh, don't cry, Venetia. I know it seems hard now, but it will be for the best, you know. You'll find someone older who'll marry you, not dump you to pursue his own career. More stable.'

'You mean less sexy,' I say, blowing my nose. We both laugh as she tries to get out of that one.

'Well,' she says, 'you can't go on throwing your heart after cowboy carpenters, can you?'

Do not confess to her how very much I wish I could do that, nor do I tell her that it was me who dropped David for precisely the reasons she was outlining. Cannot cope with the searchlight on my emotional life, and can't wait for her to go home now that she has had her say, so I can go and sit in the dusk in the garden and immerse myself in plangent cowboy music.

189

July 8th

Two long rubber vines arrive by Parcel Force in a wooden crate. The delivery man is clearly the last in a long line of handlers who have all been convinced that the box contains live reptiles. He hurls it on to the doorstep, beeps his horn for a signature and drives away twice as quickly as usual. Giles staggers in with the box. It is plastered with labels which say things like *Toxic*, or *Not to be touched by humans*, or *Customs Alert*.

'It's probably another parrot,' I say, eyeing the crate suspiciously.

Giles and Felix, eyes popping with excitement, prise open the lid and speak as one. 'Snakes. Cool, man.'

I grab The Beauty and retreat to the kitchen, shrieking, 'Call the vet. No, call the police. Call the fire brigade. Call the zoo. Call Charles and have them incinerated. Get them out of here at once. No. *Nooo.* Don't. Don't touch them.'

Have utterly forgotten that David promised swinging vines, so when Giles opens the kitchen door with a length of sinewy rubber coiled around his neck, am paralysed with dread and convinced it is a boa constrictor, suffocating him.

'It's all right, Giles darling, stay calm, Mummy will come,' I shriek, untruthfully, as I am dashing backwards out of the room. Only my brain still whirrs, with a craven desire not to have to be involved in a tussle with a snake, but to have someone else deal with this new drama.

'Can we put these in the trees and have a quick swing before school?' Giles is manhandling the so-called snake, flipping it about nonchalantly. Felix drags another in, and intelligence flickers once more as I perceive the true nature of these lengths of rubber. But how do we put them into any of the trees? Apart from a topiary yew chicken and four small crab apples in the knot garden, the trees around here are vast and gnarled. A cursory inspection from the back doorstep suggests that even the lowest branch is twenty or so feet above the ground. A more thorough investigation of the crate in which the vines arrived reveals a hastily scrawled note:

> Make sure you put these on a SAFE branch. Get an adult to test first. They need to be at least fifteen feet above the ground, so mind you take care. Gertie will love these. I'll build you a platform to swing from when I come home xxx David.

And which adult does he have in mind for branch-testing and vine-fitting? Look from the note to the upturned, expectant faces of the boys and compose withering mental email to send to David along the lines of 'Hanging is too good for you.'

July 10th

Vines unhung, email unsent, as yesterday was spent helping set up Giles and Felix's stall for the school fête which takes place this afternoon. Arrive with my mother and The Beauty to discover that we have to join a queue to get anywhere near the boys. They have created a bar with a long slippery surface, and the challenge is to try to slide a tankard full of beer along to the other end.

'It's not really beer, it's just a mixture of old tea and liquorice water so it won't smell too bad,' I hear Felix comforting a small girl with bunches, who has spilt this substance down her front.

'Oh good, a pub,' says my mother, brightening considerably from a slight sulk she was in because I wouldn't let her enter The Beauty into a 'Guess the weight of this item' stall near the entrance to the fête. 'Can we keep the drink if we win?' she asks Giles, handing him her money for a turn.

'If you must,' he says, 'but it's harder than it looks, so be careful.'

'I know what I'm doing. I've been to rather more bars than you have,' Granny responds, and slides three tankards in quick succession down to the end of the bar.

Felix leaps about excitedly. 'Well done, you've got the best score so far, Granny. Did you once work in a saloon bar?'

Duck away with The Beauty as the headmaster approaches. Do not feel equal to discussing saloons and nightclubs with him, Felix and my mother. The Beauty and I notice a washing line, and intrigued, approach the stall, which is manned by Carmel Butterstone, sister of Giles's friend Byron.

I proffer my fifty-pence piece. 'What do you have to do?'

Carmel simpers a reply. 'Mummy thought of this one. You have to see how quickly you can hang out the basket of washing on the line. The quickest wins a place in one of Mummy's Cabouchon groups, or a box of chocolates.'

How ghastly. Just do not want to have anything to do with Bronwyn Butterstone's jewellery parties, but the game sounds perfect. Amazing, though, that something so un-PC is allowed. Am very keen for a go, and am sure I will triumph and win the chocolates for The Beauty. After all, I have spent most of my life hanging out washing, so should be of Olympic standard by now.

Carmel blows the whistle and I begin, The Beauty trotting behind, handing me pegs and garments. 'Here, Mummy, do this hanky now.' Find myself fumbling a little with the first vest, but years of practice kick in and in moments I am pegging with easy rhythm. Finish, I am sure, streets ahead of all others, and return to Carmel with confidence in every step.

'Well done, Mrs Summers, two minutes forty isn't the last,' she tells me encouragingly. 'But Mummy does it in one minute fifty-two, so you'll just have to keep trying.'

She smiles sweetly and turns to her next victim, an unsuspecting father wearing a linen suit, who looks as though he has never seen a washing line before, but is guffawing away. 'Marvellous, must have a go and see if we can't beat the ladies at their own game.'

Have to move away to watch Splat the Rat to avoid the ignominy of this chauvinist pig eclipsing me at my own sport. Bronwyn Butterstone, her helmet of tawny hair immaculate, her legs like tweezers, long and bandy in gingham pedal pushers, is marching up and down with a megaphone bossing people around. Shrink away as she accosts my mother, but their encounter is short-lived. My mother is more than a match for La Butterstone, and we go to find tea with her puffing indignation.

'She wanted volunteers for the Red Cross stall which she's supposed to be running. Or rather, Red Crawss as she calls it. She said she could see I was a pillar of the community.' My mother stops in her tracks to rummage for a cigarette in her handbag. She exhales the first puff with a 'Pah!' and continues, 'Pillar indeed. It makes me sound like a colossus.' She broods darkly on Bronwyn's iniquities then adds, 'That woman is enough to turn all of us into hardened criminals.'

We find a table and sit under the green crêpe shade of a vast cedar tree, planning hideous embarrassments for Bronwyn. The Beauty removes her T-shirt and skirt, then uses the skirt as a napkin to wipe cake crumbs off her mouth. I tell my mother about David's vines, adding a final soliloquy about the hellish parrot. She shoots me a sharp look, as I foul-mouth him and his absent indulgence of the children.

'Just make sure you know what you're doing,' she warns. Am about to ask her what she means when the conversation on the next table distracts me. It is between another adult mother-and-daughter combination, recognisably related by their hooked noses and almost non-existent chins. Am looking at them, wondering which feature my mother and I obviously share, when I suddenly find myself tuned into them.

'Well everyone is saying that Hedley Sale will either marry or leave,' booms the senior one. 'And if you play your cards right, Lucinda dear, there's no reason why it shouldn't be you.'

Lucinda mutters, 'Mummy!!' in deepest embarrassment, but the mother booms on. 'Nonsense, dear, no point in beating about the bush. You've got little Archie to think of too, don't forget. And you know, don't you, that now that monstrous excuse for a man, your ex, has stopped the alimony, you've got to sort something out.' Lucinda nods, and I could nod with her, so close do I feel to the situation.

'I could be very happy spending his money,' she laughs, changing the tone. This time, I do nod. My mother nudges me reprovingly.

'Stop picking up fag ends,' she hisses. The megaphone booms the news that the presentation of the prizes is about to take place. Felix and Giles appear by our sides, and Bronwyn Butterstone starts drawing the raffle. None of us is listening. I am engaged in trying to persuade The Beauty to put her clothes back on, and in digesting the new version of Hedley as seen by other neighbours. Maybe they don't mind the temper. Or maybe he doesn't show it to them.

Suddenly Felix nudges me. 'Mum, it's you. Go on.' Bemused, I stand up, and find that the headmaster is beckoning me over and presenting me with a box of chocolates. Carmel Butterstone puts a hand on my arm.

'Sorry Mrs Summers, I made a mistake with the timing of your washing on the line. In fact you did it in *one* minute forty, which is twelve seconds faster even than Mummy. She said you must have done an awful lot of washing in your day!'

Lucinda and her mother join in the general mirth at this sally, and I am unable to think of anything at all witty or mordant to say. Victory can be the most poisoned chalice.

July 11th

My vegetable garden is of textbook loveliness when viewed from a distance with partially closed eyes. Splashes of orange and yellow from the marigolds I bought at a roadside stall last week dance out against a background of silver-green sage, bright lettuce leaves and feathers of rocket and parsley. Have taken the modern approach as far as sweet pea and tomato canes are concerned, and have a line of aluminium wiggles, each about five feet high, which make my potager appear half traditional and half like a meeting place for aliens. This, at any rate, is Felix's view. The Rousseau fantasy has long been abandoned, and I am under no illusions that my garden is for anyone but me, and of course a multitude of snails, slugs and the hens. Giles is away on a cricket tour, and I have tried to convince Felix and The Beauty that we can have quality time after tea in the vegetable patch.

'But I hate vegetables,' protests Felix, 'and I hate being made to work in my time off. I have to work hard enough at school.'

'Eughhh,' agrees The Beauty, picking up the general tone of discontent and running with it. 'It's really gross and gosting out there. I will not go. I will not.' She shakes her head in regret.

Am at a loss. Should I insist that they help me, thus creating a Solzhenitsyn-style work camp, or should I bow to their 'disgost' and let them do as they please? Mothering skills, including tolerance and especially cooking, are at an all-time low.

Am becoming like the shoemaker elves of fairy tale in having to sew or rather glue my adornments on to garments after the children are in bed in order to meet Rose's demands for the clothes before the school holidays begin. Have no sense of achievement now in finishing one jersey, as all it means is that I must do the next one. Every spare moment is occupied with the search for more outlandish trims. Yesterday I struck a rich seam when an ear of corn attached itself to my skirt while I was walking the dogs. Imagined how ravishing it would look when laid carefully on a pale blue skirt (courtesy of the Aylsham charity shop) and picked a huge bunch. Dry the wheat to a pleasing greeny-gold colour and crackling texture on the Aga, then attach stalks all around the hem, thus creating 'Free and Easy', so named because it was both.

July 13th

Mid-evening, high summer, and I would like to be out in the garden inhaling the nostalgic sweetness of night-scented stocks and contemplating my white flowers which float, perfect and ethereal, on their dark leaves at this gloaming time of the evening. However, I have just put the children to bed and am in the kitchen, sewing and listening to *Sounds of the Seventies* on the radio. Am just thinking that I may as well go the whole hog and invest in a rocking chair and crocheted blanket when the doorbell rings. Jump as if scalded, but am too late to do anything except throw a blanket over Gertie's cage to stop her saying something appalling about pants, and Hedley appears in the kitchen holding a bottle of wine. Very embarrassing to be caught in such fogeyish pursuits, as if I am some old biddy in a Trollope novel rather than a contemporary chick with my finger on the pulse.

'Hello, Hedley.'

His one brow rises quizzically as he notes the trappings of antiquity I am surrounded by. 'Venetia, what are you doing?'

'Oh, I'm listening to contemporary rock and throwing a few shapes on my kitchen dance floor,' I reply, as Don MacLean's most soppy chocolate-box song, 'Starry Starry Night' drifts out of the radio. 'What are *you* doing?'

Startled, and nervous, he shifts from foot to foot, fumbling in the pocket of his sagging trousers for a folded page of newspaper.

'Well, I thought you might like to watch the stars. Here, I've got an article about them. There's a comet exploding somewhere miles away, and we are in for a glorious shooting star show in about an hour.'

'Ohh, that must be why they're playing this song,' I remark, very pleased with my sleuthing. Hedley puts his bottle of wine down on the table and holds out the article for me to read. Bottles of wine and shooting stars. What next? Have never been pursued in this textbook fashion before, and am nonplussed. Does he think I am encouraging him? What about Lucinda from the school fête? Or maybe that is more in her mother's dreams than in any reality. That overheard conversation has certainly made me think of Hedley with new respect. But the monobrow ... the temper ... the thinly disguised dislike of small children ...

On the other hand, here I am, working my fingers to the bone over a hot needle, with a mental list of chores a mile long for which a man is needed, and I'm sitting alone at the height of summer with just the radio and a parrot to keep me company. What sort of life is that?

Sneak a surreptitious glance at Hedley, who is fiddling with a corkscrew, lips pressed together, trying to yank the cork out of the bottle without removing the foil first. Perspiration beads on his forehead and upper lip, and his jaw is tensed in concentration. His combination of choleric temperament and small, hairy and dark physique may not be ideal, but I'm sure he is quite kind, as well as cross, and his house is big enough to escape from him in anyway. But most importantly, he is here. Now.

'Have you had any supper?' Immediately wish I had. Summon an X-ray vision of what lies behind my fridge door, and it is not good. Half a tin of tuna-flavoured cat food, rejected by Sidney the cat, a cucumber, three dough sculptures made by The Beauty and Felix, and some sinister-looking sausage rolls. Luckily, Hedley has eaten. I, however, have not. Gulp down the glass of wine he passes me as if it is orange squash and have a head-rush of intoxication and recklessness. With it comes a weird sense of being outside my body, and it is from above that I see myself throwing back my head to maximise a ripple of laughter when Hedley says something extremely unwitty, along the lines of, 'It's time to watch the shooting stars now, according to the radio.' I drink another glass, this one in slower, smaller sips, thank God, but the damage is done. From far above, I look down on the top of my head, much too close to Hedley's, which has a reddish bald patch like a monk's tonsure. I try to warn myself about this bald patch, but the news is mere cannon fodder in the face of an arsenal including a summer night, a battery of shooting stars and too much alcohol. As inevitable as any wish, the monobrow looms in front of my eyes, swimming closer, and then I am in Hedley Sale's arms, kissing him as the first star bursts over the water meadows and is followed by seeping indigo stillness until the next.

July 14th

Dawn. And with it, crumb-headed sobriety. Am now fully back in my body where self-loathing and an air of defiance are at war. I sent Hedley home before anything X-rated happened, but I still kissed him. For hours; it was the middle of the night when he left, and it took all my will-power to make him go. Just could not face the idea of any of the children finding him here. Now I don't know what will happen. It really wasn't too bad. I enjoyed kissing him. (Why am I sounding so surprised?) And I very much appreciate his enthusiasm for me and for doing whatever I want him to. In fact, it reminded me of Lowly, as did the longing look in his eyes when he kissed me goodbye.

'I'll ring you later, Venetia,' he murmured, and I feigned great yawns as I put the glasses into the dishwasher, to avoid having to say anything. If he had a tail, he would have wagged it.

As soon as he left, I sprang to life. Not sleepy, I made tea in the kitchen where the clock was ticking in its friendly way, and Sidney was curled up in his favourite warm spot in the fruit bowl on top of three lemons and a pineapple. It was all as usual, and I was not. I took teapot on tray up to bed to think, tiptoeing in the hope that The Beauty would not hear me and come and interrupt.

I often set my alarm clock for very early, like four in the morning, thinking it would be so nice to do precisely this, and to absorb the unique golden loveliness of the dawn, but natural sloth-likeness always causes me to turn it off, so I miss these moments of tranquillity. Dunk a digestive, defiantly, and think: What am I playing at?

What will happen next? I am out of practice at this sort of thing. David became a part of our lives so easily, none of us could imagine him not being there from the very beginning. Anyway, David and I went away on holiday together and he moved in when we came back, so the children got used to the idea of us together in our absence.

But now, the children don't know we've split up. They are in touch with David every day, they adore him. But that is no basis for a relationship. Am becoming deeply anxious about what to do next, and in desperation, try to sleep. Just as I have almost managed to relax and doze and dawn is streaking the sky outside my uncurtained window, The Beauty totters into my bedroom, her hair tousled and fluffing over sleep-smudged blue eyes. She peeps at me, pushing back her hair with a Marilyn Monroe flourish, and says breathlessly, 'It's a lovely day, darlink. I'd like a pink drink.' Guilt becomes white hot, bed fills with sharp pins and we have to get up, even though it is only five-fifteen.

July 15th

Heatwave. The Beauty and I spend the whole day lying alternately in the hammock and the paddling pool. Much silent agonising and metaphorical moon-howling has strengthened my instinctive resolve to be an ostrich. If I tell no one, and make Hedley promise never to refer to the interlude again, surely I can pretend it never happened and get on with my life as a mother of three with no plans.

July 16th

Too hot to sew. I ring Vivienne to ask her to come and advise me on how to make fake turf look like vibrant living grass around a narrow skirt I am planning to make from one leg of the plus fours. After our conversation, I put the telephone down and congratulate myself for revealing nothing. Have become really discreet at last. Hooray.

July 18th

Vivienne appears. Before we have even sat down with cups of tea to look at the fringing, I have confessed. In fact I confess about one second after she passes through the front door, saying politely, 'So how are you?' She listens in silence, then bursts into peals of laughter.

'Oh, sorry Venetia. I know I shouldn't laugh. I told you he was after you, didn't I?'

'Did you?'

'Yes, ages ago. The only reason he's been having that stepdaughter of his to stay is to entice you over there with Giles.'

'Oh, my God, I'm so stupid.' Vivienne nods in agreement, I grab her wrist. 'No, I mean *really* stupid.

We're going camping when the holidays start, and I'm afraid I've got Tamsin excited about coming with us.'

Vivienne rolls her eyes and sighs. 'Well, you won't have any choice about what to do next unless you're secretly hoping that David will jump on a plane and come home now, will you?' She reaches for the tweed and threads a needle. 'Anyway, Simon and I both think Hedley might be rather good for you. We thought something might happen.'

Have to point out that very little has happened, but she appears to think we are as good as engaged. Anyway, have only mentioned the campfire to Tamsin, so maybe she will not tell Hedley.

Ring Rose to tell her all my news, wishing to contrast her reaction with Vivienne's, but she is preoccupied with having her house feng shuied and refuses to react at all.

'I'm sorry, Venetia, I've got to keep a calm aura in the house to preserve the positive energy forces. I think I'm going to have to get rid of the telephone, in fact. And Theo isn't allowed to have tantrums in here now, he has to have them outside the front door on the steps up from the street.'

Am temporarily sidetracked by this new flight of madness. 'What does Tristan think?'

'He's really thrilled. He says he's been trying to get me to live like this for years, but I've resisted. You should try it, Venetia, it might help to simplify your life. Is Hedley the guy who speaks Latin, with one eye?'

'One eyebrow,' I reply crossly. 'You're making him sound like Cyclops.'

'You'd better get on a plane and go and fetch that David right back here,' says Rose, suddenly crisp and forceful. 'You can't mess him around. He's gorgeous, and he loves you.'

'Well, he should come back here and prove it,' I return, and flouncing, put the telephone down. Have never known Rose to be so unsupportive. Although I suppose I should have told her I've split up from David. Anyway, she is useless. Perhaps she is having a mid-life crisis, or another baby.

July 19th

Light-headed with lack of sleep from another night with Hedley, ending when I sent him home at about three in the morning. Cannot believe I am entering into an illicit affair with a man I don't really fancy, and am sure I didn't ask him to come over last night. Am a bit worn out by the amount of Latin translating he seems able to do after intimate moments, but am determined to look on the bright side. I never knew that the word 'ululate' comes from *Aeneid* Four, where Aeneas meets Dido and their liaison is apparently accompanied by nymphs. Ululating all over the place.

In fact, am not sure I have ever heard the word ululate before, and still don't know what it means, but never mind. I think Hedley is trying to compare our romance to that of Dido and Aeneas, and can't get that excited as Dido ends up on a funeral pyre. On the other hand, am a pushover for being fancied, and Hedley does his best to convey how he feels.

'Venetia, your skin is as soft as rabbit skin,' is not my compliment of choice, but makes such a pleasing change from 'Where's my cricket bat/toothbrush/socks, and can you send me my binoculars,' that I find myself carried along on a tide of Hedley's making. Have never felt so detached from anything. It's like watching a soap opera of my own life.

July 20th

The post brings an ambient candle from Rose. It is called 'Dirt', and sure enough, when lit, gives off a faint aroma of wet dogs and dustbins. The card she sends with it has a picture of a sheep with dreadlocks on one side and the words *Get Real* on the other. Burn stupid card immediately, increasing the dirt smell one hundredfold.

July 21st

Dawn. Crisis. Hedley was here once more. It was a beautiful fragrant night, and we went out to smell the night-scented stocks. Tum-te-tum. All very lovely and fun, although I do wish he had two eyebrows and that he would whisper sweet nothings in English rather than Latin. But you can't have everything. Anyway, I must have fallen asleep, and worse, so must he. I wake with a start, with a horrible feeling of being watched, and discover The Beauty standing next to the bed, glaring at Hedley's rather hairy shoulder on the pillow behind me.

'What's that, Mummy?' she asks crisply, then wrinkles her nose, adding, 'Yuck, Mummy. It's gross and gosting.' My heart is pounding, dare not move in case Hedley wakes. On cue, Hedley wakes. The Beauty suddenly loses her sang-froid and bursts into tears. 'Oh nooo, Mummyyy, nooo,' she sobs, never taking her eyes off him as he scrambles out of the bed and into his clothes, but shaking her head and repeating, 'Oh nooo,' through her tears. I pull her on to the bed and try to cuddle her, but she is frozen, glaring at Hedley. When dressed, Hedley comes over and crouches in front of her. She redoubles her screaming.

'Go away, you are a baaad man, a baaad man.' I attempt a reassuring smile over her head at Hedley, meant also to convey my desire for him to vanish immediately, and Hedley steals out of the door, ashen and shaking.

As soon as he has gone, The Beauty stops crying, pushes her hair back from her face and says with satisfaction, 'It's all right now, he's gone. Shall we have Coco Pops right now?'

We do so, and, judging to perfection my all-engulfing desire to curry favour with her, she asks for, and achieves, ice cream with them. While The Beauty consumes several bowlfuls of this ambrosial breakfast, I try to decide what to do.

Unsuccessful. Have to admit that despite this morning's trauma, I do not wish to banish Hedley

from my life. Cannot say that he lights it up especially, but confidence is flooding back, and I can
remember again that there should be more than just
domestic drudgery and honest toil. I deserve more,
and Hedley can give me more. What I can offer
Hedley is a mystery, but that's his concern.

Come back down to earth to find The Beauty
gazing at me, nodding her head emphatically, because
I am nodding mine. Nodding speeds up for both of us
as I decide that I shall see Hedley. And I shall make
my own decisions. Yes indeed.

July 23rd

Still not managed to install the horrible snake vines in
any tree. They are dangling out of the boys' bedroom
windows and are being used by them as alternative
stairs. While I am delighted that they have learned to
abseil, I wish they would wear helmets and also that
there was something more satisfactory than their beds
to tie the ends on inside the house.

On top of this anxiety, there is the emotional
turmoil I am now dwelling in, and I have no hat for
speech day, which begins in three-quarters of an hour
and which I am attending with my mother, as Charles
is in Brittany with his twins.

'Mummy, you don't need a hat,' counsels Giles. 'It
would be much better if you could just melt into the
background. Like Mrs Dellingpole.'

Mrs Dellingpole is the worthy and extremely nice
mother of the captain of the rugby first fifteen. She is

of indeterminate age, her car is clean inside and out, and she has a small navy-blue handbag which always has a clean tissue in it. Am offended and perturbed that she should be a role model in Giles's eyes. I thought he would like having a glamorous mother with a devil-may-care attitude. I put this to him. Apparently not. And there is worse.

'Anyway, you aren't glamorous like Mrs Butterstone,' Giles says, narrowing his eyes to look at me before adding with hideous precision, 'You're more weird-looking. You never clean your shoes. And why do you always have to wear patterns and fur? You look like the Flintstones.' He looks me up and down, sighs, and then changes his mind. 'Actually, today you look like a Beanie Baby.'

Goaded, I begin to deny the shoe slander, but a glance at my feet silences me. There is a trim of mud, as if I have recently pulled my feet out of drying concrete, around my favourite ponyskin mules, chosen for speech day to complement the pale pink suit with bunny tail on the bottom and furry ears sticking out of the breast pocket I have selected for today.

'Well it's too late to find any Sta-Prest Crimplene skirts, or to have my hair set,' I snarl at him as my mother's car roars into the yard.

He tries to make amends. 'Here, give me your shoes, I'll clean them for you. But couldn't you at least cut the tail off your skirt, it's so embarrassing,' he moans, and scurries round in search of a shoe brush. He thus misses the splendid sight of my mother issuing from her car with a hat like a Mr Whippy ice cream madly askew on her head.

By the time she has fully extracted herself and her various scarves from the car, her audience includes me, Felix and The Beauty. Noticing the intent collective stare, she sticks her chin a little higher in the air.

'Felix said he wanted me to wear a hat,' she says defensively, putting up a tentative hand to readjust the angle of the giant ice cream. 'Minna's aunt brought it to the wedding, and in the end chose that dull blue one she wore, do you remember? Anyway, she hasn't been to collect it, and I thought it needed an outing.'

When arranged in the school hall it quickly becomes clear that Minna's aunt had the interests of others close to her heart in rejecting this hat. Much tutting and umbrella-shuffling greets our arrival into the rows of chairs. As the hall fills up, I look around to see if anyone is wearing anything nice and find that all the seats behind and around us are empty, even though there is standing room only on the other side of the hall. No one wants to be near us. We are pariahs, and in a moment, Giles and Felix will come in with their classmates and see, and Giles will be justified in calling me weird.

The headmaster and governors file on to the platform, and children begin to pour in through the double doors, jostling one another as the inevitable speech-day rain cloud bursts. Total humiliation is imminent, and unfair, as I have made a special effort to blend in and have even exchanged the ponyskin mules for a pair of dreary sandals I found in the car where they had been left as the unwanted part of a bag of stuff I got from a jumble sale. Might as well have myxomatosis and mad cow disease, as still no one comes anywhere near us.

Bacon is saved in the most annoying fashion possible. Bronwyn Butterstone, wearing a perfect lion-coloured suede sheath dress, which matches both her hair and her skin, leads a whole column of cross-looking parents over to the seats behind us. 'I'm awfully sorry,' she says to my mother, blinking apologetically. 'You'll have to remove the hat. No one can see, and we've got several more to seat.'

She leans over me as she speaks to tickle The Beauty playfully, then titters conspiratorially while speaking as loudly as she can, 'Venetia, I didn't know you had been a bunny girl. What fun you must have had in the seventies.'

Vile, vile, vile. Revenge shall be mine.

July 25th

Revenge was indeed mine, and I am collecting it now from the trophy shop. Felix has won a cup for outstanding genius of some sort. None of us was listening when it was awarded, so we don't know what it is for precisely, but it is his. He won it. All by himself. Giles has won one too. I think for cricket, but maybe music. Actually, I don't care what they are for. I am brimming with ignoble triumph. My children have two cups. And Bronwyn Butterstone's children have none. Ha ha. Must stop gloating now, or a mishap might befall me.

July 26th

Allow myself another quick gloat today when polishing Felix's already gleaming cup. It is more or less an Oscar, being for drama. Am so pleased that I forget that I hate David, and try to ring him. A female answerphone says that David is away for the weekend. He has run away with the electronic voice simulator, I knew it.

July 27th

Horror. The children are on summer holiday now and do not go to school again for more than fifty days. They gleefully inform me of this during a pillow fight this morning. When the pillow fight is over, Giles slumps on the floor, still in his pyjamas, and groans, 'Mum, I'm really bored, can we go to Norwich?'

'What for?'

'Oh, I dunno, just to look around at the shops and stuff. It's just so dull here. There's nothing to do.'

Horrible little ingrate, how can he be so unspeakable? Exasperation flares and I have to leave the room to prevent myself from kicking him as he rolls about at the bottom of the bed, yanking sheets down over himself in a welter of boredom. Shut the door behind me, and take a series of deep, yogic breaths, trying to do the ones which bypass your nostrils and feel as though your throat itself is breathing (much easier than it sounds). In . . . and . . . out . . . in . . . and . . . out . . .

Into my silent and tranquil space falls Felix's voice, agreeing with Giles. 'Yeah, it's so boring. It's totally chod. Let's ask Mum if we can play Nintendo if we can't go to Norwich.'

Inner calm departs and temper rises to breaking point in seconds. Outside it is already hot. We have a garden, a cricket bat, streams and water meadows around us. We have bicycles and dogs, a tree house and those sodding Tarzan vines. It isn't raining, in fact it's hot enough to make ice creams an imperative. How can they be like this? Will I survive for fifty days? Must stop looking at it like this, it is reminding me of Noah in his ark, and he only had forty days with mad animals. Decide that most dignified course of action is to ignore the children, so depart to the garden to pick roses and sweet peas. Put on a straw hat and wafty shawl for this, as wish to become Vita S. W. for a while, as she was certainly unfazed by irritating children.

Am fully in character and wondering if I should become a lesbian, when Hedley and Tamsin appear on bicycles. Abandon lesbian fantasies, as Tamsin's brave little face reminds me that dumping children for love is not on. Suppose I could take mine with me to lesbian love nest, but doubt they would come.

Am alarmed to have Hedley on my territory, as the children have not seen him since he and I became Dido and Aeneas, and I am not sure how, or indeed if, to break it to them. Hedley also seems alarmed, and keeps his eyes on the ground, mumbling in a fashion I find deeply irritating. We discuss the weather, and Hedley asks the boys if they are enjoying the holidays.

'Yes thanks,' lies Giles without looking up, then slides off with Tamsin and Felix, back into the darkened playroom to finish the next level of Peekaboo with Pikachu or whatever the frightful game is called. Realise that to them, Hedley's behaviour is normal. They never look anyone in the eye unless forced to. Hedley and I are left alone. Finally he raises his head and we look at each other helplessly.

'Tamsin's mother has left to go to Ibiza for the summer with her girlfriend, and Tamsin has turned against her and elected to stay with me. She says she wants to be here with Giles and Felix,' says Hedley finally, adding with what he must imagine to be a roguish grin, 'I feel that the gods are conspiring in favour of our union, dear Venetia.'

Union. Union. How can he say such toe-curling things? And not only do I let him, I positively encourage him. Here I go again.

'We're going camping next week at the sea. Would you and Tamsin like to come?'

He looks absurdly pleased. Only when he has wobbled off on his bike to go and hunt out his tent from his schooldays do I remember that I have also invited Rose and Tristan.

There is no way of making this seem less bad than it is.

July 29th

It is eight-thirty, and so far this morning I have received four telephone calls, three of them telling me I am mad, and one of them beeping and squeaking in an international fashion, which suggests either David or Martians are trying to make themselves heard.

The mad calls are from my mother, my newly sensible brother Desmond, and Vivienne. All of them appear to think I am an imbecile and not fit to go camping. Surely camping cannot be so difficult?

I flatly refuse to believe Desmond, who says, 'You know you'll have to boil all the water for washing-up or you'll get dysentery.'

'We won't do washing-up,' I reply loftily. 'I'm getting paper cups and plates.'

'What about saucepans?' His new-found fascination with washing-up must have something to do with being married. Most odd. I do not remember our nuptial vows having this effect on Charles. Am losing interest in the argument, and am irritated that he has missed the point: we are to be rugged hunter-gatherers and will be cooking sausages on toasting forks and spearing fish and barbecuing. Saucepans are not on my list of things to take camping.

My mother says, 'I'm in a hurry, I just wanted to say remember to take a bladder of water, if you must go camping. But if I were you I'd take them all to CenterParcs instead – that way you'll get a proper break yourself.'

Feel like adding, 'Yes, and a lobotomy,' but she has rung off.

Vivienne just sighs and says, 'Well, if you really are set on this scheme, I suppose Simon and I will have to come and keep an eye on you. Now what about packing?'

I pretend there is something wrong with the telephone and hang up, so incensed am I by her patronising tone. Still, huge relief to think of her and Simon with their peerless Boy Scout and Girl Guide skills, coming to help us rub sticks together and so forth.

Take my list, and the children, to the tiny army surplus and outward-bound shop on the coast road as soon as I am off the telephone. The man in the shop gapes wordlessly when I show him the list, then pulls himself together and says, 'And these are your fellow campers? Very bold, madam, very bold. I recommend you take these emergency flares, and I can rent you this battery-operated radio set, which is tuned straight into the emergency services.'

Felix and Giles rush at a giant black box with aerials and dials. 'Cool, they had one of these in the *MASH* video we watched at Simon and Vivienne's,' says Giles. 'It's for the Vietcong, I think.'

'What I really want is camp beds,' I wail, 'and a bladder.' May as well not bother speaking. All three children and the shop owner have vanished inside a purple tent almost as big as my house, with a card on the front announcing, *Knock-down price for shop-soiled twelve-man tent, £699.*

Chart their progress by the bulges in the side as The Beauty hurls herself at the walls, testing and breaking the surface tension. After five minutes, it is clear that no one is coming out, so I must go in.

July 31st

A bunch of inflatable plastic bananas arrives in the post from David, and a penknife. Giles emerges looking anxious from my study, where he has been fiddling with the computer.

'David sent an email saying does Mum know that storms are forecast here this weekend, and not to forget the drinking water,' he reports, frown deepening as he adds, 'and he's given me the number of a friend of his who is a lifeboatman. I think he's really worried about us. But he says Gertie will love it.'

'Oh, no! We're not taking that sodding parrot, are we?'

Giles looks pained. 'Of course we are, unless you're thinking of sending her back to the parrot hotel.' There is undisguised menace in his tone, and I am far too guilty and keen to curry favour to stare him out. Instead groan at length and throw him a box. 'Well, you'd better pack for her. And don't forget her distilled water.'

March on through the house, trying to be organised, thinking bitterly about David. He was the one who organised this summer holiday treat, ages ago before he went away. It is the kind of thing he is very good at, and I am extremely bad at, and this knowledge does not improve my mood one bit. However, there is no time for introspection, as I have to find four camp beds and a sleeping bag for me.

Have purchased a very delightful cocoon for The Beauty in the shape of a pink mini-sleeping bag. She loves it and has not got out of it except for a bath since yesterday morning, and shuffles around the house looking like a snail without a shell, or, as Felix points out, 'A raspberry slug.'

AUGUST

August 1st

Still no camp beds. Am smitten with incompetence and spend the day loafing about in the garden instead of packing. Take dogs to kennels a day early to give myself a mini home holiday from their panting, eating and sagging about in the heat. Lovely without them, must remember to do it again, as really does feel like a proper holiday but costs only three pounds per dog with a discount if I leave them for ten days. In the peace of their absence I cook a chicken and leave it to cool on the kitchen table, something that can usually only be done after exhaustive chaining-up of dogs and closing of windows and all doors. Make some ice and feel smugly sure that I am on top of the pre-camping situation.

August 2nd

Yesterday's sensation was misplaced. I am very behind, in fact, and not ready for anything. Simon has brought us camp beds and told me to take spare two-stroke petrol for the boat. Instead I pack the Scrabble board and several hundredweight of mini Mars bars.

Midnight

Torrential rain and thunderclaps like cannon fire wake me, and I have to rush downstairs and out into the gushing, streaming garden to shut the car sunroof and push the tent into the porch. Although it is raining hard, the night is hot. My nightie is soaked as if buckets of water have been poured over me; I grab a tea towel from the pile of unsorted laundry in the hall and begin to rub my hair dry. The rain continues, streaming from the guttering, bouncing mud-pie splatters of earth up from the flower beds and on to the step. The sky is soft black, with twists of silver glitter where the falling rain catches the light from the hall. Gaze out at the lawn, listening to the soft thump of raindrops landing on it, inhaling the leaf-and-water soft air. We will have to cancel our camping trip. Sudden claustrophobia and random naturist urge overcome me, and shedding my nightie and the wet tea towel, I run out into the storm again wearing only my yellow wellingtons.

'Ladi-da-di-daaa,' I warble, frisking about with my arms outstretched, warm rain drumming onto my shoulders and face as I twirl and prance on the lawn, dissolving tension and hysteria with every pirouette. Suddenly notice Giles and Felix at the open front door, gazing at me with their arms folded across their chests. Hooray, we can be a naturist family.

'Come on boys, it's lovely,' I gasp. 'Quickly, take your clothes off, you'll feel so invigorated.'

Both of them spring away as if I have rabies, alarm and consternation on their faces.

'No thanks,' says Giles politely. Felix has more to say.

'Mum. Why aren't you wearing any clothes? It's the middle of the night, someone might see you.'

Giles nudges him. 'Silly, no one will see her *because* it's the middle of the night.' Felix looks relieved and wanders off into the kitchen.

'Thank God,' he says, reaching for the mini Mars bars.

August 3rd

What insane impulse has brought us to this spot? We have gone beyond the edge of Norfolk, off into the sea to a sandy peninsula inhabited only by seals, terns and the occasional lunatic birdwatcher. We are brushing our teeth in salt water and living according to the tides. We have no electricity and no running water, just some fishing nets, a tent and an open fire to cook on. The sun is blasting down in a most uncharacteristic fashion and I have forgotten my sunglasses, so will soon develop ancient person's crow's feet around my eyes from squinting. If I don't get flu after my singing in the rain session, about which Giles said at breakfast, 'Mum, please don't talk about last night. I'm trying to eat and I don't want you to put me off.'

Rose and Tristan are meant to be here, but Tristan has managed to develop a migraine, so they won't arrive until tomorrow. They will not like it, although they both pretend that they are longing to come. Rose was not born to camp. She likes to be able to wash her hair every day and to lounge around in steaming baths, inhaling attar of roses and so forth. Her silver-blonde hair and translucent skin were never intended for dirt, and all her clothes are made of silk or cashmere, and are as far removed from salty canvas and cotton ticking as it is possible to be. I take small solace in the fact that she won't be able to observe the decline of her glamour, as there is no mirror here, unless you count the curious disc of wrinkled silver foil someone has hung on the wall of the corrugated iron hut we shall be inhabiting this week.

Am actually quite amazed that we have made it here at all, as we left home this morning at sunrise in order to catch the tide, in such a welter of anxiety that I forgot the directions and the name and address of the woman with the key. I was half expecting not to be able to come, due to the freak weather conditions, and stayed up much too late with Giles and Felix, drinking cocoa by the Aga, drying my hair and searching for packs of cards to the unabated accompaniment of furious rain. However, I awoke at the first trill of The Beauty, who rises with the dawn chorus these days, and discovered a sparkling world with rose-flushed sunrise and the orderly drip, drip sound of things trying to dry out. Suddenly had to leap into action and pack the car, rouse the children, eat breakfast and get into the car by seven o'clock. Hence the forgetting of the key holder's address, and who knows what else. Discovery of this disaster took place too far from home to go back, therefore had to bribe the children with sweets and Radio One in order to snatch a few moments in which to lie on the roadside next to the car in an attempt to meditate and therefore retrieve vital key information from my scrambled brain.

It worked. In the background, Giles's favourite song by Offspring snarled away with something about hating a bitch who's got a job, and I lay on the warm, dew-damp verge with my eyes closed against the rosy morning and attempted to exhale a ribbon of breath. Like magic, after a few false starts in which hyperventilating began, the hypnotic big breaths took over, and the name and address of the keyholder pinged into my consciousness, emerging in a rush like change in a pay and display machine. Most gratifying.

Onward to the coast, leaving verdant, heartbreaking summer country bursting with cows and flowering hedgerows behind us, in favour of glittering, Hemingway denim sea. We arrive at the coast at Felix's favourite point, the place where the hairy mammoth was found buried in the chalk cliffs, having lain for centuries beneath layers of sandy soil. He adores this piece of local history, and never tires of each detail, seeing the mammoth rather in the role of Sleeping Beauty in her briary castle, awaiting rescue. The mammoth's Prince Charming was a disobedient dog, a poodle, Felix insists. The dog was supposed to be playing catch with a ball on the beach with its owner, one winter morning three years ago. Tiring of the game, the poodle whisked away up the cliff in pursuit of a smell and disappeared into a crevice.

Felix leans back in the passenger seat, eyes shining, gazing at the cliff's edge, a serrated line cutting between the feathered golden cornfield and the sea.

'Yes,' he says, 'and that poodle must have thought he was hallucinating when he found a giant dinosaur bone. He must have felt so lucky.'

Giles interrupts without looking up. 'Mammoths aren't dinosaurs, they're Neolithic,' and keeps his nose glued to the Nintendo magazine he has been reading non-stop since his father sent it to him three days ago. Felix wisely ignores him.

'And he must have been really well trained to go and give it to his master and not just sit up on the cliff having a huge feast with it. And then it would have been really disappointing to see your bone going off to the museum. I hope they went to the butcher and bought him a good one. I wish I had a dog like that. Rags has never done anything exciting like discovering mammoths.'

The Beauty's radar has picked up the words 'dog' and 'bone', and from her seat in the back she suddenly bursts into appropriate song, in the manner of Olivia Newton John.

'Nick nack paddy wack
Give a dog a bone
This old man goes rolling home.'

Felix and I need little encouragement to join in, and we eclipse Giles's radio station entirely.

Such pleasures become a thing of the past on the quayside, where challenges to sanity and integrity pile up. Felix, Giles and I load the hired motor boat so full that the Plimsoll line vanishes beneath the water, while The Beauty assembles several buckets of stones and tries to put them on board as well, as ballast presumably.

'Just go, you'll be fine,' urges the exasperated owner of the boat, having spent almost an hour helping us shift pillows, camp beds, food, water and finally The Beauty in a smart, if tight, orange life jacket, from the car on to the boat. Everything, including The Beauty, becomes instantly wet upon settling in the boat, and I feel both carsick and seasick due to the strong smell of petrol emanating from the outboard motor and the wobbly jelly sensation of being in a boat on water.

'You know how to do it, don't you?' barks the boat owner, as an afterthought, having jumped clear of our craft, leaving us forlornly alone on the water. Nod determinedly and wiggle the handle about. Terrible strimmer-like whine starts and the boat veers, spins and heads straight for the bows of a larger, smarter sailing boat which is loading up with four middle-aged yacht-club types. Like a rabbit caught by a snake, I stare madly at the side of the boat we are approaching, so completely paralysed with terror that no messages at all are transmitting to my brain. To no avail does our boat owner shriek, 'Turn to port. TO PORT, I SAID!' It means nothing to me, my hand is locked full throttle on the handle and I can do nothing.

BANG. We achieve a direct hit to the middle of the smart boat, and at such a speed that we bounce off, enabling me to turn the way I want to go, but also to stall. It is a miracle that none of us has fallen in the water; indeed the children are all beaming, flushed with the sense of success one has when achieving a hit in bumper cars. The yachting types, however, were not braced for disaster, and have collapsed in a bobbing, orange-life-jacket heap. They pull themselves together in a trice. The leader, bespectacled, grey-haired and sporting a red baseball hat, shakes his fist and roars rhetorically, 'Can you drive that thing? The answer is no. Emphatically no. I hope you're well insured, my girl, I really do.'

I hold my breath for the grim moment of name and address exchange and insurance company details, but after peering over the side of his still immaculate and un-chipped boat, he simply grunts and turns his back on me. Another of his party bounces up to add her might.

'Are you sure you should be taking that parrot out on the sea? They catch cold very easily, you know.'

Manage not to yell, 'Sod off, you interfering old cow,' but smile sweetly at Gertie, who is sitting on

Giles's shoulder in a very professional fashion, and answer, 'She's not a parrot, she's a hologram.'

Two scarlet spots appear on the woman's cheeks, and she looks as if she would like to hit me.

Giles bows his head, muttering, 'God, this is *so* embarrassing. How could you, Mum?' and Gertie, who has been biding her time, suddenly groans horribly and starts quoting the line of Shakespeare she has just been taught by Giles:

'Hubble bubble, toil and trouble
Fire burn and cauldron bubble,'

she shrieks, much to The Beauty's delight.

I make matters a million times worse by bursting into nervous hysterical laughter. Our boat owner has assumed tortoise or ostrich position and has managed to shrink his neck so his head is invisible inside his collar as he walks away. Another wave of panic hits me. I still can't believe The Beauty, who is perched on top of a box of vegetables, clapping her approval at this sport, has not fallen off and into the sea; delayed shock at having almost killed all my children in a hideous boating accident redoubles my hysterical laughter. Felix has managed to insinuate himself between a giant packet of Frosties and a rucksack and is burrowing downwards like a crab, determined to make himself vanish.

'Just tell me when we get there and *please* don't crash again,' he mutters, adding, 'Hey, Mum, can I have the troll in this packet?' as he slides down to the

227

bottom of our heaped possessions. Giles, still crimson with shame, sighs heavily and climbs past me.

'I think I'd better drive, Mum. I've done it before with Dad on holiday.' He takes the handle, saying, 'It's a tiller, actually, not a handle,' and after wrestling for a moment with the spluttering throttle, and yanking the long string which I wish was a communications cord, he guides us out from the jetty and into deeper, emptier waters, respectfully slowly as we are travelling in the wake of the crosspatch yachting types. Manage to transfer much of my mortification into fury at David. I remember him jubilant with excitement at the outward-boundness of it all, saying, 'Don't worry, I'll deal with all the nautical elements.' Huh. Have to button my lip tightly to prevent myself from ranting about him to the children. More deep breathing, and a tiny bit of chanting 'Ooommm', dilute savage thoughts about him and we skim merrily across frilly waves towards open sea, at one with our boat, and definitely not thinking about Jaws or any other horrors of the deep, but trying to become Swallows and Amazons people.

Ozone saturates our nostrils and lungs, and light, cleansing to body and soul, bounces off the sky and on to the sea and up again. Exhilarated, I begin to relax and believe that this will be a perfect, heaven-sent holiday. However, an abrupt mood swing accompanies a rush of agoraphobia as the land falls away on either side of us and we leave the channel for the never-ending horizon of the North Sea. I am alone in charge of three children on the ocean. If the boat capsizes, I cannot possibly save them all, I don't have enough arms. Tears well and slide down my face with the enormity of this, and Felix, watching me, quietly delves in my handbag for our mobile telephone.

'Here Mummy, why don't you ring David and ask if he can get here after all? He always meant to come camping with us, didn't he? Or maybe you could ask someone else. Get Hedley to come, or Uncle Desmond. In fact I'm sure Helena would let Daddy come if you said we really need his help. Or I could ask her for you, if you don't think she'd do it for you.'

Tears now course freely, but I manage to smile at the same time, speech impossible though, as I am pole-axed by his very sensible request for a man. Any man. I must try to supply one. The Beauty is a tiny sea dog high on a wave of clothes behind me, in her own small boat of vegetables, podding broad beans and delicately picking out each tiny green ear-shaped morsel; Giles is reading a How to Sail manual in order to discover the meaning of the various bobbing buoys we are passing; Felix and I fall upon the telephone. Before we can so much as dial a number, the outboard motor gurgles and slows to a murmur, and looking up from my fevered perusal of my address book, I am delighted to see that we have reached the peninsula.

'Oh, we're here now. Let's not bother ringing them until we're desperate,' I suggest to Felix.

'I think we're desperate already,' he replies, gazing at the oozing mudflats spiked with bright green samphire shoots into which the boat has subsided. 'It's too muddy, can you carry me to the house?'

I decide it is best to ignore this absurd request, and affecting deafness towards him, I scramble to find the anchor under our possessions and hurl it into chocolate-mousse mud. Giles cuts the engine and we hear silence first, and then the cry of gulls, hissing of mud and the gentle slap of water.

Ahead, up a winding path between beds of sea heather and gorse, lies the air-raid-shelter dwelling David has chosen as the base for our summer holiday. A tiny breeze-block construction with one small window and a red front door, the house has a curved iron roof, grooved and rust-coloured like an old pair of corduroy trousers, and looks distinctly uninviting. But the sight that elicits a strangled shriek of joy from me is so welcome I am afraid it may be a vision, like the time the Virgin Mary appeared in a pizza to a very exhausted woman in San Diego. There is Vivienne standing in the doorway, and off to one side the crouched figure of Simon, for once appropriately dressed in his favourite giant Boy Scout outfit of shorts and knee socks. He is fanning a fire upon which a pan of bacon sizzles.

'I can't believe it. You've come. Thank you. Thank you,' I yell up the path to them. The relief on the children's faces is dazzling. I am unfit to be in charge of them, and they know it. So shaming.

'Breakfast,' beams Simon, 'and then a swim with the seals for me.'

Felix and Giles are aghast at the swim notion.

'No way are we doing that,' Felix mutters, discarding the sleeping bag and pillow he has deigned to carry from the boat. 'There are probably sharks in the sea now, it's so hot. Let's go and play with the Game Boy after breakfast.' Once again, I choose deafness as the easy option. How I wish I was more hearty.

August 4th

The boat has broken down, and we have nothing for supper. The tide is defying all natural laws and seems to be out most of the time, so even if we had a boat we couldn't use it. Look across the mud-riven channel at the masts and rooftops of civilisation and fantasise about chips. Vivienne tries to rally my flagging spirits. 'Come on, let's leave The Beauty with Simon and Gertie to do her bedtime story and walk to town with the boys. We can give them chips and buy something for our supper.'

The boys brighten considerably at the chance to set foot upon tarmac, and we set off.

Town turns out to be much further than it looks. We meet a woman walking a fat black pug. 'Oh, it's seven miles I should think,' she says, waving vaguely along the beach. Felix, who has been lagging behind muttering crossly, collapses in a heavy stuntman fall at these words, and lies on the shingle moaning.

'I can't walk any more, my legs ache, it's too far,' he whines. I too have trembling, exhausted limbs, and snap back at him.

'Well, either you can lie here and wait for a gull to mistake you for a worm and eat you, or you can stop making such a fuss and come with us. I don't care which.'

I march on with Vivienne, who nudges me and whispers, 'You could get a job in the Foreign Office with those diplomacy skills. He's coming now, don't look.'

We arrive finally at the village, panting and faint with exhaustion and find that the Spar shop closed ten minutes ago. The only place open is an organic teashop, so Felix, Giles, Vivienne and I sit down firmly at the table, shedding the waterproof coats I insisted were necessary, even though outside the evening is warm and lit yellow brown, like an African dusk. We stuff ourselves with vast Victoria sponge slices, cinnamon hot chocolate and flapjack. The waitress, herself very organic-looking, with two teeth missing and a scar on her neck, takes a keen interest in our greed, and upon discovering that we are starving campers on the Sand Bar, shrinks in horror.

'Oooh, I wouldn't stay there if I were you. There's a lot of undead up on the Bar.' She shudders dramatically, enjoying the sensation of having an audience rapt. 'Long ago we had pirate wreckers off the shore here, and they kept a lookout from the Sand Bar for ships to wreck. They wrecked them by beckoning them in at night with lights across some rocks hidden under the sea. The ghosts of those poor souls on the ships are everywhere about here now.'

She stops, pursing her lips expectantly, and Felix sighs, 'Totally cool. I hope we see them tonight. I've always wanted to actually see a real live ghost. Can we sleep on the beach, Mummy?'

'They're not alive. They're undead,' says Giles the pedant, and an argument flares about degrees of deadness.

This is not at all the reaction the waitress likes, and she wanders off to another table, somewhat deflated. We persuade the café to sell us a pint of milk and tramp back up the shore, scanning the horizon eagerly for signs of wrecks, feeling fat and guilty that Simon and The Beauty shall have no supper.

Simon, however, sees it as a challenge, and sets to with a penknife and some silver foil to make a mackerel line. He then rows off with Giles, who insists on taking Gertie on his shoulder, into the hazardous, wrecking, dusk-lit sea in his inflatable dinghy. Vivienne and I watch from the beach as he casts his line, now decorated like bunting with slivers of foil every eighteen inches, and winds it in. This pattern established, and unbroken by the appearance of any fish on any of the six hooks, they gradually shrink away down the shore, into softly lapping dusk. We return to the hut, where I realise I have put The Beauty to bed with no supper, just a dollop of toothpaste. Amazingly she has fallen asleep. Do people really need three meals a day?

August 5th

We have become savages in less than forty-eight hours. The Beauty has gone back to nature in a big way, and refuses to wear any clothes, just a pebble with a hole in it on a piece of string round her neck and a tea towel on her head. She has not used a knife and fork since we arrived here, which saves on washing-up, but adds to her cavewoman demeanour. I think she has also forgotten how to speak, as all I have heard for a day now is high-pitched squawking as she emulates the gulls, or roars of rage at Felix, who keeps trying to remove her tea-towel hat. He and Giles are halfway through the standard early summer holidays malaise. This is the same every time, no matter where we are or with whom, and involves a week of whining, 'I'm bored' and 'I hate you' at every-one in their path. There is usually a bit of fighting too, and The Beauty, who likes to be part of everything, has taken to pulling their hair if they sit down anywhere near her. Torpor is a big part of the daily routine, so being here and not having to wash is great, while not being able to watch television is truly ghastly. Giles roused himself this morning, though, when he heard that Hedley is coming today with Tamsin, and slunk off with the mirror from my make-up bag to try to smooth his hair into shape.

Vivienne and Simon departed at dawn for civilisa-tion, taking with them the broken outboard motor engine, so I am now Robinson Crusoe with my three children and our parrot until the arrival of Hedley, Tamsin and what the boat owner promises to be 'a top-class outboard for you'.

Rather worried about being on a desert island with Hedley, as am not at all sure how we should conduct ourselves. Have discussed this with Vivienne, who says any romance must be suspended until we are back on dry land. We conclude that I shall put my faith in single camp beds and sleeping bags, 'Better than condoms,' said Vivienne bracingly as she departed.

I have become expert at lighting fires, and using very few plates, knives and forks or indeed saucepans. Desmond would be delighted, I think, with our economy on this front, if surprised. Am keen to live in this more streamlined fashion at home, where far too much time is wasted on washing-up, putting away and laying the table. Much better to eat off a slice of bread than a plate, and more filling. This morning was a record. I managed to feed all children and myself with just one fork and a frying pan. Surely this is female emancipation in its highest form? Can't wait to share my wisdom with Rose, and wish it was her and not Hedley coming in with the next tide. She has not been in touch again since the migraine, which is pretty feeble if you ask me.

The channel from the sand bar to the harbour begins to fill with bright sails as the tide creeps in, the water aquamarine and glittering as the sun intensifies. Giles takes his book down to our beached boat, determined to be the first to see Tamsin and Hedley. The Beauty and Felix run past me with water pistols.

'Let's be aliens,' suggests Felix.

'Yes, yes, yes,' squeals The Beauty, and they whisk into the tent to find torches.

Aliens, it soon appears, must have torches turned on in their mouths at all times. Settle down to read, but cannot concentrate on the improving volume of short stories translated from Icelandic and all about catching shellfish, which is my cleverly chosen seaside reading.

'Roll me over, in the clover,' warbles Gertie from her perch on top of the chimney. She has been swearing at seagulls since we got here, and is now eyeing the oystercatchers with great interest. I find it best to ignore her.

Can't help wishing I had brought a book on motor-boat engines instead, and something comforting – G. Heyer would be nice of course, but so too would a bit of Scott Fitzgerald, or Jane Austen. Anything about a civilised way of life before outboard motors and camping were invented, and preferably with clothes and food as well as a love story. The cookery book I have picked up, 'One Hundred Ways with Mussels', is not working for me. Have noticed, though, that just as I always pack clothes for holidays by including all the garments I have never previously worn, found at the back of my wardrobe and chosen for the holiday because it'll look good over a swimming costume or it'll look much better when I am brown, so do I pick my holiday reading from the giant pile of books I ought to read. This is a very dusty tower on the floor by my bed, much bigger than the pile of books I want to read, which in turn, good intentions being what they are, quite eclipses the pile of those I have read.

A thin cry interrupts my musings. Giles is jumping about by the water, gesticulating. 'Look Mum, they're rowing. They haven't even got a motor.' He points to a small black insect, jerking towards us through the shimmering glare of midday sun. Its progress is painfully slow, particularly when a large catamaran slices past, throwing the tiny craft about in its wake, making the oars shake and wriggle like beetle's legs. Someone on the boat groans, and screwing up my eyes to look more closely, I see to my horror that it is Rose. Rose and Tristan with Hedley and the lovely Tamsin. What a terrible combination. Suddenly wish Jaws, or the Loch Ness monster, would come and get them all right now. Rose is bound to be on head commandant form as far as Hedley is concerned, and she's very outspoken. She'll never believe that Felix needed a man here and Hedley was the only one I could get. She knows me too well.

August 7th

Everything is going much better than I expected. Hedley and Tristan have discovered that their sisters were friends at school, or their dogs were both born in November, or some equally tenuous, but to them cement-strong link, and it has served to unite them as hunter-gatherers and firewood-providers. The centuries have rolled back, and Rose and I have settled happily into our role as Stone Age home and hearth-keepers. It is easy to be gracious about this as there is no housework beyond the occasional shaking of a sand-filled shoe, and the once-a-day washing-up ceremony. Do not know whether to be relieved or insulted that Rose sees Hedley as a joke figure, and beyond saying with a giggle, 'Really Venetia, what were you doing with him? Such a lapse of taste!' clearly considers my interlude with Hedley to have been an aberration. Perhaps she is right. I too am finding it hard to believe I ever managed it, or that anything more will happen when we reach real life again. Worried that the boys might notice something, I have taken care not to be alone with Hedley at all, and am becoming increasingly skilled at avoiding meeting his eyes.

Tamsin and Giles, with much snatched laughter and accidentally-on-purpose bumping into each other, have taken over the cooking, which is achieved on the open fire, while Felix bustles around, experimenting with a Spanish accent and writing fantasy menus. Best so far was the one which offered coffee and Indian or China tea for forty-five pence or fifty pence if stirred, and as the main course, steak and chips with the vegetarian option of 'carrot puera'.

Theo and The Beauty have found an anthill and are playing God the Old Testament way with the inhabitants, re-routing ant motorways and pouring water, laboriously gleaned from the sea in small Barbie buckets, over ant villages. Gertie potters around them, cracking open her supply of pistachio nuts and heavily into character now. We have taught her 'What shall we do with a drunken sailor', and also the words to 'In the Ghetto'. The latter is performed as a duet with Felix, whose mission this week has been to learn to strut and gyrate like Elvis. To this end, he has requisitioned the only pair of sunglasses, a pink glittery pair belonging to The Beauty, and performs several times a day, usually wearing swimming trunks and using a baguette as a microphone.

Rose and I lie on the shingle, and the warmth of the sun on the stones penetrates my shirt as the shingle shifts slightly with the contours of limb and spine. Mention to Rose that it feels like a particularly sybaritic New Age health treatment.

'If you call this sybaritic, remind me never to do anything spartan with you,' retorts Rose, putting a stop to any delusions of sophistication I had been harbouring. Have to take this lying down as I am so grateful to her for not having begun an open campaign to embarrass me with Hedley. However, almost as the thought enters my head, she lifts her head and peers around. Finding that we are quite alone, she stops behaving herself and launches into me.

'So what's really going on?' she demands. 'You've got to do something about your situation, you know, Venetia. You're not getting any younger, and your boyfriend is on the other side of the world. You don't know when he's coming back, or even if he's coming back. It would be different if you were married, but as it is now, you may as well cut your losses and go for Hedley. His eyebrow really isn't too bad, especially if he wears a hat.'

I squirm like a salted slug as she continues, half furious that she's speaking to me like this, and half miserable at the jabbing accuracy of her observations. The marriage bit is particularly below the belt, and I just manage to prevent myself saying in retaliation how disgusting I find Tristan's toenails. On Rose goes, talking about responsibility to my children and them deserving the security and role model of a happy relationship. She stops when she sees I am in tears, and hugs me.

'Don't worry Venetia, something will happen, you'll see.' The sympathetic version is definitely worse. I wonder if she's been talking to Vivienne?

August 9th

The last night. We have to leave at an ungodly hour tomorrow in order to do our refugee thing with the boat and all the stuff. Have packed up the house, taking with us pockets full of stones, bladderwrack and old crabs' legs, and now we are sitting around the fire, trying to dodge the wind which has the ability to blow in every direction at once in the manner of a localised whirlwind, even though the rest of the Sand Bar basks in a silk-still evening. The babies are in bed, Tamsin and Giles are stalking an oystercatcher to find her nest, following one of these comical birds with its orange road-cone beak as it totters through the heather to its babies. They have already helped another one's chick out of its egg, and are diligent in their midwifery. Felix is toasting marshmallows on the campfire, gloating because he has got a whole packet to himself and there won't be any left by the time Giles and Tamsin come back.

The rose-petal sun, veiled by diaphanous heat haze, slips towards the sea, sending a ribbon of pink dancing across petrol-blue waters. A couple of miles to the east the sky darkens to violet and grey above the cliffs, the stormy light bringing vivid depth to a fringe of grass above the dusty chalk face, and all the way up the length of beach from the cliffs to where I stand, the sun sweeps a gold velvet beam, like a searchlight across the sands. Thunder rolls in the distance, but the clouds are moving inland and will not come here.

I strip quickly and run into the sea, splashing and dispersing the pink path to the sun. Am swimming in a pair of David's old boxer shorts and one of Giles's T-shirts, having lost my swimming costume, and several other beloved garments some months ago, when I became muddled and sent the wrong pile of clothes to the orphans in Hungary. Have been unable to face the grim prospect of buying, then acclimatising my body to another since then, and am rather pleased with my casually flung-together alternative, which is comfortable, and, I like to think, makes me look like a relaxed supermodel. Wallow unrestrainedly, enjoying the flung sounds of Tristan and Hedley building up the fire, and the murmur of Rose and Felix talking. Colour is fading with the sun, and although the storm clouds have gone inland to unburden themselves, most of the light has gone from the beach now, and I hear Tamsin and Giles walking on the shingle before I see them. Am just about to call out when Giles speaks.

'I don't mind Mum and Dad being divorced, but I think Mum needs to be married to someone. I don't know why David's left her, but she can't go on saying he's working in South America, can she?' Tamsin says something I can't hear, and Giles replies, 'I know. She's always trying to be young, but she needs to get on with being grown-up and being married and stuff. Even our Uncle Desmond is married now, and he's wild. I had to be a pageboy, it was sordid.'

The sea is suddenly full of lights. Shaken by Giles's remarks, I think I am giving off electrical charges into the water, but steady myself and remember it is just phosphorescence. I lift my arm and liquid green runs down. Everywhere the tiny plankton dance in an underwater galaxy. I splash my way towards Tamsin and Giles, gasping, mouth full of water, and trying to hold up the slapping weight of my boxer shorts. Gravity proves too much for the ageing elastic, and the waistband pings, adding sagging trousers to my traumas. Rush to the shallows, interrupting them. 'Hi there, you two, where did you spring from?'

Tamsin shrieks, 'Urgh! What's that? Why is it luminous? What's it doing?' and grabs Giles's arm.

He rolls his eyes and says in a despairing voice, 'Oh my God, it's Mum,' and I know I have let him down in every way possible.

August 10th

Inevitable result of all the home truths was that I became very drunk. Rose's wine is paint stripper with cochineal in it, but it also contains a merciful dose of oblivion. Cannot remember saying anything untoward, but Giles is not speaking to me. Rose is not much better; her demeanour is that of a brisk but kind nurse, and all I can get out of her is the odd flashing smile and the promise to deal with me later. I fear I must have done something awful to Tamsin or Hedley, as they couldn't wait to leave, and went on the boat with Tristan when he took the first load of our stuff back to the car park.

Have noticed that the main symptoms of hangover are an itchy nose and an air of irresponsibility comparable to that of being a teenager. The latter earns a sharp ticking-off from Tristan when he returns to get us and sees The Beauty, who is playing cat's cradle with a crab line.

'For God's sake, Venetia, look after that child, or we'll be in hospital.'

Everyone is against me. It is time to take stock and improve. Shall do so at home this evening.

August 12th

Very peculiar to be living in a house again. Everything eerily clean, except us. Have had to start wearing a turban, as hair has become hideous floss, like a hank of sheared sheep wool. Something has happened to the colour as well as the texture, so instead of lovely white-blonde elegance of my dreams, have yellowing rug which looks as though the dogs have wee'd on my head. Have only just remembered the dogs, and have decided not to collect them yet, as doglessness at home is like an extended holiday. None of my shoes fit any more, as my feet have become giant and black-soled. The boys say the same, and we all pad barefoot across the gravel without feeling it. All four of us have pronounced freckles, mad, staring eyes and smell dank and muddy. This is a reasonable price to pay for a superb and healthy energy which comes from all that ozone. Cannot get over the heavenly comfort of my bed after a week sleeping on my yoga mat, or the civilised, pampered silence of a summer country garden compared with rushing waves, crunching shingle, the wild sea wind and the constant cry of gulls. The children are similarly lulled; none of us woke up until nine this morning, a lifetime record for The Beauty.

August 13th

Terrible lowness, caused mainly by the departure of Felix, Giles and The Beauty for their annual week's holiday with Charles. The Beauty has been looking forward to this high spot of the year, and has had a small pink suitcase packed and waiting since May. However, when Charles arrives to collect them, two hours late and wearing a forbidding and disagreeable expression, she changes her mind, and clings to the banister howling.

'Sorry about the time,' Charles coughs, locking his car with a remote-control key, quite unnecessarily as it is parked in our garden, outside our front door. 'I had to take Helena and the twins to the seaside, and we couldn't find anywhere to buy a parasol. It seems absurd, there are plenty of umbrellas for sale, but Helena insists on a proper parasol.' He looks at our sun-baked faces and shakes his head. 'It's not something you would have that I could borrow?' he asks hopefully.

'Dad, this is Norfolk, not the Bahamas,' says Giles witheringly, throwing down his case by the car and holding out his hand for the keys. 'That's why they sell so many umbrellas.'

Cannot help noticing the nervous way Charles glances at each of the children when they are not looking, or how out of place he looks among them with his knife-creased slacks and newly trimmed hair and nails. Giles and particularly Felix have ragged Man Friday hair and frayed T-shirts and look as if they are off to Junior Glastonbury rather than Club Med in France. The Beauty has beaded plaits and is still wearing her pebble on a string, which contrasts with her glittery Barbie clogs, bought from Woolworths this morning to replace the shoes she lost a week ago in the sea.

'Mummy come too, don't make me go,' she howls, embarrassing Charles profoundly. Wedge her into her seat in Charles's giant people-moving vehicle, where she perks up, taking the air-freshener smell and individual seats as an indicator that she is at the hairdresser, a place she loves.

'Shall we have a haircut, Mummy?' she asks politely. 'Or just a trim?'

Giles climbs into the front, retunes the radio to pulsing dance music and closes his eyes. Felix, grumbling about sitting next to The Beauty, suddenly gasps, 'Cool. You've got TV in the car. Now I won't have to buy more batteries for my Game Boy.'

Charles's mouth is now fully downturned with irritation and disappointment. He mutters, 'Yes, in fact they're computers too. I had to buy a new vehicle to transport you and the twins this summer.'

'Nice one, Dad,' says Giles, scrambling into the back next to Felix and The Beauty. I stand back, feeling rather sorry for Charles in his role as chauffeur to these three children whom he no longer really knows, but to whom he is bound by his sense of duty and some wavering cord of love. Am sure my own sense of relief at having nothing to do with him any more must seep down to Giles and Felix.

It certainly informs The Beauty, now quite happily munching crisps and watching the screen in front of her. She waves an airy hand at me, then kicks the back of Charles's seat, shouting, 'Come on. *Drive* me.' Must try to present Charles in a more positive light when they return.

Wave them off, craning to see the car disappear round the bend and out of the village, my awful, fixed smile made more rictus-like by imagining the horror of their journey to Cambridge with sandy, sticky toddler twins. The only mitigation is the air-conditioner in the person mover (cannot understand why they can't just be called cars: is it because they need to sound bigger?), and Felix's astonishing discovery of the individual computer screens in the back of each seat. Splendid that Charles should have installed such a feature, as it will act as a defence against the awful barbed comments that Helena can never resist.

Last time it was, 'Do send nappies for The Beauty, won't you, Venetia. I don't always remember now the twins are potty-trained.' This was particularly below the belt as the twins are nothing of the sort, they can't be, they're not even two, and The Beauty is a year and a half older than them. My private fantasy of Helena, arch pushy mother, telling absurd lies just to mortify me and being caught out, is confounded by Giles.

'Mum, when is The Beauty going to learn to go to the loo? It's so embarrassing now that Holly and Ivy can do it, and Helena always points it out just to be mean.' Perhaps there are potty-training classes, like puppy-training classes, that I can take The Beauty to. Thinking of puppies reminds me that the dogs are still languishing at the kennels. May as well leave them just for the moment, as I need to do a bit of gardening now the children have gone.

Later – three hours later

Made the mistake of drifting into my study, where I thought I had left my secateurs a few days ago, and have only just surfaced. It is six o'clock, and now too late, once again, to get the dogs. Resolve to set my alarm clock early and be there before kennel breakfast in the morning. Session in study is partly rewarding. Opened avalanche of post to find three different cheques for my clothes. Hooray. I am a top businesswoman. Humming and planning vast spend-up in every area, including leaving the dogs at kennels for another week, I continue to open post. Euphoria is short-lived. Horrible reminder from accountant that second instalment of tax should have been paid two weeks ago. The total amount the Inland Revenue wants me to give them is three pounds more than I have just received in cheques. So unjust. All plans are as dust. Particularly dashing as I had moved on from selfish mental purchase of frocks, pedicures and hairslides, to new bikes for all three and even a tiny stipend to be set up for paying Vivienne to do some sewing and thus expand my business.

Abandon the post and my study, without bothering to look at email as there will only be nothing and I will become more depressed. Notice the flashing answerphone and set it to listen, idly wondering if it is the kennels. It is not. It is David. Had quite forgotten how sexy his voice is.

'Hello there, all of you. Thanks for the latest email, Giles, and don't worry, I'm on the case. We're getting close to a wrap on the film, but there are one or two projects being discussed that I have to sort out. Call me, or email. Bye.'

Burst into white-hot, rage-filled tears. Have to go outside, where marching up and down like Lady Macbeth only redoubles my confused misery. He shouldn't still be leading the children on in this way. They think he's coming back to us, and he's not. Nothing about me. I am not even mentioned in the message.

I am working myself up into a frenzy of vengeful fury now, and have conveniently forgotten that it was not David who ended our relationship, but me. He must have found someone else. And why not? He is free after all, and I have found someone else. This thought is curiously unedifying.

Fortunately, as the children will not be back for a week to puncture my self-absorption, the garden looks so bedraggled and untended that pacing and sobbing quickly becomes heavy breathing and crouching. An urgent desire for horticultural order eclipses my emotional turmoil, and I start pulling thistles out of a plump clump of Johnson's Blue geranium. Delicious smell of damp earth mingles with that of evening dew on grass, and very soon thistles are heaped around me as I discover a pair of gardening gloves under a water butt and become absorbed in a task I should have completed weeks ago. Most satisfying to grasp a large thistle at the base of its stem, twist and then pull a long parsnip-like root out of the ground. Tension and worry simply ebb away. Amazing and emancipating to be able to do repetitive job for hours on end without interruption, and it is not until darkness has cloaked the garden and spread across the lingering sunset that I can tear myself away.

Lie in the bath, steam dripping from the ceiling, enjoying the bath lotion Rose has sent me. It is called 'Air Dry', and according to the label promotes 'a sense of well-being by taking you back in time to the days when laundry was dried Outside'.

I love the idea that 'Outside' has become a luxury commodity, and plan a cardigan to complement this bath range. It will be palest blue with tiny phials of 'Fresh Air' sewn on as buttons. In fact, I have all the stuff here, as I can use tiny homoeopathic pill bottles as phials, so I may as well start it after my bath.

August 15th

Cannot believe how easily I go off the rails without child-led routine. Work on the cardigan kept me up into the small hours, and have now woken late, and once again missed kennel breakfast. Is it worth collecting the dogs today? I can't feel that it is, as I have no dog food, and will therefore have to go and buy a sack of Canine Gold or similar. The sack will cost fifteen pounds, and the dogs' day rate at the kennels is only seven pounds fifty for the three of them. Work out that I may as well leave them there for two more days as an economy measure, and fax the kennels accordingly. Anyway, Gertie is enough of a business to look after. Come to think of it, I wonder where she is? Haven't seen her at all today. Begin rushing into rooms shouting for her, heart pounding because even though I hate to admit it, I adore her now as much as the children do. She suddenly squawks up from behind the sofa, where she has been preening in a patch of sun. 'What is it, darrr-link?' she asks, solicitously, in her Hedda Gabler voice. 'Would you like a pink drrrink?' Recognise The Beauty's influence.

The day continues to loom ahead, empty of events now that I have dealt with the dog issue. Would like to do hours of gardening, but the thistle-pulling has made my back ache, and jabbing away with a trowel after breakfast results in another ailment I christen Gardener's Wrist. Apply smart white towelling wrist-support bandage belonging to Giles, and am investigating a persistent nappy smell in the drain outside the kitchen window when Hedley appears, on foot.

'What are you doing?'

'I'm looking down the drain,' I reply, madly irritated by his appearance, for no particular reason.

He slaps my bottom, irritating me further, and laughs, 'So you are. I thought I'd walk over and see if you would like to have lunch with me,' he continues, wiping his face with a handkerchief, somewhat out of breath and pink with heat in his thick checked shirt. 'There's something I want to ask you.'

I find that curiosity overrides most other emotions, and so agree straight away. 'Oh yes please, that would be lovely.'

'Good. I'll pick you up at twelve.' He stares at my feet, apparently lost in rapt contemplation of them. In turn, I stare at his neck, at the point where the black hairs sprout from beneath his shirt collar to meet drops of perspiration below the scalp's hairline. Am about to suggest that he gets a hat before lunch, when he looks up, monobrow concertinaed in a frown, and barks an embarrassed cough.

'I think you should find some shoes by then,' he says hastily, before turning on his heel and marching out of the gate again. Finish looking at the drains, and begin rodding them, all the time musing as to why he wants me to wear shoes, and why I mind.

August 16th

Curiosity killed the cat. Have not slept for a single second. Am trying out ways of making the following words palatable or believable:

I have agreed to marry Hedley.

Hedley asked me to marry him.

Hedley and I are getting married.

I am engaged to Hedley.

Still haven't collected the dogs. This sentence does have the ring of truth.

August 17th

Have not adjusted to my new status as fiancée yet, and have told no one. Have also refused to see Hedley, but have telephoned him six times today to check that he has not told anyone either.

'I must tell the children first,' I insist, voice wavering pathetically because I am missing them so badly. In fact, am in no rush to tell them, and keep hoping that whole proposal thing was just a nightmare. How did it happen? I must have been drunk. I should have known when he said the word 'shoes' that the outing was a mistake. We went to lunch in a restaurant which was part of a country club, and the look with which the receptionist greeted my flip-flops confirmed my worst fears.

'Would madam like to select more appropriate footwear, or does she have something in the car?' asked the manager, opening a cupboard to reveal three pairs of Queen Mother shoes for midgets. None of them would go on, despite vigorous pushing on the part of the manager. I did not have anything in the car, and feeling very like an Ugly Sister, I followed Hedley and the manager to the table selected for us. We were placed, with much ceremony, in the corner of the room behind a partition with a swing door opening into the men's loo next to us. Shrank in horror from the dainty table display, with swan-sculpted butter and napkins folded like waterfalls, or perhaps water lilies, the heavy crystal glass and the cloth carnation in a narrow vase.

'Urgh, Hedley, I think we should go. This sort of place gives me the creeps.' Assumed he would feel the same and that we would giggle and depart, but he was sitting down, unfolding his napkin with a satisfied smirk.

'What was that, Venetia?' he said. I shook my head, realising it was useless, and sat down. Our small talk lasted for about three minutes, and then, in the silence which followed the waiter taking our order, Hedley suddenly leaned towards me and seized my hand.

Thinking he was about to chastise me for shredding the petals of the carnation, I tried to snatch my hand back, muttering, 'Sorry, sorry.'

He didn't let go. Surprised, I tugged more, and met his gaze. It was ardent. And with a terrible sense of inevitability, I knew what he was about to say, and I understood why we were here. The moment before he spoke hung, suffocating, between us, broken by the waiter's return with two fizzing glasses which I would rather contained Alka Seltzer than celebratory champagne.

What is so odd is that I didn't say no. I thought about rodding the drains, I thought about Lucinda at the fête and I thought about being married instead of being single with my children. I saw my computer empty of emails to me from David, and I said, 'Yes.'

August 20th

The children return today. I have discovered a new virtuous me since the engagement, and the house is spotless. Am convinced that if my surroundings are in order, my life will become calm, and the merry-go-round confusion in my mind will cease. This morning, though, I realise I have gone too far. Am still in the bath, having soaked for hours and washed my hair, and have just let the water out. In order to save time and effort later, I decide to clean the bath from within, so reach for the scourer and green scrubby thing and address the porcelain. Finally get out, having had to have a second mini-bath to remove spattered scouring cream, wrinkled but triumphant. There is no dirt anywhere to be seen, and no clutter. Have done a DIY feng shui, and am now a convert to the minimal lifestyle. Subsequently attack piles of paper, bowls of odds and ends and the kitchen cupboards.

The dustbins are groaning and looking very un-feng shui'ed, but Rose says dustbins don't count. They do to the dogs, who returned yesterday from the kennels at a price far exceeding the total value of the three of them, and are sniffing about in the bin shed hoping to find food. They cannot know that I have not cooked anything since the children left, but have been on a self-cleansing programme as rigorous as the house-work campaign. Anyway, only have two saucepans left as I took a Zen view on the others and got rid of them for having blackened bottoms and dented sides post-camping trip. Never mind. Getting married will improve my saucepan stock. Not content with clean-ing the house, I also pick lettuce and fry bread to make Caesar salad for lunch. I am openly sucking up by doing this, as it is the boys' favourite – appropriate and pleasing considering the enormous lettuce reserves in my vegetable garden at present.

Have got everything ready and am sitting in the shade of the lime tree sewing a heap of Barbie's plas-tic shoes around the armholes of a pink T-shirt, when a car purrs up to the house. In it is a furious-looking family I have never seen before. Jump back and assume crouched position behind the flower bed, peering between borage and feathery fennel leaves at them. They are thumping around, moving things and beginning to climb out of the car. With a start, I real-ise that some of them are my children, but they all have white panels down their noses and look as if they belong to a bizarre sect. Helena has brought them, and she is first out of the car, hopping on to the gravel and stretching like an ill-tempered gull. Holly and Ivy, her dear little toddlers, are also wearing beaks; they open their door and hurl items of The Beauty's luggage on to the ground. I wait for a moment until Helena's back is turned so she doesn't see that I have been hiding in the bushes, and jump up and scuttle round to greet them.

'Darlings. What has happened to your noses?' The Beauty reaches me first, and I see that the marks are not so pronounced on her, but are still visible and are the residue of a week of being forced to wear sun-protection beaks. Giles and Felix have even less of a mark, but from the poisoned glowering expressions focused on Helena, it is clear that the holiday was not a success.

'Must go, I don't think they've forgotten anything, but do ring and let me know if they have – actually, don't ring, a postcard will do fine,' she trills, scrabbling to get away before I come too close. However, I am keen to see her odd markings properly, and make a grandmother's-footstep-sized leap across the driveway and am instantly at her side. Hah! She has a sunscreening plastic beak still attached to her nose. This accounts for the precise edges of her luminous white scowl.

She forces a smile, and hisses, 'I can't get it off. That child—' she breaks off to hurl a vile glance at The Beauty, who is sweetly hugging Lowly on the sun-warmed doorstep, 'that child mixed Super Glue with my very expensive organic suncream. I have been stuck with this . . . this . . . this *beak* on my face all week, and I am going to the private hospital in

Cambridge this afternoon to have it removed.' A sob chokes her, and in sympathy, dear little Holly and Ivy begin to whimper in the back. Not wishing to delay her a moment from her operation, I wave her away, affecting contrition for The Beauty's behaviour by keeping my head humbly bowed.

Turn to embrace my children, and find they have vanished, so follow a trail of sweet wrappers and shoes into the house and through into the playroom, where all three are in a row on the sofa, and looking oddly unlike themselves, as they often do when returning from Charles. They also seem to have grown; The Beauty's skirt, which when she left was knee-length, is now a micro-mini, and Felix's shorts are similarly diminished on his long legs.

'Oh my loves, I've missed you,' I warble, sinking down in front of them, arms outstretched, knowing that I must keep going and not allow myself to wind down to silence. 'And I've got some very important news to tell you.' My heart is bumping in my chest, and I have to grab The Beauty to prevent myself from running out of the room.

'Mind out, Mum, I'm trying to do this brilliant cheat.' Felix pushes me out of the way of the television screen and settles his control gun on his knee.

'We've got a magazine that tells you loads of brilliant ways to get up a level on the Dinosaur Death game,' says Giles kindly, as if I am a child clamouring to join in.

'Mummy look. Mouldy Baby's burned her nose,' The Beauty pipes from the sofa where she has

257

felt-penned a red line down the middle of her doll's face. She waves the doll to show me, shaking her head and turning down her mouth in mock misery. There is never going to be a good time, and at least if they really freak, I can change my mind, I think weakly to myself, before closing my eyes and launching into the cold, deep water of confession.

'Anyway, I think you should know – no, anyway – it's really exciting, I've decided – no, anyway – the thing I want to tell you is that – no—'

Giles suddenly switches off the Nintendo and there is a horrible whine ending in silence. 'Come on Mum, spit it out,' he says, grinning encouragingly.

I shut my eyes and do as he tells me. 'Hedley has asked me to marry him and I have said yes. But if you don't want me to—'

'Yesss. Look at that Giles, I've done it!'

Open my eyes, and find that none of them is looking at me. Felix has turned the Nintendo back on and is rapt, doubled over the controls, Giles is helping him, and The Beauty wasn't listening in the first place, and is now in the depths of the dressing-up box, her bottom high in the air as she delves. She turns back to catch my eye, dabbing now at Mouldy Baby's nose with a hanky. 'God's sake Mummy,' she says briskly, 'Mouldy Baby's got really horruble nose trubble.'

Tempted to tiptoe from the room and attack the brandy bottle, but Giles is paying more attention than it would appear.

'Why did you say yes?'

'Mum, I don't think you want to marry him. He's quite old and I like his house, but we prefer to be here, don't we?' Felix glances up for a moment to make his point, then turns back to the screen for another assault on the next level.

Giles pushes back his fringe to stare uninterrupted into my eyes, and his level gaze has me squirming.

'Why did you say yes, Mum? I thought you would marry David. Don't you think you should see if he wants to before you go off with someone we hardly know?'

What a sensible boy Giles is. Wish I had asked him what he thought earlier. Sensation of shattered porcelain, glass, hearts, trust and television screens interrupted by wailing from the depths of the dressing-up box.

'Mummyyy, ooohh nooo!! I done a pooo!! Mummmyyy. Right now, I said.'

Oh, God. Unbearable. Perhaps I should email David and crawl to him, begging him to come home forthwith.

August 21st

Wilt, wilt, wilt. I am so sick of the summer and of being hot. The days are much too long, and there is too much evening in which to brood. Hedley has brought Tamsin to tea and he is wearing a bow tie. Giles is scarcely speaking to me and has taken to locking himself in my study doing the internet and probably visiting dreadful unsuitable dysfunctional-family websites. He claims to be checking out the stock market, and wants me to give him my credit-card number so that he can invest. 'I'll give you the cash and you give me the number,' he urges. 'I promise it will only be thirty pounds. That's all I've got.'

He does not congratulate Hedley, but walks straight past him, and Tamsin, who has had her hair woven into hundreds of tiny plaits and looks about seventeen suddenly. Giles pulls his bike from the tangle of punctured tyres and lawnmowers in the barn and begins to glide away. Hedley looks forlornly after him, the mono-brow furrowed and wiggling like a black caterpillar.

'I'm going to see Granny,' say Giles, and I nod and cower, cravenly accepting any words he deigns to throw my way. Try to pretend this is standard behaviour and call after him, 'All right darling, splendid. See you later.'

Must now try to convince Hedley that all the children are delighted, despite the contrary evidence of Giles's departure. Felix's remarks do not back me up, and he delivers them with pithy regularity.

'Hedley's too old to get married. He's had his day,' is the ice-breaker, followed by: 'I think weddings are for saddos,' uttered darkly with a nasty look. Sudden animation takes over, and Felix leaps up from the grass where he has been lying with various war lords and warriors. 'And you needn't think I'm going to be a soppy pageboy, because I'm not. I'd rather swim in shark-infested waters.'

The telephone rings, and I gratefully rush to answer it, leaving Felix to turn his remarks into interrogation of the wretched Hedley.

'What is the point of you marrying Mum anyway? She's got us. Why don't you find someone more your own age who hasn't got anyone? Miss Snape at school would be good. I'll introduce you, if you take me to school when term starts. It doesn't matter that she's got a few hairs like a moustache and looks like a witch, because she's very nice and she could shave. And anyway, Mum says looks are not everything—'

It is my mother on the telephone.

'Giles is here, in a very odd mood. He says I must ask you what the matter with him is.' She sighs an expulsion of cigarette smoke. 'I do wish these boys weren't so moody,' she complains. 'What can be wrong with him?'

Am thus forced to tell her the news in a defensive and furtive manner rather than arriving with Hedley and a lubricating bottle at her house to tell her triumphantly. 'I think he wants me to tell you I'm getting married.'

Her surprise is palpable. 'Goodness. Are you sure you are? Don't you mean that you have been married? And now you aren't? You must be confused, Venetia, it's the sun, you know.'

Grit my teeth. 'No, I don't mean that. I am getting married *again*. To Hedley Sale. All right?' The earpiece and my head fill with one of her irritating roller-coaster noises.

'Mmmm, well I never. Quick work, Venetia, I must say. I do think the boys need a man around, but Hedley . . .' she sighs, then repeats incredulously,

'You . . . You and Hedley . . . Oh, well. Poor Giles.' She puts the phone down, leaving me seething and embarrassed.

August 24th

Giles has not returned from visiting my mother since he cycled over there three days ago, and Felix and The Beauty respond to the unsettled air in the house by mounting a campaign of exploitation and racketeering that could be taken as a blueprint by international mafia bosses.

They have set up a stall on the road by the gate and are doing a brisk trade in Giles's CDs and other stolen goods. I remain blissfully unaware, humming in my study and attempting to create a filing system that will mean something to me for more than twenty-four hours. Filing actually means 'piling', as I do not have anywhere to put papers except in unresolved heaps on the floor. Should I put the Rare Poultry Society leaflet in my garden pile, my vet and inoculations pile, or should I start a new mound called simply 'places'? Have similar trouble with the guarantee and instructions leaflet for the computer, and with the rota, already sent, for parental nursery-school duties next term. In the end, move these and several other items like them from the desk to the floor without sorting them at all. Am beginning to realise that it is not filing I need to do, but wallpapering. If I could stick every bit of paper I need on to the wall in my study, I would be able to look at them while on the telephone, and would thus be constantly ahead of paperwork. Have a rush of enthusiasm for this plan until I realise that what I am thinking of is just a larger noticeboard, and I have three of these already, layered with much flapping and unlooked-at paper, and I should now spend half an hour sorting them. Somewhat defeated, I clear a space on a chair by the window and immerse myself in an old newspaper in the log basket. Am interrupted, after a while, by the arrival of the postman, chuckling. He tells me that I should be proud of my little entrepreneurs.

'What little entrepreneurs?' I ask suspiciously, cursing inwardly because I knew I should have been attending to the children instead of fiddling about in here.

'Well two of your kids are down on the corner selling CDs, very reasonably. I bought this one from them; I gave them a quid, I thought seventy pence was robbing them.' He splutters with laughter and waves my favourite and rarest Waylon Jennings album triumphantly.

I lean into his red van and snatch the CD.

'I'm afraid that wasn't theirs to sell. You'll have to ask for your money back.'

Disconsolate, the postman reverses away down the drive, muttering, 'You should keep an eye on those children, they're dangerous.'

I follow, moments later, allowing an interval to elapse for the return of his money as I know there will be an ugly scene about it. Can tell that this was the case when I arrive at the marketeers' stall. This consists of a small hexagonal silver paper table from the playroom and an upturned bucket upon which are displayed various pieces of my jewellery and other miscellaneous possessions of mine and Giles's, as well as David's cordless drill and a selection of other tools. The hectic flush on The Beauty's cheeks indicates that her brush with the postman was furious, and Felix, appropriately dodgy-looking in a greasy old pork pie from the dressing-up box confirms this: 'She bit the postman's finger when he asked for his money back. You shouldn't have interfered, Mum.'

Deliver a crisp lecture on theft and fraud while squinting anxiously at the tables, wondering what precious or embarrassing items have already been sold to gleeful passers-by. Cannot tell from the kitty, as The Beauty is sitting on the money tin, wagging her finger in the direction the postman has taken.

'No, you may not have your pence back. You gave them to me,' she is insisting with much energy.

Felix also entirely ignores my sermon, and with cheeks quite as pink as The Beauty's shouts, 'Well it isn't stealing, because the neighbours were really happy to get back their gnome which Lowly pinched and chewed on the lawn.'

'But did they pay for it? Or did you give it back?'

'Of course they paid for it. This is a shop.' Felix jumps up and down, emphasising his point. 'They were pleased, actually, because it only cost fifty pence, and they said it was a bargain because gnomes are really expensive new.' Suddenly his rage diminishes, and he stops and shifts from foot to foot and stares at the ground.

'Anyway, Mum, what are we supposed to do? If you marry Hedley we won't need this stuff any more, because we've got to go and live at his cruddy house where there's no Nintendo or anything good. I thought we could buy one to take with us with the money from our sale.'

Anguished to think of their confusion and turmoil, but at least the Nintendo needn't be an issue. 'But you can take yours with you,' I point out.

Felix throws me a look combining pity and scorn. 'Don't be silly,' he says, 'we're leaving it for David. How do you think he's going to feel when he comes home and none of us are here and he hasn't even got a Nintendo?'

His welling tears, his clenched defiance, catapult me back to the year Charles left, and I am engulfed by familiar pain and paralysing guilt. All wavering resolve is strengthened. Of course I must marry Hedley. He will never leave me for a masseuse, like Charles, or head off into the celluloid sunset like David. He is a rock, admittedly a slightly red-faced one, but he will solve all these emotional nightmares and allow me to concentrate on the children. And the cardigans, he's keen on the cardigans.

Open my mouth to begin translating this into language suitable for the under-tens, but am cut short by a commanding 'parp-parrrp' as my mother's car slews into sight around the bend, her hair beneath a pointed purple hat visible above the steering wheel, string and a plastic bag issuing from the closed driver's door. Her arrival has a temporarily edifying effect on Felix, who climbs on to the wall to wave.

'Look, Granny's wearing a witch's hat.'

'Granneee, ooohh hellooo. Stop your car,' screams The Beauty, leaping up and dashing into the road in kamikaze style. 'Come and see the shop. Come and buy stuff, right now.'

Very admiring of her sales pitch, I am caught smirking indulgently as my mother coasts to a halt, having cut her engine some yards back. Giles is in the car with her, and both have wraparound sunglasses on: fine for Giles, but disturbing and Blues Brotheresque on my mother. She winds down her window and leans out to greet me.

'Venetia darling. Has it come to this? I thought you were becoming a fashion designer.' She waves her cigarette at the roadside stall.

Giles leaps out of the passenger side snarling, 'Mum, how could you let them take my things?' and snatches a handful of CDs.

The Beauty bursts into tears and kicks him on the shins, while roaring, 'Stop fussing about, you silly idiot.'

The scene of mayhem is too much for Felix, who suddenly loses his head and vaults over the wall and back into the garden, turning his head to yell, 'God this is it. *This is it*. I hate my family. I wish I was dead.'

It is all too much, a real gas-oven moment. I slump in a heap on the upturned bucket and burst into tears. Am sobbing away with abandon when warm arms creep around my neck, and Giles is there whispering, 'Please don't cry Mummy, we can sort it all out, I know we can.'

Redoubling of tears for a moment of self-indulgence before I pull myself together, and scooping the Rescue Remedy from its position at the front of the stall, I consult the card propped next to it which commands: *Skweeze some drips on your tunge when you are crying – only 10p a drip*. Duly squirt a whole pipette full into my mouth and instantly stop feeling so unravelled. Sniffing, I stand up and hug Giles back.

A car towing a caravan and sagging with occupants and luggage passes, slowing and opening the windows for a better view of us. One of the children in the back produces a camera and waves it out of the window. I hear him yelling at his mother, 'Look, gypsies! Please stop, I want to take a picture of them.'

Am cheered by this, as have always wished to lead my life in a picturesque Romany fashion, and immediately begin to imagine spending the dwindling dog days of this summer driving a fat cob and wagon down leafy byroads with happy children wearing neckerchiefs. If only we had done that at the beginning of the holidays, none of this would have happened.

My mother has clearly cast a spell on The Beauty, and she is neatly and silently packing up the stall, lifting items up to gaze at them wistfully before returning them to piles designated to each member of the household. All piles are wedged into the wheelbarrow, and Giles pushes it back into the yard, The

Beauty kneeling precariously on top, her expression resigned yet wary, like a small refugee.

Praising God in His wisdom for inventing computer games, and promising my conscience to deal with issues of hypocrisy and inconsistency later, I grant permission for Dinosaur Death Run to be played, and drag a chair close to the kitchen table in order to sit with head buried in hands.

My mother busies herself with the kettle, and sitting down opposite me she places a cup of tea in front of each of us, ignoring for once the clean glasses and corkscrew on the window sill.

'I want to talk to you, Venetia,' she says, and I shift uneasily, dreading what is coming next.

'You are making a huge mistake,' she says, her eyes never leaving my face, her expression grave and penetrating, and her whole demeanour so unlikely that if it were not for the purple turban, I would find it difficult to believe it is her. 'Hedley will not make a good father for your children because they already have a father. They need you to be happy, they do not need you to clutch at straws.'

Manage to protest, 'Hedley isn't a straw,' but am quelled by a glance as she continues, 'I don't often interfere with your plans, and I would not have done so on this occasion were it not for Giles. He is terribly upset. He says you don't love Hedley, you're trying to get back at David. He says you should be marrying David.'

My head, which I thought I was shaking in disbelief, suddenly starts nodding involuntarily, as the truth of her words seizes me, and furious mortification floods in. Instead of meekly agreeing with her, I slam my fist on the table and retort, 'I can't marry David. He hasn't asked me. He never rings, he doesn't care about me. For all I know he's been eaten by a crocodile. We haven't seen him for months and I have reason to suspect that he has found love with the snake-handler on the Tarzan film.'

'Don't be ridiculous, Venetia,' my mother snaps. 'He's done nothing of the sort. And if you live with someone, you cannot go around getting engaged to other people without sending so much as a telegram.'

Thoroughly incensed, I leap up and begin pacing about. 'I did, I had a conversation with him months ago and we agreed that it wasn't working. All he's done is send horrible insects and pygmy heads to the children, not to mention that parrot.' I jerk my head in the direction of Gertie, who is sidling along the window sill, head on one side, listening to the muffled tone of the radio.

My mother is sitting calmly, her hands clasped in Rev. Trev style on the table. 'Go on,' she says.

Press my palms against my eyes, and have swirling, drowning sense of panic.

'I agree with you that they need me to be happy in order to be happy themselves. And I am usually very happy,' I say, indicating otherwise as tears roll down my face. 'It was Minna and Desmond getting married, or maybe it's a mid-life crisis, but all my instincts have become protective and I feel that by marrying Hedley I can make a secure environment for the children.'

'Why can't you make one on your own?'

'I can, but it's very hard. I thought that marriage to Hedley would be better.' Gloom lifts, and suddenly have a sunburst sensation as if I am Vivien Leigh in the last moments of *Gone With the Wind*, chin rises, and I insist, 'And I still think it will be better.' Very important to stand up for myself in these matters.

My mother still doesn't light a cigarette. This is the longest I've ever seen her not smoking, apart from when she's asleep, and I know that she has not finished with me yet.

'I thought you had more strength of character than that,' she says quietly. 'When did you ever expect it to be easy?'

Have not been carved up in this way since my divorce. A flame of righteousness flares within me. I snap: 'Look, I'm marrying Hedley and that's that.' Stalk off to attack the garden, and, presumably in denial of some sort, begin brooding over the role of the postman in today's dramas. Hope he gets transferred soon.

August 25th

The school second-hand shop is open today, and it is a triumph of filing that I know this. Came across the leaflet while searching for the puncture-repair kit in a drawer I like to think of as 'Domestic'. The family height chart by the kitchen door reveals that Felix has grown two inches since April, and Giles has grown three. This means a great many larger items will be required for both of them, and many name tapes will have to be sewn on. Busy myself with maternal chivvying, largely ignoring my mother, who has elected to stay on, as Peta is hosting another of her medieval meditation evenings on the grass between her caravan and my mother's front door. At breakfast time, I vengefully pass my mother The Beauty, who is moaning gently, having developed a cold in the night. To my irritation, both are very happy with this arrangement, The Beauty snuggling into my mother's embrace like a kitten.

The boys and I having spread school clothes all over their bedrooms, drive off with a lengthy list which I hope to deal with at the second-hand shop, and they hope will require a trip to Norwich. For once, I am the first to turn up the dance channel on the radio, and it is a perfect thought-killer.

August 26th

Still in denial. Considerable satisfaction gleaned from tearing down dried-out sweet-pea plants and dead-heading the roses. Decide to attack the box hedging with secateurs, but am quickly disheartened by the fact that it is so tiny. Cannot believe that it needs pruning as this is only its second year, and instead turn to the easier, more cerebral work of wandering around planning my autumn planting. Having endowed my garden with several thousand pounds' worth of fantasy, my spirits lift. There is nothing like mental gardening to enthuse oneself again, particularly when the reality is falling so dismally short of expectations. New projects include the planting of a great many old roses, all with glamorous Proustian names like Mme Victor Verdier and Souvenir de Philemon Cochet. An exhaustive catalogue perusal leaves me with a list of thirty-seven roses where I need six. Whittling commences, and is painful, as I most particularly want to include the exotic Tipsy Imperial Concubine somewhere, and it is not the colour I need, being pink with yellow and red tones. Imagine it to look like a tequila sunrise, and decide it can have a home next to the summer drinking table in the most sheltered part of the garden. Attempt to turn my thoughts to the chaos of my emotional life, but find my brain is jammed on gardening mode and will not accept other thoughts. Shall try again after dark.

August 27th

Spent three hours yesterday evening trying either to telephone or email David, but am convinced that there is a gremlin or widget in my computer, as all the numbers and addresses I try make weird alien noises, then go dead. Am now attempting to write a letter, but cannot get past *Dear David* as situation is so dire. Against my better judgement, I reread the emails between us pre-Hedley. This is a mistake. My eyes fill with tears, blood rushes to my head and a terrible nostalgia for my life as it was then pervades. In trying to trace the moment when I lost touch with David, I review the past months and cannot remember why I was so sure we should split up.

The postman arrives, and I cannot bear to speak to him. Throw myself on the floor in my study and crawl behind a chair in order that he cannot see me through the window. Of course, he has a parcel, so rings the bell. I hear the slap of The Beauty's small bare feet on the hall tiles, then the creak of the door, and her voice piping, 'Sorry about that, Mummy's not well. She had too much vodka drink with Granny. She's hidin' in her study so she can't see anyone, but I know where she is.' The Beauty, having finished slandering me, pauses for effect, then laughs her fake laugh and delivers the punchline, 'She's lyin' on de floor.' Both she and the postman fall about with mirth at this sally, and it is some moments before he departs, having allowed The Beauty to sign for the parcel. She marches with it into the study, whipping open the door so I am caught still crouching under the window. She gives me a knowing look.

'Come on Mummy, let's open it,' she commands, tearing at the brown paper. In the parcel are three cardigans I ordered from a cashmere factory seconds shop. The sight of them is quite lowering.

'Let's ring Vivienne,' I suggest weakly. 'Maybe we can ask her to help with these.' Reach for the phone, then change my mind. I cannot speak to Vivienne until I have untangled the mess. I must see Hedley. I mean, I want to see Hedley. But I must also do these cardigans within the next twenty-four hours, and more immediately, I really should get the children and myself out of pyjamas and into day clothes and make lunch. This last thought occurs as The

Beauty totters off to the kitchen to return, moments later, munching handfuls of dry Coco Pops straight from the bag she has removed from inside the cereal box. Letter to David must wait and be dealt with later.

August 29th

Have been dodging the telephone since my mother's pep talk, in case Hedley rings, as he is always better face to face. Am also dodging the children. This is surprisingly easy considering how large they are and how small the house is, due to their very predictable habits. Left alone, Giles and Felix wear pyjamas and eat cereal in front of the television with the curtains drawn all day. The Beauty takes the biscuit tin and all her dolls into the dogs' castle and makes a boudoir deep within it. There she bosses babies and dogs to her heart's content.

When I sneak past on tiptoe, she is arranging a wedding between Mouldy Baby and Lowly, with Gertie as clergyman.

'No, no, no,' she insists, 'don't eat it, Lowly. You have to wear the crown and so does Mouldy. That's right. Now Gertie, say a prayer.'

Move on stealthily to hang out the washing. Folding the dry clothes, I close my eyes and inhale deeply, loving the fresh-air scent, enveloped in it. Things have moved on from fresh-air candles, and now Rose tells me that in America, the vogue is for sheets to be 'Line Dried', an expensive process involving specially altered tumble driers, perhaps indeed broken ones able to let fresh air in.

'Of course, what everyone there longs for is a washing line. There's something so grounding about actually pegging out your clean laundry every day.'

Sometimes Rose goes too far.

Anyway, my limbo life cannot go on. Hedley has left nine messages on the answerphone, most of which are rants, due to the delivery of thirty tons of pig manure outside his front door. He has been engaged in a boundary dispute with a neighbouring pig farmer, who believes that actions speak louder than words. From the choleric nature of the messages, it is clear that Hedley has not even noticed that I am avoiding him. His voice transmits a tone of massive ill use and fury, which he seems convinced I will share.

It is another hot, windless day, with the sun high and bright and the sky bleached pale blue. Nothing is moving in the hedgerows, but beyond, the fields are in turmoil as great yellow combine harvesters charge to and fro, trailing clouds of dust and shards of bright straw, as they perform their alchemy by devouring the last of the corn crop in order to deliver sliding mounds of gold into the waiting trailers.

Drive everybody to the weekly auction in Aylsham as a delaying tactic for work as well as life. Have run completely out of inspiration, and in the hope that they will just vanish, have taken to leaving the as yet unworked-on cardigans on the bench in the hall. The result of this is that The Beauty has started wearing them, but with her legs rather than her arms in the sleeves.

'They're just soft pants,' she explains, when asked what she is doing. 'You try them.'

Park at the auction by wedging the car in between a van full of caged ferrets and another delivering seven sludge-green lavatories to the outdoor part of the sale. 'Can we have one?' yell all the children in one voice, but looking in different directions at different objects of desire. Giles has seen the ferrets, Felix the bicycles just beyond, and The Beauty is entranced by the green loos being tenderly wrapped in blankets and deposited on the concrete outside one of the cavernous saleroom sheds. A bell rings; milling people herd towards a smaller shed for the fur and feathers sale. We join them, blinking to acclimatise to the clanking, sawdust-scented darkness of the shed. The usual bedraggled and demented chicken line-up, with the occasional proud, single cockerel, is augmented today by a big array of ferrets. Become transfixed by family of spectral white ferrets, slinking and rolling in a wooden box with a mesh top. The biggest one has yellowing fur at its neck, but the young are dazzling white, tumbling and playing, breaking off to uncoil their bodies and stand up on their hind legs to sniff the air. Can feel myself succumbing to their fascination, so concentrate on their rat-like pink eyes to put myself off and turn away towards the more harmless guinea pigs and rabbits. Discover The Beauty clinging like a rock climber to the mesh wall of cages, stroking a fudge-coloured rabbit.

The auctioneer opens the cage, reaches in to grab the occupant and holds the hapless creature up for a quick last-minute look before beginning his melodious bidding murmur. Giles looks at me.

I nod, weakly, relieved he isn't attempting to buy the ferrets, and whisper, extremely generously as I perceive it, 'But not more than five pounds.'

'OK.' He hoists The Beauty on to his shoulders to wait for the bidding to open.

The auctioneer, a fellow parent at The Beauty's nursery school, grins in an avuncular fashion, wipes his face with a red spotted handkerchief and begins, 'Three-fifty, who'll give me three-fifty, three-twenty then.'

The Beauty's hand flies up and she yells, 'Me. I'm doing it. Shuddup Giles.'

The auctioneer winks at her and accepts her bid, and we are off: 'Starting at three-twenty with the young lady, three-twenty, three-twenty, thank you, three-fifty, three-fifty, three-seventy, four.' A thin man with blurred pale skin and yellow dyed hair is bidding against her.

The Beauty glares balefully at him, and Felix tugs my sleeve to whisper, 'That man looks like a banana.'

Felix and I begin to snort with laughter, distracting those around us and, most fortunately, the banana man, who misses the final bid. 'It's four-four, four-fifty, five-five, five – any advance on five pounds? Five pounds then, selling at five pounds . . . *sold* to the young lady.' The auctioneer whacks his hammer against the cage and moves on.

We stand, flooded with euphoria, looking at our purchase. Bunny has resolutely turned her face to the corner of her cage and shows no sign of wishing to meet us.

'It's called Fat Rabbit,' says The Beauty. 'But it's a bit lonely. Shall we get another one? Right now?'

'She's right, Mum, it'll be lonely on its own. We should have two, you know. There are some really sweet lop-eared ones just coming up now.' Felix could be a rabbit social worker with the level of concern he is displaying. I am completely taken in by the pleading, serious expressions on all three children's faces, but make a last-ditch attempt to save myself.

'Who will do the mucking out? Who will feed them and gather hogweed every day?'

'We will, Mummy, honestly. We've always wanted some rabbits,' says Felix.

'But you never take the dogs out,' I remind them.

'We're older now,' coaxes Giles, 'and anyway, you never ask us to take the dogs out. We look after Gertie.'

'Well that's because Gertie likes doing what you do. She even eats cereal with milk and sugar now.'

'No she doesn't, she eats—'

'Look, look, what a sweet poppet rabbit,' shrieks The Beauty, pointing as a small grey lop-eared bunny is hoisted from its cage. The bidding has already started, but Giles and Felix insinuate themselves like smoke into the tight-pressed crowd around the auctioneer. They push The Beauty forwards and she shoots up her hand as the bidding reaches three-fifty. Praying they will stop at five, and quite unable to squeeze myself past anyone to be near them, I hang around at the edge, trying to see over a dirty baseball cap to where the children are.

'*Sold*, to the young lady and her brothers for nine pounds,' shouts the auctioneer. I hear him in disbelief. Nine pounds? They can't have bought a rabbit for nine pounds, it's absurd. I told them they could only go up to five pounds. What are they thinking of? I raise my hand to try to lodge a complaint, but the children emerge at my side, lit with excitement and clutching three small grey rabbits.

'Fat Rabbit can be yours, Mum. We're having one of these each. And there are two more in the cage, which I thought we should give to The Beauty's nursery when term starts again,' says Felix.

'That was why it was nine pounds,' explains Giles, stroking the ears of the rabbit disappearing into his crooked elbow. 'Actually it's a real bargain. Five for nine pounds is less than two pounds each.'

Six rabbits. How ghastly. 'Can't we just leave a few of them here?' I ask hopefully. 'I'm sure some nice person would rescue them.'

Giles and Felix both look shocked. 'Mum, you couldn't abandon them in the saleroom, could you?' asks Felix.

Have to do deep breathing and struggle to reach a higher spiritual plane in order not to snap back, 'Yes, I bloody well could.'

Beaten down, and keen to leave before we purchase any other life-changing errors, I meekly suggest that we take them home to settle them in.

August 30th

The rabbit house is palatial. Giles suddenly remembered his museum, untouched for several months and now home to several mice and probably a few rat squatters too. The construction, cocooned by cobwebs and dust, consists of four chest-high walls made by David and painted to look like a Roman temple, with glass cases found in a junk yard propping them up from the inside. The rabbits were installed yesterday and immediately vanished behind the artefacts we gave them to play with. The boys too vanished, muttering something about skateboarding into the village, and promising vaguely to do the rabbits later. The same has happened today.

Take comfort from the fact that The Beauty is still interested, and we have had the bunnies at home for a whole twenty-four hours. She will not come out of their run, but is sitting on a small chair she has dragged in, breathing heavily and looking around for rabbits to boss. She spies a cottontail behind the tattered Mary Poppins umbrella that was one of the feebler museum exhibits and shrieks, 'Aha! Found you. Don't worry, sweet poppets, I won't tell anyone.' She bends forward to talk to them, hands clasped in her lap in the manner of a playgroup leader. Three of the rabbits hop over to her and sit up on their back legs.

One places a tentative paw on The Beauty's knee. Am really coming round to the sweet little fur bundles. Am sure I have read somewhere that it is good for stress to have something to stroke. I shall have a rabbit as my executive toy, and stroking will start immediately. It works. Ten minutes of calm rabbit-stroking and I am ready to face anything.

Telephone my mother and ask her to come and oversee the children.

'I've got to go and see Hedley, and I'm sure they won't want to come, given their views, so I wondered if you would like to drive over and let them show you their new rabbits?'

'Rabbits, how awful,' she says. 'I expect the dogs will eat them. God, no. Don't take the children with you. Absolutely not,' she adds with feeling. 'Have you spoken to David, though? I really think you should.'

Surprised to hear myself snap back with a blatant lie, 'I know what I am doing.'

She ignores me. 'All right, I'll come. But I will not hold the rabbits. I hate rabbits. I'm not gathering any dandelions for them, or putting water into those awful bottle things they have.'

'No, no, the children will do that. See you later.'

'When have your children ever looked after their animals?' she retorts before hanging up.

Horrible hourglass sensation of stomach sinking into shoes has faded now, thanks to bunny-cuddling session. The Beauty is busy burying Barbie in her sandpit, the boys are not back from the village and I am able to arrange myself in the hammock with the newly developed photographs I collected this morning. Hammock creaks in protest but does not give way, and the dappled canopy of the tree is soothing. Tear open the pack of photographs in happy anticipation of reliving the camping trip, and instead find myself staring at David. David, very brown, his eyes clear silver-grey, grinning broadly in front of a log cabin. Goose pimples rise on my arms and my heart leaps thumping into my throat as I flick through the snaps, not stopping to look at any one picture properly because I so desperately want to have seen them all, to know what is in there. Reach the end and sigh; apart from the first one, they are all of monkeys, parrots and other jungle miscellanea. Recall a postcard arriving some time ago rolled around a film. These must be the pictures he sent the boys of life in the jungle. Throw the photographs on to the ground and lie back with the David picture in my hand. Am very shaken by seeing him where I did not expect him. Or am I shaken by seeing him at all? Had forgotten the electric effect of his smile, and the particular way he inhabits a crumpled white shirt.

'Mummy, what you doin'?' Brought back to earth by the piercing gaze of The Beauty, and find that I have the photograph almost resting on my nose, so closely am I examining it. Hurl it to one side and hug The Beauty tight, making her squeal. While she waves her toes and coos, I reach my arm out in an impossible stretch and grab the photograph, stuffing it in the pocket of my skirt. My mother appears, fanning herself with a straw hat.

'Just go,' she sighs. I go.

'Who is he smiling at? Who took the picture?' These questions create the rhythm for the short journey to Hedley's house, and wrestling with them occupies every scrap of ingenuity I possess. Sniffing vaguely, I park my car, wondering whether anyone ever takes Hedley's rubbish out for him, or if it always smells like this here at the end of the summer.

Hedley struts out of the front door, shouting into a telephone, gesticulating wildly. He sees me, his gestures become more expansive to include me, and his brow tilts up to the left. The brow appears to have got bushier in the days since I last saw him. Mobile, as it is now, due to the frenzied conversation he is having, it reminds me of those fluffy neon worms on transparent wire that they sell in joke shops.

'Well get it moved today or he's toast,' yells Hedley, and jabbing at the off button he hurls the phone into the heart of the vast heap of manure I have finally noticed.

'Oh, God, no wonder it smells here,' I exclaim. 'Still, it's useful for the garden, although I wouldn't normally start doing mine this early. It's not as big as I thought it would be, though. Have you got him to take some away again?'

This is the wrong thing to say. Hedley's eyes bulge, and he is about to scream at me when the phone begins to trill from the depths of the muck heap.

'For Christ's sake,' Hedley yells, charging like a tiny bull at the muck heap, and burrowing into its steamy heart. He finds the phone without much difficulty, but the ringing has stopped. Wiping it on his trousers he advances towards me, clearly expecting to kiss me.

'Now Venetia, tell me what you've been doing, dear heart,' he beams. I dart backwards behind my car, trying to make light of my desire to escape.

'Oh goodness,' I gabble, 'I think you need a lovely glass of something to cool off, don't you? Let's go and look in the fridge.' From behind the car it is a simple stride in through the front door, and I am on my way to the kitchen, Hedley in pursuit, smelling fulsome and delivering a monologue against lawyers who insist on sending weedy letters instead of allowing action.

'. . . And I told them I meant it, and I am prepared to tie myself to the railings for my principles,' he fulminates, leaning against the sink, shedding crumbs of well-rotted manure around his feet. The kitchen has the celestial and yet clinical smell and appearance of a room which has just had the benefit of a cleaning lady's bleach-and-mop technique, and the aroma of Hedley is unbearable in it, as indeed is the sight of him coated in pig sewage in this pure, contemplative space. Pour him a glass of iced water from a jug in the fridge and open the kitchen door into the garden, taking a reviving gulp of air before turning back to him.

'Come on. Let's go and sit outside.'

Hedley follows me into the garden, mumbling, 'Why on earth can we not just stay in one place?' I pretend not to hear him. I sit down at a table brushed by the skeletal leaves and flowers of a herbaceous border, which is in collapse now until autumn.

'Actually, this bed could be dug over now, you know,' I say brightly, but Hedley is not taking the bait.

'There's something on your mind,' he says brusquely.

With the sense of stepping out over the edge of Cromer Cliffs, I shut my eyes and hear myself answer, 'I'm sorry, I can't marry you.'

Am actually quite amazed, as I had thought I was coming to confess that I had not yet told David I was getting married, and that I must do so before Hedley and I could fix a date, so would he mind waiting a bit. I was going to talk about slowing everything down, allowing time for adjustment and then maybe a wedding next year sometime. And yet here I am, saying it all over again.

'We're not suited, Hedley, and my children would drive you insane.'

He swallows, shakes his head, and clasps his hands tightly together. He coughs.

'I don't think they would,' he says quietly.

This is terrible. He and I are stuck in his garden, with shock and silence between us and the sun burning angry through the trellising and on to Hedley's face. I do not know what to say, or how to leave. My sense of relief is overwhelming. Part of me would like to leap up and dance around the garden, but I also have a sense of hot shame at causing this mess. I stand up, and the heat on my skin breaks into dots of perspiration. My throat closes in claustrophobia. I must leave. I am shaking, and my mouth is dry.

'I've got to go, Hedley. I'm sorry,' I mutter, and without touching him, I turn and walk up through the garden to the green door in the wall which leads to the front drive and my car.

August 31st

Drain-rodding is not usually an evil of the summer, but this morning finds me lying in the yard with my arm down a manhole, wiggling the rods in what feels like treacle. I am tentatively enjoying my freedom, but am wondering if I will ever have a moment to think about it properly. The weather has changed abruptly, and a brisk cool wind is catching the yellowed leaves and twirling the first of them off the trees and down on to the lawn. The Beauty, appropriately clad for wet work in her rubber ring and dark glasses but no clothes, is helping me, oblivious to the mottled blue of her limbs. Two of the rabbits are galumphing around us. Giles glides past on his skateboard, faintly interested in my work, and surprised to see the rabbits, whose existence he has still not acknowledged since their return home from the auction.

'What are they doing here?'

Scrabble to my knees to make the most of a chance for an acid riposte.

'You bid for them at the auction,' I say sweetly, 'and now they live here. They have two meals a day, non-stop water and a hogweed delivery during the morning.'

'Excellent,' he says vaguely, and scooping one foot along the ground he skims away towards Felix, who is sitting on the doorstep strapping pads to his knees. 'Come on Felix, you don't need those.'

'I know I don't, but I like 'em,' Felix grins back, 'and I need to wear them before we go to Dad tomorrow, in case they don't fit and I have to get him to take them back.'

They swoop off down the road towards the village, their voices a low murmur, occasionally amplified when one makes the other laugh. I watch them until they slide round the corner, and return to the drains, grinning goofily with pleasure at their friendship.

Am under a spell of love for them at the moment, which makes me oddly benign in view of their useless animal husbandry. I just don't care. They were both so gentle and solicitous when I told them I was not marrying Hedley, that I wept. They hung around me, hugging and offering to bring me Rescue Remedy, and I howled.

'Mum, you can still change your mind if you really want to, you know,' said Giles, passing me a handkerchief after a couple of minutes of my sniffing sobs. 'We'll manage.'

And in his determined voice I could hear his fragility and his strength, and I wept even more.

'We'll find you someone else,' said Felix, stroking my limp hand against his cheek. 'There's bound to be someone nice, a bit like David but here more of the

287

time.' He sighed. 'It would be really good if David could just come back, actually.'

Sobbed for several moments more, during which time Giles kicked Felix, grimacing and trying to prevent me from hearing him as he whispered, 'Don't go on about David.'

Recovered by stages, until I could sit up and smile at the two of them and The Beauty anxiously watching me. I blew my nose and took a deep breath. 'We're fine on our own, aren't we?'

And in the same way that uttering the words 'I can't marry you' to Hedley informed me and set my fate on a new course I was not aware of seeking, asking this of the children, watching their vigorous agreement, confirmed it for me. We are fine. We will continue to be fine and I am free, and both lucky and happy to be with my children.

The Beauty potters by my side and I experience a real sense of empowerment and fulfilment that is increased by the removal from the drain of one shoe (The Beauty's), one rubber gnome (the neighbours'), and a pair of sunglasses which I know were once mine, and very expensive. Glugging noises and a foul smell suggest that the drain is now functioning properly, and in triumph The Beauty and I remove to the bathroom for a deep-cleansing session. This takes longer than expected, as The Beauty insists on washing my hair for me, and it is only as we come downstairs again much later, that I remember the rabbits. They are loose. So are the dogs.

Empowerment splinters, dread surfaces and I race into the garden expecting genocide. However, a miracle has been worked. All three dogs are lying under a tree panting, flat out on their sides, dead to the world. The rabbits, who had been assisting us with the drain-rodding, are hopping on the grass beneath the washing line, looking like exemplary Beatrix Potter rabbits, perfect in every way. The others are snug in their Roman palace, with no murder by the Senate or other high-ranking notaries having taken place at all. Adrenalin returns to normal levels and, having put the rabbits away, The Beauty and I return to the house to pack for their weekend with Charles and Helena, the first since the not-to-be-spoken-of holiday.

SEPTEMBER

September 1st

Charles comes early to collect the children. Am just performing an experiment with some pairs of silk long johns I have dyed. Inspired by The Beauty's sartorial genius, I am trying to make soft pants to wear as alternative leggings or pedal pushers. Have washed these to shrink them, and have paid Giles and Felix a pound to model them for me while I decide how to adapt them.

'Good God, what are you doing to those children?' Charles demands, a hectic flush spreading across his face and reminding me of Hedley. Giles and Felix are playing the fool, and both scream with laughter and collapse on the grass.

'We're supermodels,' flutes Felix, wiggling along in front of us, one hand camply on his hip. 'We only get out of bed for ten thousand pounds, so give us it now.' More wild sniggering, and then, to my horror, The

Beauty trundles up to Charles, and without so much as saying 'hello', turns her back and flicks up her skirt to reveal no knickers.

'I'm a mooneee, a mooonneee. Mooo, mooo,' she squeals, and lurches forward into a somersault and then a curtsy. Charles is aghast.

'Really Venetia, have you no control? The twins would never behave with such an absence of decorum. Unless under that child's influence,' he adds, glaring at The Beauty, now rolling with her brothers down the slope in the lawn. I watch the soft pants gathering grass clippings without regret. They will not do. Perhaps something shorter, like old-fashioned swimming trunks, might be the answer? Charles strides off towards the children and stands over them, cupping one hand and slapping the back of the other as if he is a boxing referee counting the combatants out.

He fails to persuade any of them to get up, and picks his way back to me, his every movement suggesting distaste. He coughs and, fixing his eyes firmly on the roof, says, 'I know it's no business of mine, but those children would be a lot better off if you found yourself a husband. I don't know what happened to that fellow David, but he had a good effect on them. Especially her,' he says with relish, removing his gaze from the chimney pots in time to see The Beauty pull down her eyes and push up her nose to make her favourite ghoul face at Felix.

'They're all a bit exuberant at the moment. They'll calm down once they get to Cambridge,' I say soothingly.

'That's the trouble,' says Charles, his voice doom-laden. 'We're not going home to Cambridge. We're going to a country house hotel for the weekend with Helena's parents. I nearly said no when they asked us, but then I thought it would be a nice change for the boys. They seem to get rather bad-tempered around the house otherwise.'

Cannot imagine their tempers being improved by a hotel, but the children all appear thrilled.

'Has it got a swimming pool and a tennis court? Can we have room service? When are we going?'

Even The Beauty catches on to the mood of extravagance, and rushes to fetch her small suitcase, shouting, 'Shall we go in a helicopter?'

Charles is touchingly thrilled by their enthusiasm, and drives away chatting animatedly with all his passengers. Wave them off and return to the garden for aimless wandering, and to avoid feeding remaining four-legged and feathered dependants. This is a failure. As soon as I am alone, contemplating the simple beauty both to eyes and nose, of a small area of the garden where purple-headed lavender gives way to floating ghostly blooms of Rosa Alba and then to a dense green wall of yew, now in its prime and sprouting mad AstroTurf sprigs of impossibly bright new growth, my ears are assailed by the rattling groan of enquiring hens. All of them, usually busy at the compost heap or out on the road begging from passers-by, are now at my heels. The leading hen and her spouse have twisted their heads round so that one eye can look up to watch me, and the other eye can scan the ground so as not to miss a choice worm or caterpillar on the grass. They do not even peck at the borders, as the ground has become too dry and cracked for anything but dust-baths this month.

It is quite impossible for me to achieve serenity when surrounded by a posse of moaning hens; so am forced to return to the yard and resume my usual role of provider. Have to focus on the colour blue to prevent bad temper. Do not entirely succeed, and dole out corn in a fit of graceless irritation, brooding on my circumstances.

Everything to do with domestic life takes for ever, and is endlessly repetitive. Full of optimism and nesting instincts, we surround ourselves with it when in the first flush of love. Look at Desmond and Minna. There they were, a few months ago, with nothing more to worry about than whether Minna should have her nails done, and whether to listen to Waylon Jennings or an Elvis bluegrass set in their car. Now they have a mortgage, a window box to water, a cat called Ghetto and a vast stack of photograph albums to fill. A baby will be next, and all their Elvis memorabilia will be put in a box in the attic to gather dust.

Have fed the hens now, and refilled the old sink that they drink out of. Will just give the dogs something quickly, and can then go and lounge in the garden with work to do and ill-tempered thoughts to think.

An hour has passed, during which I have fed the dogs, and been impelled to worm them, as could no longer stand for another moment the way Rags glides across the kitchen floor on her bottom. Have also de-flead them and washed their beds, then unblocked the washing-machine filter because their hair clogged it. Sudden zeal for dog hygiene on my part is fuelled by guilt, as Digger has developed dreadful swellings on his back and I have not noticed. Perhaps they have only just come. Must take him to the vet on Monday.

The telephone has rung six times, but have not been in the mood to answer it, as wish to wallow in self-pity and frustration a bit longer. Must stop this negative thought process and get on with the day. Some yoga in the garden should do the trick, but first must change into appropriate Zen gear, as combination of Chinese pyjama top and an ancient print dress worn as a skirt because the top half has so many holes, is now hopping with fleas and also revealing too much of me through gaping seams and missing buttons.

Turn to go upstairs and improve appearance, but too late. A car pulls up, and I panic, madly thinking it might be Hedley. Fears of being caught out and mortified in Miss Havisham mode evaporate when the car expels the unalarming figures of Vivienne and Simon. Simon's perpetually cheerful expression is lit up further by my shambolic appearance, especially the bits where cloth gapingly reveals thigh, and a bit of stomach with a blotch of faded camping suntan still visible. Vivienne, however, is appalled.

'Venetia, what have you been doing to yourself? You must get some new clothes organised, you're supposed to be a fashion designer now.'

'These are fashionable clothes,' I insist. 'They just need mending a bit.'

'We've got a business proposition to put to you,' says Simon, brandishing a bottle of champagne.

'Oh good.' I am eyeing the champagne, which suddenly becomes exactly what I need to give me a bit of courage and uplift. Have no trouble in understanding how women become alcoholics, especially mothers. In fact, find it much harder to understand why so many don't.

'We'd like to put some money into your company so you can expand and start manufacturing on a bigger scale,' Simon continues.

Vivienne, looking wonderfully cool, like a pistachio ice cream, in a pale green top and a beige skirt made of waffle towel material adds, 'Yes, and I'd like to take over some of the administration for you, if you didn't mind, Venetia, so you could get on with designing the things, and so it doesn't all collapse every time a child is ill or on holiday. But let's go and sit down, we can't talk about it without a drink.'

Am thrilled and irritated in equal measure by their offer; thrilled that my sewing of trolls and wishbones on to jumble-sale clothes all summer has resulted in a takeover bid by the giant conglomerate that is Vivienne and Simon; irritated that they have noticed the areas of inefficiency and lack of cash flow in something I was convinced was going according to plan. Must admit, though, have not been altogether clear about the plan. Can only just keep up with decorating the garments at the moment and rather thought I would sort it out after the children go back to school.

'I'm sure some champagne will help us all think more clearly,' says Simon, popping open the bottle with practised ease. Cannot feel that the kitchen, which has something unidentifiably sticky on the floor, making it difficult to move off once feet have settled in one position for a few seconds, is the place for us to have a business meeting, so ask the others through into the garden.

Lead the way, having gulped most of my champagne in one slug, in a spirit of confident happiness. I am about to close a deal and become hugely successful in my own right. Hah! Am striking a blow for demented housewives living in the country. In fact, maybe that's what the company should be called.

'Let's drink a toast to The Demented Housewife,' I yell, looking back as I do, to beam at Vivienne and Simon behind me. They are not there. They have stopped and are gazing in horror across the yard.

'Something awful has happened,' says Simon.

I swivel my gaze around the yard and scream, 'Oh, my God. I forgot to put them back in when the children left. Oh, no, oh, no.'

At the bottom of the wall in the yard, beneath the bowed blood-red heads of my Dublin Bay rose, are two of the rabbits, lying stretched out, lifeless. The Beauty's dolls' pram is beside them, and her babies and their clothes are strewn about the yard. Another rabbit, or rather the legs of another rabbit, are sticking out from beneath my car, its top end tucked beneath the wheel as if it has been run over. The scene is gruesome and nightmarish.

Scream rhetorically, 'Those bloody dogs. How could they?'

Cannot stop thinking to myself how annoying it is that I have just bought two big sacks of rabbit food, but at least there are still three rabbits left. Simon comes out of the barn, still holding his drink, and shakes his head.

'They've had the ones that went back in as well. Why have you got so many rabbits, anyway?'

'Simon,' Vivienne admonishes, but I answer him.

'Oh, because we have. Or rather had,' I snap in exasperation. Rant and stomp about for several minutes, not wanting to approach the corpses, but looking around vengefully for a dog to kick.

Simon carefully puts his glass of champagne down next to The Beauty's pram, and crouches over the nearest rabbit. 'Not a mark on any of them,' he says, having completed his examination. 'I think you'll find that Rags and Lowly egged one another on. It's classic terrier behaviour, I'm afraid. I doubt Digger had much to do with it.'

'Digger doesn't have much to do with anything,' I mutter, and Digger, skulking behind us, thumps his tail in recognition of his name.

'Thank goodness the children aren't here,' says Vivienne, sighing as she picks one of the corpses up off the ground. 'What do you want us to do with them?'

Am suddenly overwhelmed with exhaustion and nausea, but do not wish to appear as unravelled as I feel. Manage nonchalantly to pick up a limp body myself, selecting the back legs to hold it by. The dead weight sways, then lolls, as if dripping, from my arm. I must put it down before I scream. Look wildly around for somewhere for them to go.

'Just pop them in here for now,' I say briskly. 'That way we can think of something to do with them a bit later.' Simon's mouth gapes, and he watches me slump the horrible flopping thing into The Beauty's dolls' pram.

'You can't mean to leave them in there?' he says, deeply perturbed. I am now anxious to get back to business, and would much rather not dwell on the macabre happening, as I feel it implies an inability to cope, and does not suggest a top business organisation or a company chairwoman with a brain.

'Oh, yes,' I say airily, 'we always use the pram for dead bodies. We call it the hearse, in fact.' Chuck another bunny in and smile serenely, avoiding Vivienne's eye, willing myself to appear in control of the dreadful circumstance. 'In fact, rabbit fur makes a very good trim for bags and skirts.'

Vivienne gasps, 'Venetia!' in shocked accents, as if I have confessed to being a bank robber, but Simon laughs, picks up his glass and continues towards the garden bench.

'You may as well make use of it,' he says. 'Now, what about our idea?'

The drama of the past minutes has given me valuable breathing space, and has deflated some of the champagne-spiked confidence I felt for the idea. Am now a little wary, and not at all ready to commit myself. My business may be small and fragile and disorganised, but it's mine, and I need time to consider a step which will lead to my giving it up or sharing it. Mentally edit this and say to Simon, 'Let's not rush this. I'd like time to think, please,' and he nods, smiling and avuncular, as if he had thought so all along.

'I thought you would say that. Think about it, just think about it. Have a chat with Charles when he brings the children back. Or ask Hedley, he's got a sound business head, and you'll probably see him, won't you?' Simon pauses to give a knowing wink, and I wish passionately that I lived in an inner city, or a Miami condominium where no one knows anything about their neighbours, nor do they care. Comfort myself that although they may know about the affair, at least none of them knows about the awful engage-ment interlude.

He drains the last of his champagne and passes the glass to me. Vivienne follows him towards their car, and they depart. It is only as the sound of their engine dwindles in the hot, still air that I remember I have six dead rabbits in a dolls' pram. Wheel them into the larder where it is cool and shut the door.

September 2nd

Of course, forgot about the rabbits yesterday, and made no visits to the larder to jog my memory, as just ate lettuce, radishes and chopped chives from the garden. This was a triumph on the grounds of health, self-sufficiency and virtue, but was spoilt by the discovery of half a yellow caterpillar clinging to a sorrel leaf on my almost empty plate. No amount of seaching revealed the rest of the caterpillar, and the experience marred my world-view for the day.

In fact, spirits sank like the mercury in a barometer after lunch, and I was forced to take to the road in order to regain a sense of purpose in life. Driving between high banks where skeletal dried-out dandelions poked above tired grasses, I longed for autumn. For new beginnings, bonfires and the prospect of the children happily occupied at school all day. The sky, a sickly yellow-grey all morning, and partially responsible for my gloom, pressed down as I drove, and the first rain for months fell out of it in splashing drops on to my gnat-smeared windscreen. The splashes quickened and became a drumming torrent on the car, flooding the road, beating down from a relentless sky. I turned the radio up, revelling in the plangent misery of an old Suzanne Vega song, and drove on into the purple wall of rain.

Most therapeutic. Reached Cromer, where the sun spilled out across the swollen sea, and the clouds shook final drops of rain on to the beach. Skipped about, skimming stones, then gave into a primitive urge and took off everything but my pants and T-shirt and ran into the water. Even more therapeutic. And a very good reason to eat cream tea, which I did, without a trace of guilt, on the way home. Followed Charles's car the last half-mile back to the house, and leaping out to embrace my darling children, I experienced joy for the first time in ages.

September 3rd

Am certainly not experiencing joy today. Finally remember the rabbits at teatime, and break the bad news.

'Oh,' says Giles, not looking up from the ketchup bottle he is reading.

'What rabbits?' asks Felix, jabbing away at his Game Boy. 'Oh, *yes!* Giles, look, I've caught the Tortle.'

Am momentarily diverted. 'What do you mean, you've caught the Tortle? What's a Tortle?'

Am ignored, and now both boys are jabbing away at the Game Boy. Try again with The Beauty. 'I'm afraid your rabbits have gone to heaven, darling,' I say gently. 'Shall we go and bury them?'

She puts her head on one side to consider for a minute, then shakes her head.

'No, I'm busy,' she says heartlessly, adding, 'Is heaven next to Holt?'

Suddenly can't stand their heartless, zomboid, screen-filled existence. Grab the Game Boy and clasp it to my bosom, ranting, 'You children are subhuman. Do you not understand that the dogs have eaten your rabbits and we've got to bury them?'

Hurl sodding Game Boy out of the window, causing blood-curdling shriek from Felix. The Beauty spouts instant tears in sympathy, and Giles walks out of the door and into the yard to retrieve the treasured item, his hands in his pockets, muttering, 'Why do you have to get into such a psych? And anyway, if the dogs ate the rabbits, we can't bury them, can we?'

'We can bury the rest of rabbit,' says The Beauty, brightening.

Felix stops crying as the Game Boy is restored to him. 'Cool. Have they got heads or not?'

Lead them to the larder, where thankfully, the thick walls and flagged floor keep the temperature low, so no awful decomposing has begun. Wheel out the pram with its dreadful cargo.

'Yuck. It's not very nice, Mum. I don't think The Beauty should see this.' Giles stands in front of the pram, blocking his sister's view.

'You shouldn't have used her pram, Mum,' says Felix, taking her hand and leading her away. 'Come on, Beauty, let's get some flowers and have a funeral.'

The Beauty, thoroughly enjoying the solemnity of the occasion, goes with him meekly. 'They're only dead and good for nothing now,' she says as they potter off to the garden for wreath materials.

Why are my children so callous? On the other hand, I should be pleased, as this is the most interest any of them have shown in the rabbits since we got them. Must make the most of their ghoulishness and use the experience to teach them something. The ritual of mourning, perhaps? Giles and I trundle them down to the wood, armed with spades, and begin to dig, our spades clanking as if against steel once we have removed the layers of leaf mould, so dry is the ground.

After a minute or two of getting nowhere, Giles speaks my thoughts. 'Do we have to have separate graves for all of them?' I nod. 'Thought so,' he says gloomily. He looks at me again after a moment, measuringly.

'You're sure we can't just do a couple,' he suggests. 'Then we could just chuck the others away in the wood. It would be good for the circle of life.'

'No. How could we choose?' I answer, breathless already. We continue panting and digging, my efforts even less successful than Giles's due to the collapse of my flip-flops as I attempt to lever the spade into the earth. The Beauty and Felix materialise with cardboard shoeboxes and flowers.

'Here are the coffins. They've got to share,' announces Felix, brilliantly relieving us of half the workload with his practical undertaker's approach. Lay the hapless bunnies in their coffins, and try not to shudder and scream when The Beauty lifts one from the pram, hugs it and rains kisses upon its forehead.

Giles rolls his eyes. 'She'll probably get myxomatosis,' he says.

Am becoming very sick of the whole dead-animal saga now, and after what feels like hours but my watch says is a mere three minutes, have dug a hole too small to put a tulip bulb in, never mind a hefty trainers shoebox containing two rabbits and a garland of campanula and pulsingly bright pink cosmos. The dogs are sniffing about. Find myself wishing they had eaten the rabbits rather than just killing for pleasure and leaving us with the toil. Seize the pickaxe that

Giles has leaned against a tree, and begin a Grim Reaper attack on the bone-hard earth with it.

Start to quite enjoy the profound ghastliness of the scene in the wood, where the peaty smell of leaf mould mingles with a gamey essence of hung flesh, and where, of course, no one is helping me, the children having run off to play hide-and-seek. I lean on the pickaxe handle and gaze out at the countryside, so familiar it is my sanctuary as much as this garden and this house, my home.

Yesterday's storms have not broken the taut line of low cloud above the water meadows, and although the sun is out, its light is heavy and indolent, creating rich tones in the tawny trunks and green-gold leaves, but absorbing any movement to leave the view still and silent, glowing as if it has just been painted. Autumn is creeping in on the faint mauve mist above the stream which threads through the fields, and in the soft smoke tint the wood beyond has assumed. Voices bounce off the trees around, recalling me, and the echo and the flurry of feet falling in leaves fills our small wood with more than just the children and me. I look towards the house. The windows are lit orange in every pane, flames licking the stretched glass. Everything inside me lurches in dizzy horror and I fling down the pickaxe. I almost run back across the lawn to save the house, but, before I have finished forming the thought, I have stopped again. The house is melting in the low evening light, burning the reflected sun as it sinks to the horizon.

The children rush up behind me, and Felix grabs my skirt and crows, 'I'm safe. Mum is base.' Giles runs away to hide again. His voice swoops laughter back towards me. In the still moment while Felix counts, a pigeon claps up into a branch and begins to coo.

School starts tomorrow, and we will fall back into the ritual of routine. I will miss them in the day, but The Beauty will attend her nursery three days a week, unless she is expelled, and I can work. My life is not in pieces, as I have sometimes thought recently. It is a happy whole. Apart from having these corpses to deal with.

I am about to turn back to the wood, with the half-hearted compromise that I will bury one shoebox tonight, when Felix has finished hugging me and counting. The dogs stop hurtling in circles on the lawn, and suddenly charge as one beast to the gate, barking manically. They fall silent as if they have been switched off, and I swing around, my heart pounding as I hear a step on the gravel and a man's voice saying, 'Down. Come on you lot, it's me.'

Digger has rolled over and is lying panting with pleasure, his legs wiggling like a centipede's. It can only be David. My hands become clammy, and I stand staring, not even able to breathe, as still as stone with a bumping heart. But it isn't David. It's Desmond. Snap at him most unfairly.

'What are you doing here, and why did you walk?'

He gives me a severe look. 'One of these days you're going to turn into a real old curtain-twitching busybody,' he says. 'I walked because Minna and I are having a drink in the pub, and there's a fantastic cricket match going on. I thought the boys might like to come down and watch it.'

The boys are already on their skateboards, Giles towing The Beauty who has climbed into her pram, and they are out of the gate and on their way to the village.

'Hurry up Mummy,' commands The Beauty. 'You can have Coke and crisps if you like.'

'But we haven't buried the rabbits,' I wail. No one answers.

'Come on Venetia,' urges Desmond, 'it's only a drink. I'll go and shut the dogs in. You go on ahead.'

My mother and Minna both look slightly aghast when they see me, but they quickly explain that it is only due to my staggering gait, caused by broken flip-flops. Minna goes into the pub to procure drinks for all.

'Isn't it time you got some sensible shoes?' asks my mother. 'You're supposed to be a businesswoman.'

Decide not to rise to deliberate provocation as am so enjoying the restful, civilised air of the evening.

'You're not the first person to say that,' I remark amiably. 'I'm going to change my appearance completely when the children go back to school tomorrow.'

'The end of summer,' muses my mother.

'And not a moment too soon,' I retort tartly, grabbing a drink off the tray Minna is placing on the table. We sip gin and tonic and watch the cricket, all of us bathed in the last glow of the sun, while dark blue shadows creep from across the green towards the cricketers. Desmond joins us, smirking unnecessarily, and sits down next to Minna.

He passes me an envelope.

'This is for you.'

'Oh, right. Thanks.' Take it, and assuming that it is a bill or similar, put it in my pocket without looking at it. Have another slug of gin, and notice that everyone at our table is looking at me, not at the cricket. Even my children have all stopped cramming their mouths with crisps and are gazing, unblinking, at me. Creeping sense of disquiet tingles in my fingers and begins to course through my body, no doubt causing my face to turn scarlet. No one speaks. They all continue to stare at me. I can bear it no longer; I am now experiencing non-specific guilt. Stand up and glare back at them all.

'What? What have I done? Why are you all looking at me like that?' Gesture towards The Beauty. 'And why is *she* looking at me like that?'

'I'm not *she*. I'm *me*. How dare you,' mutters The Beauty crossly, breaking the tension because both my mother and I snort with laughter. Giles leans on me.

'Mum, why don't you look at the envelope Desmond gave you.'

Pull the envelope out of my pocket again and look at it. It is just an envelope. Sealed, but blank. Glance up to say, 'So what?' and find they are all at it again. Staring.

Have now completely had enough. Slam the envelope on the table and march off, shouting over my shoulder, 'You've all gone mad. I'm going to the loo for some moments of sanity. Could you please all be normal when I come back.'

Lock myself into wonderful chamber of peace and contemplation and begin a leisurely perusal of old copies of *Hello!*. Some time passes. I must take the children home and clean them up for school. Am just flicking through a fifth magazine, promising to myself that it will be the last, when there is a fumbling at the door, and the now battered envelope creeps in, pushed by a small hand from the other side.

Yell, 'Oh, for God's sake,' and hear the familiar echo of The Beauty relishing her favourite blasphemy as she trails back to my mother. Grinning, I picture her shaking her head and muttering, 'Godssake, godssake, godssake,' all through the pub. Anyway, opening the envelope is a good delaying tactic. Inside is not a bill. Instead there is a letter from Giles to me. Weird. Scan it quickly. Then read it again. And again.

Dear Mum,

I don't think you wanted me to do this, but I told David you were going to marry Hedley in an email and he said I shouldn't intafere but I've done it again. I told him you weren't going to marry Hedley after all, and now he's come home. He's at home at our house right now, and he wonders if you would like to marry him instead. I know it would be better if he asked you, but I thought I'd better·write it down in case he didn't get round to it again. He says he must be mad not to have done it before this

summer ever happened. Sorry I intafered. Granny
said I should, but that's no excuse is it? Sorry.

Love Giles

ps David said he would bury the rabbits.

Only because I am locked in the loo and no one knows
can I admit that my first coherent emotion, as numb
shock passes and the light fades, is huge relief that the
rabbits have been dealt with. Otherwise am utterly
pole-axed and suddenly coy about returning to the
table outside the pub and my mad, staring family.
Concoct a cunning plan involving climbing out of the
loo window in order to return home by the fields, but
am thwarted by heavy breathing and a loud thud on the
other side of the door. It is Felix, the family emissary.

'Come on Mum, we know you're in there. Granny
wants to go home now. Can we all go with her and
watch *Grease?* Is The Beauty allowed to stay up?
Please, she'd love it and I want to see her dancing
along to the songs.'

The heavy breathing ceases while The Beauty
announces kindly, 'Course I am.'

I must pull myself together. Open the door, blinking in the bright strip lighting outside the cubicle, and
inspect the watch on Felix's wrist. Oddly, it is still
early.

'All right, you can go. I'll come and collect you in
an hour. You can miss baths. We'll just pretend you're
very suntanned at school tomorrow.'

'Cool,' yells Felix, and hurtles back outside to the
others who are already packed into my mother's car.

Wave, and walk back to my house through the dusk, suppressing hysterical excitement, determined to be the poised epitome of languid sophistication when I see David. In the event, this is not possible.

ALSO AVAILABLE BY RAFFAELLA BARKER

COME AND TELL ME SOME LIES

Gabriella lives in a damp, ramshackle, book-strewn farmhouse in Norfolk with her tempestuous poet father and unconventional mother. Alongside her ever expanding set of siblings and half-siblings, numerous pets and her father's rag-tag admirers, Gabriella navigates a chaotic childhood of wild bohemian parties and fluctuating levels of poverty. Longing to be normal, Gabriella enrolls in a strict day school, only to find herself balancing two very different lives. Struggling to keep the eccentricities of her family contained, her failure to achieve conformity amongst her peers is endearing, and absolute.

Come and Tell Me Some Lies is Raffaella Barker's enchanting first novel – a humorous, bittersweet tale of a girl who longs to be normal, and a family that can't help be anything but.

THE HOOK

Christy Naylor was forced to grow up quickly. Still reeling with anger after the death of her mother, she abandons college in order to help her father uproot from suburbia and start a new life on a swampy fish farm out in the sticks, a prize that he won in a shady game of poker.

Amid this turmoil, looms the mysterious Mick Fleet, tall, powerful and charismatic. Unsettled and unsure of herself, Christy is hooked on his intense charm. She knows nothing about him yet she feels like she is being swallowed up in his embrace and she plunges into a love affair blind to the catastrophe he will bring . . .

HENS DANCING

When Venetia Summers's husband runs off with his masseuse, the bohemian idyll she has strived to create for her young family suddenly loses some of its rosy hue. From her tumble-down cottage in Norfolk she struggles to keep up with the chaos caused by her two boys, her splendid baby daughter and the hordes of animals, relatives and would-be artists that live in her home. From juggling errant cockerels, jam-making frenzies and Warhammers, to unexpected romance, Bloody Marys and forays into fashion design, *Hens Dancing* is like a rural *Bridget Jones's Diary* as it charts a year in Venetia's madcap household.

B L O O M S B U R Y

GREEN GRASS

Laura Sale has grown tired of her life. Her daily routine of dividing her time between pandering to the demands of her thirteen-year-old twins Dolly and Fred and their challenging conceptual artist father, Inigo, has taken its toll. She longs to remember what makes her happy. A chance encounter with Guy, her first love, is the catalyst she needs, and she swaps North London for the rural idyll she grew up in. In her new Norfolk home Laura finds herself confronting old ghosts, ferrets, an ungracious goat and a collapsing relationship. As she starts to savour the space she has craved, and takes control of her destiny, Laura finds it lit with possibility.

A PERFECT LIFE

The Stone family live a fairy-tale existence in their home in rural Norfolk, complete with adorable children, glamorous parents and postcard-perfect seaside picnics. Nick, Angel and their family lead a charmed life. And yet beneath the surface all is not as it seems.

Why is Nick away so often? Where's the laughter? And what is happening to the children?

We all want a perfect life, but at what price?

POPPYLAND

On a freezing cold night in an unfamiliar city, a man meets a woman. The encounter lasts just moments, they part barely knowing one another's names, they make no plans to meet again. But both are left breathless.

Five years on they live thousands of miles apart and live totally separate lives, except that they both still think about that night. So when they meet again it seems clear that they will do all they can to try and stay together. But can it be that easy? Will they be able to escape their past? Will they be able to take the risk they know they should?

BLOOMSBURY

FROM A DISTANCE

April, 1946. Michael, a soldier, returns to Southampton on a troop ship. Brutalised and in shock, he cannot face the life that awaits him at home. Impulsively he boards a train to the western tip of Cornwall, where his life is shaped by his heart and the fragmented Britain he has come back to.

More than half a century later, Kit, an enigmatic stranger, arrives in Norfolk to take up an inheritance he doesn't want – a decommissioned lighthouse, half hidden in the shadows of the past, now sweeping its beam forward through time. According to Kit, his life is complete, and he doesn't wish to see anything the lighthouse's glare exposes. But the choice is out of his hands.

Luisa, a second generation Italian, has so far lived through her children and has reached a point of invisibility. The constant push and pull of family life has turned like the tide, and she is suspended, without direction. Kit and Luisa meet and neither can escape the inevitability of Michael's split-second decision at the Southampton docks

Moving between the post-war artists' colony around St Ives in Cornwall and present-day Norfolk, Raffaella Barker's new novel explores the secrets and flaws that shape our interactions across generations. *From a Distance* is a tender and compelling story of human connection and the yearning desire we have to belong.

'I love Raffaella Barker's books – so funny and acerbic'
MAGGIE O'FARRELL

ORDER BY PHONE: +44 (0)1256 302 699; BY EMAIL: DIRECT@MACMILLAN.CO.UK
DELIVERY IS USUALLY 3–5 WORKING DAYS. FREE POSTAGE AND PACKAGING FOR ORDERS OVER £20.
ONLINE: WWW.BLOOMSBURY.COM/BOOKSHOP
PRICES AND AVAILABILITY SUBJECT TO CHANGE WITHOUT NOTICE.

WWW.BLOOMSBURY.COM/RAFFAELLABARKER

BLOOMSBURY